D1520943

COMING HOME

Whiskey River Road Book 1

KELLY MOORE

Edited by
KERRY GENOVA

Cover by
DARK WATER

TITLE

Coming
HOME
WHISKEY RIVER ROAD

KELLY MOORE

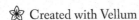 Created with Vellum

I'd like to dedicate this book to two people. Jennifer Thomason for all the countless hours she spends reading my books, making suggestions, and writing editorial reviews for me. You make me a better writer. Thank you.

Dave Thomason...you know what you did.

PLAYLIST

My playlist of songs that inspired me to write Coming Home.

Don't Want to Write This Song by Brett Young
    Wild Horses by The Sundays
    What if I never Get Over You by Lady Antebellum
    Prayed for you by Matt Stell
    Fight Sony by Rachel Platten
    You Say by Lauren Daigle
    You Are the Reason by Calum Scott and Leona Lewis

CHAPTER ONE
CLEM

I park the truck on the edge of the concrete slab that has two other pickup trucks on it. Slowly getting out, I blow out a lengthy breath while trying to convince myself that I've done the right thing by coming home. I smooth down my long, chestnut-colored hair and adjust my simple army-green dress. Ethan gets out and walks around to my side of the truck.

"Are you ready?" He holds out his hand, and I take it. We head to the steps of the house, and he stops dead in his tracks.

"Why is there a shotgun leaning on the wall by the door?"

"That's not a shotgun. It's a rifle. I don't know, maybe they had some coyotes out here last night."

"Coyotes?" His gaze skims the area around the house.

The front door thunders open and my daddy, Chet Calhoun, steps out onto the painted wooden porch. "What the hell are you doing back here?" His heavy voice blares as his Adam's apple bobs. His silver hair and mustache haven't changed, but I don't recall the deep-seated wrinkles that now hang at his gray eyes. He's older but stands just as tall and brooding as he always has.

"I wanted to come home." I shrug one shoulder, unable to come up with anything else to say.

"You're not welcome here." He reaches behind him and grabs the rifle.

"Oh, Daddy, you're not going to shoot me." I brush the rifle downward, and he raises it again. "Then how about him." He waves it in Ethan's direction, and he scoots behind me.

EIGHTEEN HOURS EARLIER...

"DOES YOUR FAMILY EVEN KNOW WE'RE coming?" The springs creak in the seat as Ethan climbs in the passenger side of my old pickup truck. The knobs rattle as he shuts the door and he immediately tries to roll down the window but struggles with the broken crank.

"No, and trust me, it's better this way." I turn the key over, and nothing happens. With a slap of my hand on the cracked dash, the engine sputters as it comes to life. My lucky charm always works. Its old bones make all kinds of noises, including a backfire that has Ethan jumping in his seat and banging his head on the bare ceiling of the truck.

"What the hell, Clem? Why do you still have this old truck anyway? Even the bumper doesn't look like it wants to hang around on it. It's holding on by one bolt. It's a piece of shit. Is it even going to get us to Kentucky?" He rubs the side of his head.

"Ahhh, cover your ears, Lizzy." I gasp and pat the dash like I'm consoling her. "She and I have been through a lot together. I'm pretty sure she'll outlive me. Besides, once we get to the ranch, she'll fit right in." The sound of the gears shifting into drive drops heavily into place with a sharp grind. The engine gives one last hiccup before it jerks into motion. I glance over at Ethan, and he's already digging through the bag of junk food and drinks that he bought when I stopped to fill up the gas tank.

It's early, and the heat is radiating off the sunbaked long, narrow highway. The glass in my window makes a rubbing noise as I exert pressure to turn the window crank. It stops at halfway and won't go any further, but it's enough to let a breeze flow through once I open the sliding back window. The wind sends my dog tags hanging from the rearview mirror into a tornado spin.

Over the sound of the wind whipping through, I hear Ethan slurping his drink through a straw. I cut my gaze to him, and he shrugs.

He starts feeling around the seats and the center console. "Where are the cup holders?"

"You'll have to hold it between your thighs because there isn't any."

"Jesus, Clem. Why couldn't we have driven my new car?"

"Because that thing is pretty and a Corvette has no place where we're going?"

"You make it sound like we're going to *The Hills Have Eyes*."

I giggle at his reference to the scary movie. "Have you ever been to the hills of Kentucky?" I add, in my not so frightening southern drawl.

"No. You know I'm a city boy from New York,

but you're scaring me just a little." He pinches his fingers together.

"How did you and I ever become best friends?" I can't help but laugh at him.

He finally gets his window rolled down and hangs his arm out. "I helped you get through basic training, and then you wouldn't quit following me around." His smile goes from ear to ear.

He's right. I didn't know a soul and was terrified once I enlisted. I had no idea why this charming city boy helped me, but he did. I could've easily fallen for his good looks and lean body. He has that all-American boy thing going on that all the women love. Jet-black hair, perfect teeth, and smile. Bright blue eyes that could make any normal girl's libido rage.

I was still reeling from walking out on Boone on our wedding day. I haven't spoken a word to him since. I wasn't ready to jump into another relationship, much less a fuck fest with a hot soldier boy. I wanted to find out who I was besides a girl that was raised to be prim and proper but born with a dirty mind. After having my mouth washed out with soap enough, I learned to keep my thoughts to myself.

"It was you who kept pursuing me." I snort.

He reaches over and spins the volume on the radio. He immediately starts humming to the country song playing. I introduced him to it, and now he's a die-hard fan. I tap the steering wheel to the beat of the music and enjoy listening to him.

It isn't long before I glance over and see his head lying against the doorframe with drool coming out of the corner of his mouth. Not a sexy look on him. It will be a boring eighteen-hour drive from Fort Carson to Salt Lick, Kentucky if he's going to sleep half the ride.

I pull my dark, round sunglasses from the visor and focus on the drive. I can't help but wonder how my family will take me coming back. I was just a young girl when I left. Returning at twenty-eight, I have a better perspective on what I want out of life, and the things I once hated about the ranch, I now think fondly of and have an aching in my heart to return. My older sister Ellie and I have written for years, and she's kept me somewhat in the know about Mom, Daddy, and our two brothers. The last email I got from her was pretty nonspecific. She said there was trouble at the ranch, and Daddy's health wasn't the best. I figured now was the best time to return. I'm free of the army and can start a new life. But first I need to make some amends.

Daddy and I used to be close, but I'm sure Boone's heart wasn't the only one broken that day. I love my father, but he was always so controlling of his family. *"We're cattle ranchers and racehorse breeders and trainers. That's what we do, and that's what each of you will do."* I can still hear his firm voice in my head. He was the one that insisted that I marry Boone. He'd hired him as the lead trainer when I was sixteen years old. My love for the horses had me following in his shadow like a little lost puppy dog. It didn't help that I was a horny teenage girl, and all I could think about was what was under the fly of his faded blue jeans. He was five years older than me. He only thought of me as the boss's baby daughter until I turned twenty. I was a late bloomer, and my girls didn't blossom until then. That's when he started to look at me like a man looks at a woman, and I ate it up.

He taught me everything I know about training racehorses and other things. I was comfortable with him and enjoyed his company. There was a raw sexual force between us that I didn't understand. My father saw that. Well, not the sexual part. He would've skinned my hide. He pushed us together. He said we'd make a powerful team in the industry.

Boone was sweet in a rugged sort of way. He'd flex his biceps, and my sex drive would approach a meltdown level. I was in a constant state of a puddled mess between my legs just looking at him. He was a true cowboy from Texas. The song, "Save a Horse (Ride a Cowboy)," always skirted around my mind when I was near him.

My dad found him hanging around the tracks and took him under his wing. His dark-brown sexy, soft curls and killer smile made it easy to fall for him. I loved him, but I wanted more out of life, and he deserved someone that didn't feel stuck. In hindsight, I picked a really bad day to decide I couldn't be who he or my father wanted me to be.

Seven years in the army, I grew up. I traveled overseas and learned the cybersecurity industry. I only ended up in Colorado six months ago. It was the first time I'd been in the same place as Ethan since we were assigned to an army base in Europe. I stayed there, and he went on to Germany. By then, I only saw him as a friend and not someone I wanted to hop in the sack with.

I know I should've made more attempts to talk to my family after I left, but Daddy was so angry. He told Ellie to tell me to never come home again. He wouldn't take any calls from me, and he forbid my mom to talk to me. My older brother Wyatt is thick as thieves with my father. He lives and breathes the business, so he only does what he's told to do.

My brother Bear, who's only a year older than me, was too busy being a ladies' man to care what was going on with anyone's life but his own. Ellie's always been a sweet, innocent girl and loved the ranch. She swore she'd never leave.

I've been lost in my thoughts for hours, listening to Ethan snore. I reach over and shake his leg. "Hey, I need to stop for fuel and to use the ladies' room."

He wipes the drool off his face with the back of his hand. "How long have I been sleeping?"

"Four hours. You never even woke up the last time I fueled up." I pull off the highway into a mom-and-pop station. Ethan helps out by pumping the fuel while I run inside.

When we get back onto the road, Ethan is driving. He keeps trying to adjust the seat to fit his lengthy legs. "You really haven't spoken to Boone since you left him at the altar?"

"No. Ellie said he didn't want anything to do with me. I can't blame him."

"You've remained pretty closed-lipped about the story other than the basics, even from me. Why don't you tell me the details, being that I'm going to meet all of them? I think you should spill it."

Resting my head on the back of the seat, I let the wind cool my face and bring back clear memories. "I remember Ellie zipping me up and watching me in the mirror. I'd been in my own head, frantic about what I was about to do. The dress suddenly felt like hot glue on my skin. My head started spinning, and I felt woozy. Pictures of my future flashed before my eyes. I recall telling my sister, 'I...I can't do this.' I ripped the veil and the flowers out of my hair that she had spent the last hour fixing.

"She asked what I was talking about. She kept telling me that Boone and half the town was waiting for me in the church.

"My chair scooted across the floor as I fought to stand because my legs felt like wet noodles trying to hold myself up. My dress got caught underneath one the legs, and it ripped a layer of frill off. I screamed for her to unzip me. I twisted my arm over my head to tug at the zipper, but my hand was shaking so much I couldn't get a grip on it."

I stuff my hands between my legs and look down. "Ellie kept saying she didn't understand. I can still feel her pulling the zipper all the way to my lower back, and I shrugged out of my dress.

"I told her that I did love Boone, but that I was only twenty-one years old. I wanted more out of life than the ranch and racehorses. If I had married him, it would be all I'd ever know. Traveling from horse track to horse track would be all I'd see of the world. I needed more, I wanted more, and it was such a confusing time for me.

"She cried, telling me that I'd been born and bred into this. That Daddy told her I'd become one of the best horse trainers he'd ever seen.

"I couldn't get in my skinny jeans fast enough. I remember telling her, that's what he wants for my life, and what about what I want? That never mattered to him. She tried to convince me that it did, but I knew better. Then she kept repeating the question, what about Boone?

"I told her that was just it. I didn't know what I wanted, but I needed to figure it out before I settled down into a life I would regret."

I look back up to see Ethan watching me from the corner of his eye. "I finished dressing as she kept trying to convince me to stay. She knew I'd spoken to a recruiter and had been talking about it for days. I tugged my cowgirl boots on and worked on pulling the hundreds of bobby pins out of my hair. She couldn't believe I was really walking out. A runaway bride. I grabbed the suitcase that I had packed for my honeymoon to nowhere and my purse. I asked her to help me. When she didn't answer, I told her I was leaving one way or another and marched to the back door of the church. I was terrified when I peeked out the door to make sure no one would see me. I ran to Lizzy that was parked underneath the shade of some trees.

"I was so afraid I'd get caught because Ellie was running behind me screaming my name ,begging me not to leave. I yanked the Chevy door open, and the last thing I said to her was to tell Boone I was sorry. When I drove off, I saw her in my rearview mirror, waving frantically and tears streaming down her face. When I got to the end of the dirt road, I hesitated only for a second. I clearly remember whispering the words, goodbye dirt road. I never slowed down again."

He's quiet for a moment as if he's mulling around what I've told him. "Does Boone still work for your dad?"

"Yeah. I've been reading in the racehorse magazines that the horse he's been training for the past three years is winning at all the tracks. Sounds like he's got a good chance at the Kentucky Derby this year."

"Wow. Has your dad ever had a winning horse before?"

"Back in 2009, he had a horse that won. The

racehorse he has now, Whiskey River, is from the same bloodline."

"Where do they come up with horse names. I mean, some of them sound like royalty." The truck bounces over a pothole.

I grab onto to the rough dash. "Some of them are considered royalty and treated as such."

"I'm looking forward to seeing what your life was like growing up on a ranch."

"I didn't appreciate it enough."

"Do you regret leaving?"

"I don't regret going into the army and all the experiences I've had. What I do regret is leaving the way I did. I hurt my family and Boone. If they'll let me, I want to make it up to them, but my dad isn't the most forgiving person in the world. He's perfected holding a grudge to high levels."

"And what about the man you left at the altar? Do you want to make things up to him too?"

"There's no way I ever can. He's moved on with his life and so have I."

WE STOPPED AT A SMALL HOTEL FOR THE NIGHT and ate at a rowdy steak house. We got up early, bought our coffee, and hit the road.

With two more hours to go, we start getting into farmland. Broken wooden fences on one side of the narrow road, barbed wire on the other. Clumps of dandelions and foxtail border the bluegrass fields between the road and the fencing. Harvested round hay bales are sitting in a crop stubble. Cows graze near an old rotting barn structure forgotten in a field. The sky always seems bluer here and filled with birds flying overhead. A hawk is perched on a wooden fence post, waiting to find a field mouse for its supper.

We pass a farmer wearing overalls, who's pushing a wheel barrel and chewing on a stalk of sweet grass. Off in the distance, there's a tractor throwing up a plume of dust in its wake.

"Are you getting nervous?" Ethan has his arm out the window, making waving motions with his hand.

"A little, but I'm bound and determined not to let Daddy keep me away from my family any longer."

"Good for you. I'll be by your side unless he has a shotgun, then you're on your own." He laughs.

"Oh, my father has a multitude of guns."

His eyes get round as saucers. "He's not going to shoot you is he?"

"I don't think he'll go to that extreme, but you might want to wear a bulletproof vest," I tease him.

"Ha-ha, not funny."

Gravel crackles under my tires as I turn onto a long, winding drive and stop by the green street sign.

"Whiskey River Road," Ethan reads and then shoulders the door open to get out. "That's where the horse's name came from."

I step onto the gravel and drag my sunglasses to the top of my nose and look down the road that leads to my family. The fragrance of the lavender flocks smells like home, and I can taste the pollen filtering through the dry air. The road turns to red clay dirt about a quarter mile down. I recognize the familiar tracks in the gravel from a horse trailer being hauled by an oversized truck.

Ethan's army boots scuff in the rocks. "Take my picture under the street sign." He points to it and smiles.

I take my phone out of the side panel in the door of the truck and snap his picture.

"You're almost home." He climbs back in the passenger seat.

I put Lizzy in gear and slowly head down the

uneven road. Ethan fiddles with the radio and stops when he hears the song "Sweet Home Alabama."

"Wrong state, but it'll still work." He turns up the volume.

I laugh and join him in singing it. The potholes along the dirt road jar my teeth and seriously mess with my rendition of the song, but I refuse to let it ruin the moment. I need to keep the good mood I'm in to be able to face my family, more specifically, Daddy.

CHAPTER TWO
CLEM

As we get closer to the ranch, I see the winding creek that I spent many a long day playing in its cold water with Ellie. When evening would come, we'd spend hours trying to catch the fireflies that hung out in the tall grass along the water's edge. Rows of white fences border the pastures, and cattle graze in the sharp-colored bluegrass.

I slam on my brakes when an ATV races across the dirt road, sending a spiral of red clay in the air in front of me. When it clears, I see Bear staring back at me from behind a green bandana tied around his head. He tugs it down, and his crooked smile hasn't changed a bit, but he's no longer a boy. He has a dark-colored beard marring the rest of his face.

"It's about time you found your way home." He puts the bandana back in place and pushes the clutch, jerking forward then taking off down the road in front of us.

"Who's that?" Ethan asks.

"That's my brother Bear."

"Bear as in grizzly bear? Is that his real name?"

"No. His real name is Bradley, but I can't remember a time he wasn't called Bear."

I stop the truck when I see the ranch entry sign. "That family sign has hung there as far back as I can remember."

"Calhoun Ranch," Ethan reads.

"This place was my grandfather's. It started as a cattle farm and branched out into racehorses. The only thing here at the time was the main house and a rundown barn. My father has built these three hundred acres into a magnificent piece of property. He owns as far as the eyes can see to the west. There are horse stables, two barns, an official size horse racing track, and fifteen different houses tucked into the land. At least that was seven years ago."

"Now I know why they call it bluegrass country. It's beautiful." Ethan takes my hand in his. "Is that a chicken?" He points with the other hand to a stray brown chicken pecking at the bits of grass poking from the clay surrounding the thick wooden post holding up the ranch sign.

"Yeah, Momma loves chickens but every now and then one gets out. Personally, I hate those little buggers. Believe it or not, they're very protective. My mom has a rooster that perches in her lap, and if you try to get near her, that thing will attack you like a woodpecker pecking wood."

"Thanks for the heads-up. I'll make sure to stay clear of your mother. I don't want my eyes pecked out." Ethan releases my hand and covers his eyes.

I laugh at him. "I'll keep you safe, I promise."

Pressing slightly on the gas pedal, the truck rolls forward slowly. Now that I'm here, I'm not in a hurry to face Daddy's wrath. The white pristine two-story house is as I remember it. Rocking chairs rest on the front porch wrapping around the house. Navy-blue metal shutters frame the windows.

I park the truck on the edge of the concrete slab that has two other pickup trucks on it. Slowly getting out, I blow out a lengthy breath while trying to convince myself that I've done the right thing by coming home. I smooth down my long, chestnut-colored hair and adjust my simple army-green dress. Ethan gets out and walks around to my side of the truck.

"Are you ready?" He holds out his hand, and I take it. We head to the steps of the house, and he stops dead in his tracks.

"Why is there a shotgun leaning on the wall by the door?"

"That's not a shotgun. It's a rifle. I don't know, maybe they had some coyotes out here last night."

"Coyotes?" His gaze skims the area around the house.

The front door thunders open and my daddy, Chet Calhoun, steps out onto the painted wooden porch. "What the hell are you doing back here?" His heavy voice blares as his Adam's apple bobs. His silver hair and mustache haven't changed, but I don't recall the deep-seated wrinkles that now hang at his gray eyes. He's older but stands just as tall and brooding as he always has.

"I wanted to come home." I shrug one shoulder, unable to come up with anything else to say.

"You're not welcome here." He reaches behind him and grabs the rifle.

"Oh, Daddy, you're not going to shoot me." I brush the rifle downward, and he raises it again. "Then how about him." He waves it in Ethan's direction, and he scoots behind me.

"Who's at the door?" Momma brushes past

Daddy. When she sees me, tears instantly fill her eyes, and her hand covers her mouth. "Clementine." She rushes over and wraps her arms around me, nearly knocking me down.

"Momma." I hug her back until she releases me, holding me at arm's length so she can take a gander at me.

"You're so skinny, and your hair is darker." She glances over at Ethan. "And, who is this handsome young man you've brought home with you?"

"Don't be getting all friendly with them. They're not staying!" My dad drags her back to his side, and his weapon resumes its stance in my direction. "Get off my property."

"I'm not leaving, Daddy." I defiantly cross my arms over my chest. "I know you don't want to see me, but I want to see my family."

"You should've thought about that before you turned your back on us seven years ago."

"I know, and I'm sorry. If you'll just give me a chance..."

"A chance for what? For you to leave again?"

"No. I want to be part of this family."

"You don't have to stay in this house for that to happen."

"Fine, I'll stay in town."

"She'll do no such thing," Momma chimes in. "She's our daughter for gawd sake. You've kept her away long enough." She yanks the rifle from his hands.

"She is not staying in this house!" He points at me as raises his voice at her.

"Fine, then she can stay in one of the houses on the west side of the property."

Daddy growls and then a smug smile covers his weathered face. "You can stay in 102."

I'm scared to ask why he looks so pleased with himself. "Okay then. We'll get settled and come back when you don't have a weapon close by." I march down the steps like a petulant child.

"Why don't you two come back for dinner. I'll have supper ready at six," Momma yells after us.

I hear the scuff of my dad's boots walk further out onto the porch. "You may want to think better of the invite. Boone sits at our table every night."

I climb back in the truck and Ethan slams the door so hard I think it's going to fall off its hinges. "What the hell was that?" He tries to crank up the window, but it only goes a quarter of the way up before the knob falls off.

"I told you he wouldn't be happy to see me." I

drape my arm over the seat and turn to look behind me to back out.

"Who pulls a shotgun on their own daughter?"

"Again, it's not a shotgun. It's a rifle! And that was my father," I say dryly.

"Do you think it was loaded?"

"It's always loaded."

"Why are you not freaking out about this?"

"Because I know he'd never really shoot me." I gnaw on my lip. "I don't think."

He pulls out his phone from his shirt pocket. "I can get us two airplane tickets to New York. My family would love to have us come visit them."

"I'm not going anywhere. I need to do this. He'll come around eventually. I understand if you want to leave." I pull the truck out on to the dirt road and head toward the west side of the property. I'm trying to picture 102 in my head, but I'm drawing a blank at the moment.

"If you're staying, I'm staying. I can't leave you in crazy town, or should I say crazy ranch?"

"We'll get settled, change out of these clothes and find my sister. I need to get to the bottom of her encrypted note." As I make a turn by the horse track, I see Boone sitting on a short stool in front of a beautiful silky black Thoroughbred horse. He's entranced in whatever he's doing and doesn't see me roll by in the truck. I glance back at him in the mirror. I can't see anything but the side of his face. His shoulders look broader, and he's still wearing the same old dark brown cowboy hat that I remember. That thing must stink more than a pig wallowing in slop. He bought it for our first real date, the one that led to us having sex in the back of his pickup truck. I wore the hat, he wore nothing. It was the first time I'd had sex. I smile at the memory of it and my nether parts warm thinking about it. He was so sweet and gentle for a big gruff guy. Too bad it was the beginning of the end for us.

"You're lost in thought over there. You second-guessing staying here?" Ethan looks worried.

"No." The truck bounces over a pothole. I hold steady and continue over a hill. I see the houses in the distance.

"Wow, those are nice." Ethan whistles. "Which one are we staying in?"

"I don't remember which one it is." I continue driving over the hill until the road splits. There's a small wooden sign with house numbers listed on them.

"It says 102 is that way." Ethan directs me to the right.

I veer in the direction the sign indicates, and the property opens up to a gorgeous blue pasture. There's a ranch-style home with a car parked out front. A small sign on the side of the drive has an arrow with 102 pointing toward the back of the house. I make the sharp turn and follow the drive.

"I remember. There was a cute little cabin back here my sister and I used to come play in as kids. We'd pretend it was our castle."

"Please tell me that's not it." Ethan's mouth hangs open.

It's a rundown wooden shack. The front door is hanging from its hinges, and the one and only window it has is shattered. The roof that's covered in dead leaves and twigs droops in one corner. An abandoned bird's nest is in one of the eaves. In the small gravel drive in front of it, is a rotten old sign that says 102 Whiskey River Road.

"Some castle," Ethan mutters.

I shift the truck's gear into park. "Not exactly how I remember it."

"It looks like someone used it for target practice. There are bullet holes in the wood." He looks like he's ready to run.

"No wonder my old man smiled." I climb out of

Lizzy and reach behind the seat and grab my suitcase.

"We're not seriously staying here, are we?" Ethan gets out and gawks at the shack.

"Think of it like hell week in boot camp. You'll be fine." I pat him on the back and head to the hellhole.

Wildflowers are growing against the walls of the wooden shack. I lift up on the knob of the old red door to keep it from falling all the way off. It creaks and drags, scraping the half-rotten step as I move it out of the way. A musty, damp wood smell fills my nostrils as I step inside.

Ethan flips a light switch. "At least there's electricity." The light on the ceiling flickers but remains on.

"This is not at all like I remember this place. I wonder why Daddy let it get so run down?" I brush a cobweb from my face.

"I don't know, but I think we should stay in town." Ethan brushes his hand on the back of an overstuffed chair that has its innards bulging out, and dust flies into the air. He coughs to clear his throat.

"It's my punishment, and I'm staying. I understand if you don't want to." There's a slight give in the plywood floor as I make my way further into the room.

"Is there more or is this it?" Ethan looks around the small room.

"That's the kitchen." I point to an old wood stove and a sink. "And there's a rickety loft up there." There's a ladder that leads to a small opening.

"Please tell me there's a bathroom?" The look on his face is horrifying.

"There is...it's just out back." I lift both my shoulders.

"This place is a nightmare. Good thing I still have my tent packed. I'm going to set up under a patch of trees I saw next to the cabin."

"You might want to sleep with a gun unless you like being a coyote treat." I'm totally teasing him.

"I'll take my chances with the dogs." He stomps back outside.

I'm determined I'm not going to let my dad run me off. I can fix this place up in no time. He's got a huge shop near the house. I'll borrow his tools, and make this place like I remember it. The first thing I need to do is fix the door and the broken window.

I walk out front and Ethan has already dragged his tent out. "Are you always such a Boy Scout?"

"I bring this with me wherever I go. Good thing,

because from the looks of that loft, there's not room for two." He sets it in a shady spot.

"I'm going to find some tools to fix the door and Visqueen to cover the window. Will you be okay here by yourself?"

"I'll be fine, but don't stay gone too long in case your dear old dad shows up with his shot...rifle again," he corrects himself.

Climbing in the truck, I head in the direction of the four-car garage that is separate from the main house. One side houses all his tools. I take the long way around so that I don't have to drive by Boone again. I'm not ready to face him. I may even have to skip out on dinner if he's going to be there.

I pull up, and Bear is parking his ATV. He heads my direction as soon as he lays eyes on me. "I thought I'd catch up with you at the house." He slams into me with a hug.

"I didn't get a warm welcome." I laugh.

"Well, what did you expect? You've been gone a long time." He holds me at arm's length to get a good look at me like Momma did.

"You've grown up." I tug at his beard.

"Yeah, a lot has changed since you've been gone."

"Did any one woman ever catch that big heart of yours?"

His brows scrunch together. "That will never happen." He mutters something under his breath that I can't make out as he walks beside me as I go into the shop. "What are you needing in our father's precious shop? He's one person that hasn't changed a bit except for being grumpier every year. He'd tan your hide for being in here."

"I think I'm beyond the years of hide tanning." I use air quotes. "I need tools to fix a door and something to cover a broken window."

"That truck of yours needs more than a Band-Aid."

"You leave Lizzy out of this." I playfully swat his arm. "It's for the shack he put me in."

"Oh, shit. Did he send you to 102?"

I nod. "What happened to it?"

"He knew you loved that little place, so he refused to keep it up. I think he and Boone used it for target practice a few times."

I open a drawer and find a small tool set with everything I'll need for the door. Bear grabs duct tape and plastic sheeting.

"You wouldn't happen to know where Ellie is?"

"She lives in the house in front of your little

rundown shack." He runs his hand over his beard. "She's not the sweet, innocent girl you remember."

I scowl at him. "What do you mean?"

"You'll see."

"What's going on around here? She sent me a letter saying things weren't good, but she wasn't specific."

"You know I'm not one to be in anybody else's business, never have been. The only thing I can tell you is that Dad had a heart attack a few months back."

"She never mentioned it. She did say his health wasn't the best."

"Yeah, Momma has him eating fruits and veggies." He laughs. "I hear him cussing from the other side of the house that he's a steak and potato man and that's what he expects for dinner, along with his glass of whiskey."

"You're right. He hasn't changed. How is Wyatt?"

"Still has a big old stink bug up his ass. He thinks he's better than all of us since he's become a lawyer."

"That's right. When I left here, he was taking the bar exam. What about you? What are you doing?"

"I've pissed our father off by becoming a grease

monkey. I'm part owner of a garage, and I have my own band."

"Get out of town!" I push his shoulder. "You aren't working with the racehorses?"

"The horses have never been my thing."

"Wait, Dad lets you live here and not work for him?"

"I don't live here, but I manage the cattle. Dad needed help after his heart attack, so I promised Mom I'd handle them."

"Where do you live?"

"I have a small apartment over the garage." He walks me out to my truck. "Did you run into Boone yet?" My door hinges squeak when he opens it.

"I saw him at the track working on a horse's hoof, but he didn't see me."

"He's going to shit when he gets a load of those fawn-colored eyes of yours." He tweaks my nose like he did when we were kids. "You look good, Clem."

"Does he really have dinner at the main house every night?"

"I don't know about every night, but he's bringing his gal friend with him tonight."

"That's good. I'm glad he's moved on." If that's true, then why did I feel a small twinge of jealousy? I have no right to feel anything for the man I walked out on seven years ago. "I brought my best friend with me. If you're going to dinner, you can meet him then."

"This sounds like it's shaping up to be something I don't want to miss." He kisses my cheek. "I'm glad you're home, Clem."

"I think you're the only one that feels that way."

"Let me know if you need any help at 102." He slaps the top of my truck.

"I'm sure I will."

CHAPTER THREE
CLEM

When I make it back to the cottage, Ethan's tent is up, and the flap is wide open, but he's not inside. I grab the toolbox and the Visqueen from the bench seat of the truck and place them down underneath the broken window. I hear voices coming from inside. Through the cracked glass, I see Ellie.

The door makes a terrible scraping noise when I open it. Ellie and Ethan both stare at me as if I've interrupted something. Ethan looks a little guilty—like he was caught with his hand in the proverbial cookie jar.

"Clem!" Ellie rushes over to me. "I'm so glad you came home."

I hug her, then take a step back to check out the

woman standing in front of me. She's not at all the girl I remember. She was always on the pudgy side. The woman before me is thin, with curves and jugs that she never had before. Her hair is dyed from its mousey blonde to bright, golden strands of curls. Her eyes even look a shade darker green.

"Gawd, I've missed you."

She twirls a piece of my chestnut hair between her fingers. "You haven't changed a bit, just a tad older."

Ethan clears his throat. "Ellie was telling me that she lives in the house on the front of the property."

"That's what Bear told me. I'm surprised you don't live in one of the fancier houses closer to Mom and Dad."

"I like it back here. More privacy." She winks at Ethan, and I squint at him.

"This place is a disaster." I gaze around the room.

"Yeah, Daddy took his aggression out on this place, but I'm sure you'll have it fixed up in no time."

"Speaking of which, I took some of his tools. I need to get the door fixed and return them before he discovers they're missing."

"Dinner's at six at the main house. We'll catch up then. I've got to review the books for the week," she says, tossing a piece of hair over my shoulder.

"You handle the books?"

"While you were gone doing gawd knows what, I became an accountant. I handle all of the numbers for the ranch and the racehorses." She waves her hand in the air.

I'm on her heels as she heads for the door. "That's not something I ever pictured you doing."

"It has its benefits." She winks at Ethan again before she walks to her house.

I turn around, and Ethan is staring at her ass. I grab him by the ear and drag him inside.

"Ouch! What was that for?"

I let him go, and he rubs the side of his head. "I leave you alone for a minute, and you're ogling my sister's backside!"

"First of all, you were gone longer than that. Second, she came over and started hitting on me. Third, why didn't you tell me your sister was hot!"

I smack him in the stomach. "You keep your rocket away from her."

He snorts. "I'm sure your sister can handle herself."

"Just control your boy toy and help me fix the door."

I open the toolbox, and he holds the door in

place. "I never knew you were so handy or had such a potty mouth." He grins.

"My father expected us girls to be able to do anything his boys could do. I've been the one that's kept Lizzy running all these years. I can change the plugs, oil, and repair the engine. And, as far as my mouth goes, I sometimes have a hard time keeping the words in my head from slipping out of it."

He laughs. "I like this side of you. But evidently, that skill doesn't apply to anything beyond the engine. The outside is a piece of shit."

"Shhhh, Lizzy will hear you." I lower my voice like the truck has ears.

"Are you seriously going to stay here?"

"Yes, and I'm going to rebuild this place, and you're going to help me."

"I wasn't planning on sticking around all summer, but since you have such a cute neighbor, I think I will."

"You're an ass."

"That may be, but I'm the only one around here right now that has your six, so I think you should be nice to me."

He has a point. He's my only ally. We get the door hanging straight, and it doesn't drag on the ground. His phone vibrates, and he walks out of earshot. I roll out the Visqueen and cut off strips of duct tape long enough to secure it in place.

I step back and look. "That'll have to do until I can replace the glass." I go inside and take out my laptop to check the Wi-Fi and find there isn't any. I'll have to see if I can log in to Ellie's so that I can work. My plan is to start up my own cybersecurity business. I already have tons of leads from my commander. I could've taken a high-paying position with an established company, but I wanted to do it on my own time so that I could come back here.

I open a narrow closet by the front door and find a ragged-looking broom with the old straw bristles barely hanging on. "It will work for now." I take the scrunchie off my wrist and knot my hair into a messy bun. I have the uneven floor swept by the time Ethan comes back inside.

"Everything okay?"

"Yeah. It was my mom wanting to know when I was coming home for a visit."

"What did you tell her?"

"I told her I was staying here for the summer and maybe I could fly home one weekend for a visit."

"I don't know, you being a city boy, I'm not sure you'll make it here all summer, especially in that tent."

"I think the army took the city right out of me. I've learned to adjust to a lot of things." He walks around the small area, looking around. "Do you think there's a shower in here?"

"It's out back by the outhouse."

"Did you say outdoor shower? Jesus, it's bad enough the bathroom's outside."

"Yes, Mister I've Learned to Adjust," I mock him.

"Fine. I'm going to get cleaned up for dinner."

"Ah, dinner, that should be fun." I roll my eyes.

"I'm sure your dad is not going to make it easy on you."

"That's only the short of it. Boone is bringing his girlfriend tonight."

"That's a good thing, right? That means he's moved on."

"Yeah, good thing." I wave him off and hide the tiny bit of excitement I feel about being at the same table with Boone.

I know I'm the one that left, but there's still unfinished business between the two of us. Things that we've never worked through and one of the biggest reasons I left town.

Instead of showering, I fill the small sink with

water and wash my face. I pull on a pair of skinny white jeans and a pink blouse before Ethan makes it back. He looks hot! He has on a pair of blue jeans and a gray button-down with a pair of loafers. He's really good-looking, and I'd be lucky to have him, but he's never stirred my heart. I've always believed love is something that actually makes your heart beat faster when you're around the person you love. Lust, now that's an entirely different beast, yet I've never been able to separate the two. Probably silly for me to think that way, but it's the little girl in me that's still alive and believes in fairy tales. I thought Boone hung the moon, but I let fear and doubt consume me. I just wasn't ready.

I hear heavy boots outside the door and a firm knock. "Clem, you in there?" I open the door to Wyatt. He's tall and handsome. His black hair has a slight tinge of gray around his temples. He's got Daddy's silver eyes with a hint of blue in them. He's clean-shaven, and his dimple in his chin is more defined than I recall. "I heard you were back." He doesn't try to embrace me like Bear and Ellie did when he steps inside.

"I am. This is Ethan. Ethan, this is Wyatt, the oldest of the Calhoun siblings."

He shakes Ethan's hand. "You come back and

bring your boyfriend? I say boyfriend because I don't see a ring on your finger."

I don't correct him. "How are you? I heard you're a full-fledged attorney."

"I am and have been for several years now." He walks around, looking at the place.

"Is there a Mrs. Wyatt Calhoun?"

He brushes down his long white sleeves and toys with his expensive watch. "There's been no time for that. This place alone keeps me busy."

"Oh, really. I can't imagine why a horse and cattle ranch would keep an attorney occupied."

"You've no idea. Did you come back to help Boone train the Thoroughbred for the derbies?"

"No. I came back here to make amends with my family."

"Don't start thinking you're going to be written back in the will because you've finally decided to be a Calhoun again." He leans against the wall and crosses one ankle over the other.

"I wasn't aware that I ever quit being a Calhoun, but as far as a will goes, I don't care about the money." *Dickhead.*

"I don't think there's much here you do care about. This land, the horses, the cattle, this is what Calhouns are." He pushes off the wall.

"Wow! Arrogant much?" Ethan closes the distance between the two of us and bows out his chest. Ethan may not be as big as Wyatt, but his time in the military taught him how to fight.

I step in between them. "I'm part of this family whether you like it or not." I launch a rapid gunfire of eye daggers at him. There's not one lick of emotion on his face.

"We'll see about that. Calhouns don't run away. We face our problems head-on."

I hear Ethan's jaw tense behind me. I reach back and grab his hand. "We'll see you at dinner." Pride has me sticking my chin in the air. But I can't resist the urge to put him in his place. "You're living proof that some people never change."

He steps up close to me. "How's that Clementine?" He spats the last part of my name.

"Once a dick, always a dick." I shrug one shoulder.

He chuckles, takes a step back, and plasters on a fake smile. "I see that sailor mouth of yours hasn't changed a bit." He mock-salutes me before he swaggers out, cocky as ever.

"What an ass." Ethan paces the squeaky floor.

"I couldn't agree more, but he has every right to be angry with me. I deserted all of them."

"You did what you had to do, and now you've come back to apologize. He needs to pull the stick out of his ass and give you a chance."

I giggle thinking about Bear calling it a stink bug. "Unfortunately, he and Daddy share that same problem. Their balls have to be bigger than everyone else's. Come on, let's forget about him for now. I want to show you around. First stop is the stables. Have you ever ridden a horse?"

"Never."

"Let's start with introducing you to one." I take him by the hand, dragging him outside. I see him glance in the direction of Ellie's house before he ducks his head to get in the truck.

"She's not your type."

"How do you know?"

The engine ticks a few times before it comes to life. "City boy, country girl."

"They make movies about that sort of thing." He laughs.

"She's sweet and innocent, and I've seen your wild ways."

"You've been gone awhile. I don't think she's as sweet and innocent as you recall."

"You just hush up about my sister." I scowl and speed by her house, sending a layer of dust in the air.

I ride the bumps hard until we make it to the stables. It's part of the old barn that's been remodeled, so that outside still looks like an old fashion barn.

I pull up next to the tall double doors, with rough wooden walls and park Lizzy.

"Wow, this is a lot bigger than I imagined." Ethan follows me inside. There are hooks by the door that hold the bridles, leads, and halters for the horses that are too old to race. In the corner, right where I remember them, is the shovel and the pitch-fork. Daddy used to make all us kids take turns cleaning out the stalls. There are eight regular-size stalls and one large one, that would typically house the prize horse running in the derbies. Opening the simple latch on one of the empty stalls, I step inside. Straw is scattered across the floor. There's a water bucket, a feed trough, and a salt lick block that's been worn to its grooves.

"It smells like horse shit in here." Ethan is fanning is hand in front of his nose.

"What did you expect it to smell like?" I giggle.

"I don't know, as nice as this place is, I figured even the horses' shit wouldn't stink."

"It doesn't work that way." I full out laugh at him this time. "Come on." I drag him from that stall to another one that has a beautiful Spanish Mustang lying down inside. "I know you. You were just a baby when I left here." I squat beside him and nuzzle his nose and feel the dry, hairy tickle of the horse's lips against my cheek.

I turn to see Ethan watching me. "You let him kiss you?" He scrunches up his nose.

"Come here, silly." I wave him over.

He slowly kneels beside me.

"Hold your hand out, like this." I show him.

He widens his fingers and pats the horse's head. The horse shakes his head, flipping its mane from side to side.

"He likes you."

He scoots closer and scratches him between the ears. I see him inhale, breathing in the scent of the horse and the straw. "Do you ever get used to the smell?"

"What smell?" I tease.

A beam of sunlight comes through the sliding window in the stall, and it paints the horse's coat a bright chocolate color. "He's beautiful," I mewl and nuzzle him again.

Heavy boots thumping the floor have both of us on our feet.

CHAPTER FOUR
CLEM

"Who the hell left the stable doors open?" My dad's turbulent bark vibrates the windows, and the mustang stands tall and beautiful. His boots stop stomping when he sees me and Ethan in the stall.

"Figures it was you." He swipes his hat off and scratches his silver mustache. "You'd think as many times as I howled at you as a kid, you'd shut the damn doors."

Ethan almost pushes me over when he moves by me, rushing to the doors.

"Sorry. I guess I forgot. I was so excited to show Ethan the horses. He's from New York and has never ridden one. Of course, you wouldn't know where he was from because you hadn't met him before today..."

"Just quit yammering!" he snarls.

Why do I let him make me so nervous and revert back to my teenage self? He's never been one I could talk to easily. I take in a deep breath, corralling my tongue. "You don't have to be nice to me, but you could try to be a little friendlier to Ethan."

"I'm not friendly to anyone. What makes him so damn special?" He swats the dust from his jeans. "I've got too much work to do around here to be making things pleasant for *your* friend."

Ethan returns to my side and stands with his arm touching mine. "It's my fault, sir. I was the last one through the door."

"Was it your fault too that she ran away seven years ago?" He points at Ethan.

I know he's just being an ass, but Ethan doesn't. "I had nothing to do with that." He raises his hands in defense.

"He knows that. He's trying to intimidate you." I cross my arms over my chest.

Ethan leans in close to me. "It's working," he whispers.

"Good. Maybe you'll be so scared you'll take

your scrawny ass out of here and take her with you."
He changes the direction that he's pointing to me.

"Neither one of us are leaving, and we aren't afraid of you." I jut out my chin and refrain from calling him a name like Wyatt. Oh, it's on the tip of my tongue all right, but it wouldn't help in trying to win him over.

"Speak for yourself," Ethan whispers again. "He aimed a rifle at me."

"I see your boyfriend has a pair of balls." Daddy tilts his head at Ethan and grins.

"Could we leave my balls out of this, sir." He covers his crotch.

"You aren't sticking around, so there's no reason for you to be in the barn."

"We're staying. I'm going to remodel 102 and start my company."

"Bullshit! If you plan on staying on this property, you'll work for me. No freeloaders live here."

"Fine! I'll help train the horses."

"You'll muck the fucking stalls, that's what you'll do." He walks over and picks up the shovel.

"I know good and well you have hired hands that do it. Why wouldn't you use me where my talent lies?" Why's it okay for the men in this family to curse, but I'm supposed to "talk like a lady"? Momma's voice still blares in my ears.

"Talent!" he huffs. "Have you even touched a horse since you ran away?"

"Well, no."

"Then it's yet to be seen that you have any talent left in you." His face is angrier than a hornet in a Coke can.

I bravely step up next to him, yanking the shovel from his hand. "I'll muck the stalls, but in my spare time, I want to train the horses."

He brushes by me. "Fine by me, but you'll have to convince Boone to let you anywhere near his prized Thoroughbred. I don't think he'll let you within ten feet of *him*, much less his horses."

"Huh! We'll see about that!" I know he's probably right, but I don't want to give him the satisfaction of giving in so easily.

"Oh, he was being sarcastic, right? I have balls." Ethan looks at his crotch.

"Ethan!" I yell and press my hand to my temple. "Yes, he was being sarcastic. Now can we get the stalls cleaned out."

"There was no *we* when *you* volunteered to clean the stalls. I'll help you rebuild the little shit shack, and clean up the yard around it, but I...let me repeat...I am not cleaning up horse shit." He storms out of the stable.

"No, but you'll be walking yourself back to the cottage!" I holler after him. Not a great comeback, I know. Daddy has me so flustered I can't even think of anything saucy to say.

"I can give your boyfriend a ride back," Bear says as he strides into the stables.

"He's not my boyfriend, and it won't kill him to walk." I scoop up a pile of straw with the muck, cursing under my breath.

"You might want to change out of that fancy blouse of yours before you start cleaning up." He leans against one of the stalls.

"You're enjoying this, aren't you?" I wipe the sweat that's formed on my brow.

"Who do you think was the black sheep while you were gone? Me!" He pushes off the gate. "It will be nice for our father to have someone else to abuse for a change."

"Thanks for that. Thanks for wanting it to be me," I say sarcastically and realize I sound like my father.

"Look, Sis. You know he'll come around sooner or later. Your real issue is going to be facing Boone." He glances at his watch. "And if you want to have time to get cleaned up before dinner, you better get to work." He walks over to a hook on the wall and takes down a dingy t-shirt, tossing it to me. "You might want to put this on." He starts whistling a happy tune and walks out of the stable.

"First thing I need to do is buy me a pair of work boots," I mutter to myself, digging the shovel into the manure and tossing it into a wheel barrel. "For fuck's sake, how did I go from being a respected person in the military to digging up horse shit?" *Because you deserve it for the things you've done*, the voice inside my head says.

"That's not true. Yes, leaving Boone at the altar with no explanation was not my finest hour, yet I don't regret anything but hurting him, and my family. I found out who I was and what I was made of by joining the army. I'm glad I didn't get married so young."

"Who are you talking to?" Ellie, who came in without me hearing her over my self-banter, laughs and leans on a sawhorse that has a plaid wool blanket draped over it.

I put down the shovel and walk over to her. "Nobody. I just had a run-in with Daddy."

"Did you expect anything less?" She brushes a lock of hair out of my face.

"I envisioned my family taking me back with open arms. Isn't that what families are supposed to do?"

"You're a Calhoun. Really, that's what you thought would happen?" She snickers.

"He never let me explain. He took Boone's side."

"The man was broken-hearted, left at the altar."

"He's my father." I prop a hand on my hip.

"Look, I know the reasons why you left, but you still deserted all of us. It wasn't only Boone. Daddy was pissed."

"I know, I know, you're right. I have to atone for my sins, as Momma would say." I can't go back to confessional. I was banned when I was caught being a little naughty in the booth. Back then, I had no control over my body. It wasn't my fault that the priest looked like a god that fell from heaven. I was a horny teenage girl. What did they expect?

"You've been here what, a minute? I think you're expecting too much." She stands. "Now tell me about Ethan. You two aren't together, are you?"

"No. Why?"

"He looks like that type of guy I could have some fun with." She wiggles her eyebrows.

"What do you mean fun?"

"You know...a little roll in the hay."

My mouth gapes. "Oh, my gawd, I can't believe you said that!"

"Don't play all innocent with me. I know your dirty mind. Gawd, the things you used to say. What other fun things do you think there is to do around this place anyway?" She snorts and heads for the door.

"I don't talk like that anymore," I shout after her. I didn't say I didn't think them. I'm left standing by myself, wondering what all I've missed. I hear my mom's voice coming from outside. I recognize her singing. Only two times I recall her singing. One was at bedtime to help me fall asleep when I was a young girl. The other was when she'd be feeding the chickens.

I walk to the opposite end of the barn from where I came in and go out the small narrow door that leads to the chicken castle. Dad and Bear built it for her. It's a two-story chicken pen made from an old oak tree that needed to be taken down. Daddy sanded, and Bear painted on the protective coating. Its barn red with white accents.

As I walk closer, a chicken preens as it makes a fluttery ruffling noise with its feathers. Momma stops singing to see what spooked the chicken.

She puts down the bucket of feed and hugs me.

"I know your daddy was rough on you, but I'm glad you're home."

"Me too, Momma."

She steps back and laughs. "Girl, you're a mess. Supper is soon. You might want to get cleaned up, and not come in smelling like horse manure."

"Do you think you could sneak me in the house to get a shower?"

"You bet I can. Your daddy has a whiskey in his office with Boone, and Wyatt before dinner. You come to the screen door in the back, and I'll let you inside."

"That would be awesome. I better go finish up in the stables." I turn to walk away and stop. "What about Bear?"

"What about Bear?" She throws seed to the chickens.

"You said he has a drink with Boone and Wyatt?"

"Bear and Chet don't get along well enough to drink together. He thinks Bear has too many silly notions to be part of his circle. Bear joins me in the kitchen for a glass of wine. I love listening to all his ideas." She smiles like she's been getting away with something.

Bear's right; he has been the black sheep. I

stand tall and walk back into the barn. "I'll be the black sheep, so he doesn't have to be," I whisper to myself.

I'm thankful that Boone didn't bring his horse back before I finished up. I need to face him, but knee-deep in horse shit is not how I want it to be. I have no grand ideas for the two of us. He's obviously over me, and I've grown up. I've had my libido under control for years now. I'm sure he's as gorgeous as ever, but I'm not led by my desires anymore. I've learned to leash that baby in. Hopping in Lizzy, I head back to the shack. Ethan isn't in his tent nor inside. Before I go change, I open up my laptop and make notes on what all I need to order to fix this place up. I connect with my hotspot from my phone and order a pair of work boots and overalls to be express delivered.

I'll have to get up early and work in the stables before anyone else is up. Then I'll be able to put in a few hours of work around here. I know Boone's routine, if it hasn't changed, is to train the horses late in the afternoon. I'll have to put off starting my company until this place is whipped into shape.

I grab a change of clothes and some makeup to take with me. I'm nervous about seeing Boone but more worried about what he thinks of me.

"Clem, you in here?" Ethan comes barreling through the door.

"Yeah. Where have you been?"

He gives a cheeky smile. "I'll never tell."

"Didn't I tell you to keep your bits away from my sister?" I place my hand on my hip.

"Your sister is a grown woman and can make her own choices."

I raise my palm to him. "I don't want to hear it. I'm going to get a shower."

"The hot water in the shower out back doesn't work. I froze my balls off."

"Maybe that's where you left them," I say under my breath. "I'm going to the main house for a shower. I'll meet you there at six."

"I might pass on dinner and order something in."

"Please, I need you there. I could really use the support."

"Okay, but if your dad pulls out any weapons, I'm out of there."

"If you want, I'll drive back and get you."

"I think I can get a ride." He's all smiles again.

I drive Lizzy up to the barn and park behind it. I don't want them to see me pull up to the house or hear the gawd-awful noise that Lizzy makes. I feel like a teenager sneaking out of the house all those times I did with Boone. Whoever thought I'd be sneaking in the house at nearly thirty years old.

I place my hand lightly against the screen door and push my face close to it, looking inside. "Momma," I whisper.

She wipes her hands on her apron then unlatches the screen door. "They just went into the office." Her voice is low. "Use the back stairs."

I run up them, knowing they'll creak. I strip out of my clothes and climb in the stream of warm water. I take extra time making sure to get all the manure smells off me. I towel dry my long hair and brush it out. Swiping on a thin layer of makeup, I apply a little peach color to my cheeks and gloss to my lips.

My floral silky sundress rests off one shoulder, and my navy sandals match perfectly with the colors in the dress. I fish-braid my hair in the direction of my bare shoulder and lay it flat against it. Dressing like a woman is one thing I missed in the military. I love getting all dolled up in a dress. It's one of the few times I feel pretty. Lord knows around here jeans and boots are much more practical. Sunday church was about the only time I got to wear a dress and act like the lady my momma wanted me to be. Other than the times I'd sneak out with Boone.

Smacking my lips together one last time, I stuff

my dirty clothes in a bag and think momentarily about burning them rather than washing them. I tiptoe down the stairs and hear a child's voice. Momma and Bear are tipping their wineglasses together. There's a little girl with long pigtails and freckles on the bridge of her nose, standing on a stool, eating a cookie.

"Peanut butter cookies are my favorite." She takes a big bite, and crumbs fall on the counter.

I watch for a minute, taking it all in. Bear's black curls are damp at his neck along with the end of his beard. His deep green eyes match the color of the girls, and I swear she has the same lopsided grin as him.

"All clean?" Momma asks when she sees my gaze glued to the little girl.

Bear steps over and takes my hand. "I'd like you to meet, Missy, my daughter."

I look at her then back at him. "You have a daughter?"

Missy holds her hand out. "It's nice to meet you."

"This is your aunt Clem." Bear smiles at her.

"Aunt Clem," she repeats in the sweetest voice.

"It's nice to meet you too." I shake her hand.

"Daddy says he's glad you're finally home." She resumes eating her cookie.

I pull him out of earshot. "You have a daughter? Why didn't Ellie tell me?"

He shrugs one shoulder. "Maybe she didn't think it was her place to tell you everything around here."

"How old is she?"

"Six."

"You're married?"

"Was. She left right after Missy was born."

"Left? What do you mean left?"

"I would think of all people, you'd understand the meaning." He half chuckles.

I swat him in the arm. "Tell me what happened."

"She was a girl I met in a bar. We got drunk one night, and she got pregnant. When she told me she was having my baby, we got hitched." He says it all very quietly so Missy won't hear him.

"Then what happened?"

"She liked her drugs more than she liked being a momma or a wife, so she left."

I turn to look at her sweet face. "And you've raised her on your own?"

"For the most part, yeah. Mom helped a lot when she was a baby."

"She lives with you?"

"Where else would she live?" He laughs. "I drop her off at school in the morning, come here, get my job done, then go to work at the shop. The guys there adore her, so she hangs out in the garage with me after school. I have to admit, it is a lot easier now that she's in kindergarten."

I hug him. "I'm sorry I've missed out on being here for you and getting to know her."

"You're here now."

"How is Daddy with her?"

"She has him wrapped around her sweet little finger."

Daddy and Boone's voice coming down the hall breaks the moment between us.

CHAPTER FIVE
CLEM

"There's my princess." Daddy's usual deep gruff voice is soft. Missy turns around and jumps into his arms. His gaze lands on me as he kisses the top of her head. Those eyes that were adoring his granddaughter only milliseconds ago have formed deep creases around them, and his eye daggers are much more painful than mine.

"Grandpa! I've missed you." She squeezes his neck.

Boone is looking over his shoulder when he walks into the kitchen. He damn near runs into the bar top when his head swings in my direction.

"Clem, I heard you were back in town." He draws out my name. He turns to my dad. "Why didn't you tell me she was coming for dinner?" It sounds like his voice came from low in his throat.

"I was hoping she wouldn't show up," my dad hisses.

"Grandpa, you don't like Aunt Clem?" Missy tilts her nose in the air.

Bear intervenes. "Let's go get you washed up for dinner." He takes her out of my dad's arms.

All the while, I've stood staring at Boone. I want to say something, but the words are frozen in my throat. The guy standing on the other side of the island bar is no longer the young man I remember. Holy freaking smokes he's hot! Like GQ for sexy cowboys hot! I'm totally screwed. I press my thighs together to stop the low hum. I've been around hot, sweaty, horny men everywhere I've been stationed, and none of them caused my body to ache with a need that's burning in my belly.

His black hair is styled short all over with a beard that's trimmed close to his face. And that mustache. Jiminy Cricket, it makes his mouth look lustful. Not to mention his eyes that look like rain on a stormy day. A storm my suddenly famished libido wants to be blown away by.

"Boo...Boone." A stammer leaps nervously in my throat.

I watch as his jaw flexes a few times His brows merge into a savage line with not a hint of a smile. His hand raises into a fist and lightly taps the countertop a few times. "I'll be back in a few." He gazes down, then glances back up at me with his lips in a flat line. He walks out, and I've yet to say anything other than his name.

"Well played," my dad says sarcastically with a grin that turns to a smirk.

Ethan's knock on the screen door has my mom opening it for him and welcoming him inside. He joins me at the island. I must have a dazed expression. "What did I miss?" Ethan says, looking between me and my dad.

"Your girlfriend shows up for dinner and is suddenly at a loss for words when she sees her ex-fiancée." Daddy has sparks blazing in his eyes.

"That's enough." Momma steps up beside me. "You act like she's not your daughter."

"The daughter that I raised wouldn't have turned her back on her family," he all but growls.

I'm shocked when Momma stands up to him. "Well, the daughter I raised is a strong, independent woman who had some choices to make for her own life." Her nose points upward at him with a bold fierceness that I don't recall her having before.

Go, Momma! I cheer inwardly that someone is on my side.

"And those selfish choices hurt this family."

Leave it to Daddy to bring me down a few notches. Momma's mouth opens to say something, and I touch her arm to stop her. "You're right. I'm willing to say I'm sorry a million times. Every day if I have to. Will you ever forgive me?"

"Time will tell if you're really sorry." He storms out of the kitchen.

Momma grabs white plates from the hutch. "You two help me set the table."

"This was a bad idea. We should go." I want to tuck my tail between my legs.

"Don't you dare let him run you off! You ran scared the first time because you were afraid to tell him how you felt." She hands me the dishes. "Don't make a liar out of me about that strong, independent woman I was yammering on about to your daddy."

"You're right, Momma. I'm a Calhoun, and I belong here." I take the dishes and straighten my spine before I walk into the dining room. The long oak table has been in our family for years. It seats up to fifteen people, and I remember it being full of guests most of my life. I place the plates, one at each chair and Ethan walks behind me, setting down the silverware.

"This should be an interesting evening. Maybe we should have like a safe word for us to make our exit."

"That's probably not a bad idea."

He snaps. "How about Jumanji?" He laughs. "Welcome to the jungle."

His humor lightens my mood. "How are we supposed to work Jumanji into a sentence?" I giggle.

Before he can answer me, my dad walks in and sits at the head of the table. He unfolds his napkin, placing it in his lap. He doesn't say a word, only watches me finish setting the table. Ellie bounces into the room and gives Daddy a quick kiss on the cheek. She takes a seat two down from him. Next are Wyatt and Bear with Missy. Wyatt's look is icy, but Bear's is warming. I think he feels sorry for me.

"Can I sit beside Aunt Clem?" Missy wiggles free of Bear's hand and snuggles up to me.

"Sure you can." I smile at her and run my hand down the length of her hair. Bear pulls out a chair for her to sit.

I walk back into the kitchen to help Momma carry in the platters of food. The homemade fried chicken smells heavenly. I haven't had it since the day I left home. Ethan carries out the mashed potatoes and biscuits, and Momma grabs a few more trays. When we return to the dining room, Boone and a buxom blonde are sitting on the opposite side from Missy. I feel Boone looking at me as I move around the table and take a seat next to my niece. Ethan sits by me, and Momma takes the chair next to King Calhoun.

Everyone joins hands as Daddy says grace. I peek open one eye to see Boone's dark, stormy eyes boring into me. His blonde girlfriend has her head lying on his broad shoulder. My gaze travels from his face to his bicep that is stretching the gray t-shirt he's wearing.

Keep it together, girl. Sweet fucking Sally. Those eyes turn on all my pleasure switches.

"Amen," Daddy says, and everyone repeats.

I need to say an extra Hail Mary for my dirty thoughts.

The food starts being passed around as soon as the amens come out. "I think there are a few introductions that need to be made at this table." Wyatt clears his throat. "Margret"—he nudges his head in the direction of the busty blonde hanging onto Boone —"this is our wayward sister. The one that left Boone at the altar." I want to slap the smugness right off his face.

"Wyatt, shut the hell up." My mom points her fork at him, and I burst out laughing at her reaction. "You have no business speaking ill of anyone."

He glares at her.

"Don't look at me like you don't understand what I'm saying. I'm speaking idiot so you should have no problem with my meaning."

Damn! Where did Momma learn to talk like that?

He yanks his napkin from the table and tucks it under his chin.

"I, for one, am glad you left him at the altar. If not for you leaving him, he and I wouldn't be getting married." Her country twang is annoying, and so is the flip of her hair.

"Congratulations." I'm not sure what else to say other than to introduce the man sitting next to me, snorting. "This is my friend Ethan. He's from New York. We met in the army, and he's going to be staying at the cottage with me for the summer and helping me rebuild it." I'm rambling.

"What are you going to be doing for me if you're living on my property, boy?" Dad asks between bites of his food.

"I...um..."

"I've already informed your girlfriend that there're no freeloaders here."

Boone's gaze darts to Ethan like he wants to kill him. I don't correct him. Maybe it's better he thinks we're together.

"I could use help with the cattle," Bear chimes in.

"I don't know anything about cattle," Ethan says apologetically with a shrug.

"Figures," Dad mumbles and Momma's eyes throw daggers with daddy's name all over them in his direction.

"Can you ride a four-wheeler?" Bear butters a biscuit for his daughter.

"That I can do. I rode them in the army."

"Then you can help me with the cattle." Bear winks at me.

"I hear you're shoveling horse shit," Wyatt says, never looking up from his plate.

He must've gotten a degree in *dickology* along with his law degree. I ignore his snideness, at least outwardly. "I'd like to train the racehorses." I decide to be brave and put it out there.

"Would you now?" Boone crumples his napkin on the table.

"Yes. I'm sure I'm still good at it. I was a natural. You said so yourself." I keep a stiff upper lip.

"I'm not so sure that's a good idea." He looks over at Margret.

"Oh, I'm fine with it, sweetie. I'm not one bit worried. You've told me how much you dislike her," she adds and plasters on a fake smile over her painted-on, glossy lips.

"I think you should be worried." Ellie snickers.

"And why is that, pray tell?" Margret picks up her glass of tea, holding her pinky finger out.

"Because you ain't his type, and I remember how much Boone loved my sister." All our heads whip around to look at Ellie.

"This coming from a woman who can't keep her legs closed to any man wearing a pair of tight jeans." Margret's words are sharp as razors.

I reach over and cover Missy's ears. "I think we should remember there's a child in the room."

Missy shouts, "I've heard much worse!" She bites into her biscuit and honey drips out the side.

"Have ya'll seen the movie Jumanji?" Dead silence fills the room. "You know, the one with Dwayne Johnson and Kevin Hart?" Ethan is leaning close to me.

"Not now," I whisper between still lips. "I don't

think anyone here would be interested." I lightly slap his thigh under the table.

"I love that movie." Missy giggles. "The Rock is so handsome." She places her elbows on the table and rests her head on her hands. Her eyes look sparkly like a girl with a serious crush.

"Maybe we should tame the conversation a bit." Bear points to Missy.

"He's right. Can't we have one meal where someone doesn't end up leaving the table angry?" Momma clinks her glass with a fork.

"I didn't realize that roasting someone was a family ritual," Ethan says softly in my ear.

"Evidently I've missed a lot."

"I don't think I want you around the prized Thoroughbred. He'll be racing in the Kentucky Derby in May. He needs consistency, and you can't provide that." Boone's fork rakes across his perfectly straight teeth as he pulls it out of his mouth.

I remember running my tongue across those gorgeous teeth and everywhere else in between. *Focus, focus.* "I'm not going anywhere." I lift a shoulder.

"That's yet to be seen." My dad can't resist the digs.

"I've already told you I'll be remodeling the

cottage, so I'm not leaving."

"Where do you plan on getting the money?" Dad snarls.

"I've saved up some. I'll just have to do a little at a time. I think the leaking roof and bullet holes in the walls will be a priority, along with the shattered window."

"There is some tin we took off a barn outside of 108. The barn was crap, but the tin is in decent shape. I'm sure there's enough for you to replace the roof on the cottage," Bear offers. "I'll help."

"That would be great. Ethan and I can load it in the truck."

"What if I was going to sell the tin?" My dad has his fork halfway to his mouth.

"You were going to donate it," Ellie says, then turns her body in my direction. "There are a lot of things lying around here you could use and save a ton of money."

"Thanks." I smile at her, grateful for her help.

"You fix that shack up, and I'm going to sell it," Daddy grumbles.

"You will do no such thing," Momma huffs. "You'd never let an outsider own any piece of this land."

She's right. I think back years ago when one of

the neighbors wanted to expand his property. He offered a ton of money for a few acres, and Daddy was adamant about not selling one single blade of grass.

The rest of dinner is eerily quiet. Lots of glares and frowns are shared, but not any more words. One by one, they take their dishes to the kitchen. Standing in front of the sink, I see Boone and Margret having words out by her car. I wish I could hear what's being said, but the window is too thick. Momma steps up beside me and takes the dishrag from my hand, handing me a drying towel instead.

"Have they been together long?"

"Going on a year."

"Does he really love her?"

"I think he cares for her, but Boone only had one love of his life." She bumps her hip into mine.

Boone kisses Margret on the cheek before she gets in the car and drives off.

"Funny," Mom says.

"What?"

"She always stays after dinner, and they take a walk together." She's got a glimmer in her eye.

"I'll be right back." I lay the towel down and run out the screen door and down the steps. Boone is holding his hat in his hand, watching her leave.

"Hey," I say when I'm beside him. "I know you and I have some unfinished business—"

He cuts me off when he puts his hat on and walks away.

"Boone, please wait!" I run after him. "You're going to have to talk to me sooner or later. I'm not leaving."

"That's one thing you are good at." He keeps his pace.

I stop him by placing my hand on his elbow. "I'm sorry. I shouldn't have left the way I did. If I could change it, I would."

He looks at me square in the face. "We'd be married?"

"I...I..."

When I can't give him a quick answer, he starts marching off again.

"Please let me train one horse, just one." I hold a single finger in the air.

His head shakes from side to side as he keeps storming off.

"Hey, Clem. I'm going to walk Ellie back to her house," Ethan is yelling at me from the porch with her tucked into his elbow.

"At least someone has made friends here," I mumble.

CHAPTER SIX
CLEM

"You gave up too easily," my dad's voice echoes off the porch. I do a double take to make sure he was speaking to me.

He sits in a rocker as I make my way up the three steps. Three short steps to what I know will in no way turn out like I want it. He sips his after-dinner drink and props his booted feet up on the wagon-wheel table with a plexiglass top. His father made it, and I've never seen it moved from this spot.

"Sit, young lady." His crooked finger is even authoritative.

I hate being called young lady and he knows it, but I refuse to squirm. I sit in the swing chair and cross my legs, smoothing the skirt of my dress. "I'm surprised you wanted me talking to him at all," I say with a haughty tilt of my nose.

"There are a lot of things you don't know about me or anyone else in this family."

"Could we please not rehash the fact that I left?" My head hangs in defeat before we've gotten very far into whatever lecture I feel coming on.

He swirls his drink, watching the whiskey flow over the round ice ball. "Boone was a broken man when you left. It took him years to consider asking a woman out. He spent day in and day out with those horses. He kept waiting for you to come back. He never thought it would take so many years to show your face. He finally gave up, and here...the...fuck... you...are."

Warm tears build behind my eyes, and I blink to keep them at bay. "I'm sorry." My lips tremble around the words.

He sips his drink then twists the corner of his silver mustache between his fingers. "Why'd you leave, Clementine?"

I've thought for years how I'd answer his question, yet at this very moment, I struggle with the words. "I was so young and felt trapped in this place in many ways. Boone represented a life I wasn't sure I wanted."

"Bullshit. You loved the horses. You were one of the best damn trainers I'd seen in years. That wouldn't be possible if you didn't love what you did." He places his feet on the ground and rests his elbows on his knees. "What spooked you?" I swear I see a flicker of true interest cross his face.

Do I dare tell him the secret that Boone and I share? He already thinks so little of me. I decide to keep it where it belongs...in the past. "I've told you the truth. I needed to get away from here to find myself. I wasn't ready to be married."

"Then why the fuck did you agree to marry him in the first place?" That flicker is gone and replaced with a face wrinkled in contempt.

He's always so angry it's hard to talk to him. I want to, but he brings out the worst in me. "I thought I was ready, and then I wasn't." My shoulders slump, knowing good and well he's not going to like my answer.

"That's a sorry-ass excuse. No wonder he kept walking away from you." He stands, taking his drink with him.

"Maybe if you'd forgive me, Boone would soften toward me."

"I'm not going to make it that easy on you." He takes a few steps and turns back around. This time instead of seeing anger, hurt mars his weathered face. "You were my baby girl. You didn't just crush Boone's heart. You ripped mine out. I blamed myself for being too hard on you. That's why you left. I took him under my wing because it was all my fault. It's taken me until this moment to realize I wasn't hard enough on you." He slams the door behind him.

I jump off the swing to go after him, and I hear the slide of the dead bolt. I lean my body against the hard door, and my back drags along it as I sit very unladylike on the painted blue concrete floor of the porch.

"Why don't you make your way back to wher-ever you came from?" Wyatt's deep voice carries over the railing on the porch.

I stand, straightening my dress. "Why do you hate me so much? What did I ever do to you?" I storm toward him, wanting some answers from him.

"I don't hate you per se." He rubs his chin. "I just don't like what you put this family through. You didn't see him after you fled." He puts emphasis on the *D* sound.

"No, I didn't see Boone. Why can't anyone understand that I wasn't ready to get married? I'm sorry that it took me until my wedding day to figure it out!" I'm down the steps and inches from him. He hovers over me in height, but I won't be unnerved by him.

"I wasn't talking about Boone," he scoffs.

It takes a minute to register what he said. "Daddy?"

He nods. "He was so depressed he almost lost the ranch. He sold all the horses except the one you were petting today in the stable. He only kept that damn horse because he knew how much you loved him. He wanted nothing to do with the rest of them. All the studding fees he was making went away when he sold them. That money funded this ranch when the beef market was low. Then a drought hit, and he almost lost all the cattle. We all pitched in and helped save this place in one way or another. All but you." His lip quirks up in a smile. "You were off finding yourself, and we 'Calhouns,' dug our heels in deep to save the ranch. That's the only thing that pulled him out of his funk. We've sacrificed and fought for each other, including Boone. He spent his own money on finding another racehorse."

"I was out fighting for our country! Doesn't that count for anything?"

"Not in my eyes. You were sitting behind a desk, not in the middle of a war."

I take a long, hard look at him. "You were jealous." I wanted to say jealous prick. Instead, I find gashes in my tongue.

"Fat chance of that," he denies, crossing his arms over his chest.

"He started paying attention to you after I was gone. I remember him being extremely hard on you because you were the oldest. I used to feel sorry for you." I reach out to touch his arm, and he shrugs out of my reach.

"He adored you, and you could do no wrong in his eyes."

"And you hated that." I won't back down.

"Even if you're right, which you're not, he'll never see you the same way again."

"I don't want him to see me as the young girl that left here. I've grown up and can take care of myself. I know what I want now, and I don't have to feel trapped in a world that was smothering me."

"You don't think at times we've all felt smothered?" He laughs out of frustration.

My eyes rock side to side, looking at his. "The difference between you and me is that I didn't let it take over my life. You did."

"You've no idea what you're talking about." He starts backing up.

"Well, I think you protest too much."

"Just stay out of my way. And, if you hurt him again, you'll never be welcomed back here."

"Like I feel welcome now," I yell as he slams the door of his expensive pickup truck. "That's two doors slammed in my face in less than five minutes." I stomp to the back of the house. Momma is staring out the screen door.

"Try again tomorrow." She smiles sweetly.

"I'm not giving up."

"114," she says.

I scowl at her, not understanding.

"Boone lives in 114."

"I'm not dealing with him tonight. I've had enough fun for one day. I'm going back to the cottage to sulk." I climb in Lizzy, thinking that I'd like to slam the door like everyone else has, but if I did, it would be lying on the ground. Dust flies as I head down the dirt road that leads to 102.

There's no sign of Ethan in his tent, and no lights illuminating from Ellie's house. "We've been here one night, and he's getting laid. I can't even get people to talk to me without leaving in an argument!" I huff and fall down in the ragged chair. I draw my legs up, trying to lie down on something that is way too small. I press my face into the arm of the chair and choke on the musty smell. It completely unravels me. I get up and scoot it across the floor, open the door, and push it outside.

"There! Serves you right for not being perfect!" I almost yelled, "for not being the perfect daughter." An owl hoots and I run back inside, finally getting to slam a door. Childish, I know, but if the oldest Calhoun can do it, so can I.

I wash my face in the kitchen sink then head up the vertical ladder to the loft. I slip out of my dress, putting on an oversized t-shirt, and curl up on what has to be the most uncomfortable, thin mattress I've ever laid on, including the cots in the army. *Mental note: purchase a new bed set in the morning.*

I close my eyes, but my mind keeps running over what Wyatt told me about our father. I was so selfish. I never thought about how my decision would hurt all of them. Right now, I hate myself. How do I expect them to like me?

I fluff my pillow a few more times before I decide that sleep is not happening. I get on my phone and start ordering things that I need. I pay extra for overnight shipping. At two a.m., I set the alarm on my phone for six and will myself to sleep for a few hours.

The sound of revelry wakes me, and I'm confused as to where I am.

"Phone."

"Alarm."

"Home." I breathe out through a yawn and stretch my arms. "It's going to be a long day." I roll out of bed and find a pair of my fatigue pants, an old t-shirt, and well-worn army boots to work in the stables. I climb down the stairs and rush out the front door to the outhouse. On the walk back, I peek inside Ethan's tent, and he's buck naked lying face down sound asleep. I reach inside and throw a blanket over his glowing white heinie, but not before admiring how good it looks. I really shouldn't be gawking, but I'm only human. I shrug to myself.

Instead of driving Lizzy, I make my way up to the barn on foot so that her motor doesn't wake anyone. I open the barn doors wide to let in the morning freshness. Wasting no time, I grab the shovel, a pair of work gloves, and the wheel barrel, getting right to work. Before I start digging in each stable, I take time and nuzzle with the horses. I have missed this.

I'm whistling a happy tune and knee-deep in horse shit when I hear a sound coming from inside the barn. I raise the shovel, holding it to use as a weapon if need be, stepping outside the horses' gate. "Who's there?" I look to the right and nearly jump out of my skin when I hear a voice to the left of me.

"It's just me."

Boone is standing with his hands out in front of him so that I don't knock him out with the shovel.

"You scared the crap out of me." I lower the shovel, leaning it against the wall.

"Well, you were shoveling horse shit." He lets out a low laugh.

"What are you doing in the stables this early?" I remove my gloves and brush my hair out of my face.

"I've forbidden anyone from disturbing the schedule I have the Thoroughbred on, so I take care of all his needs, including cleaning out his stall."

"I could do it." I eagerly volunteer.

"Seems you've missed the part that I don't want anyone near him." He tugs a pair of gloves out of his back pocket and puts them on before he picks up a pitchfork.

"Can I at least meet him?"

He yanks the brim of his cowboy hat and turns for me to follow him. At the very end of the barn is a double-sized stall for the Thoroughbred. He unlocks the gate and goes inside first. Boone takes out a carrot he had hanging out of the back pocket of his jeans, and the silky beauty eats it out of his hand.

"He's beautiful. Is this Whiskey River? I read about him in my horse magazines." I giggle. "Good name, by the way. Where did you ever get it from?" I tease.

"This horse is going to win the Triple Crown and get this ranch back on its feet."

I lean against the stable wall and prop one foot on it. "Wyatt told me a little about what happened. He said you bought this horse with your own money."

"Wyatt has a big mouth." He runs his hand down the back of the horse.

"Have you done all his training." I point to the horse.

"For the last three years. His father was one of the fastest horses I've seen until he injured his knee."

"So he's strictly a studhorse now."

He nods. "But this beauty will do what his father couldn't if I can get him to not be so skittish. I've tried every trick I know to calm him down."

"I know one you haven't tried." I push off the wall.

"What's that?"

"How about I show you instead of telling you,

KELLY MOORE

but it'll mean you'll have to trust me." As soon as I said the words, I wanted to take it back.

"Trust you?" He lets out a gruff laugh. "You're the last person I trust."

"Okay, I deserve that, but I can help you."

He yanks his cowboy hat off. "Why don't you help me understand why you left me?" His voice is raw with emotion, and it hits me right in the gut.

"I was afraid and still hurting. Losing the baby and not being able to tell anyone was overwhelming. I needed out. I needed my life to have a purpose. I felt so much guilt because I was relieved that I miscarried. What kind of monster did that make me? I wasn't ready for a baby." I step close to him. "You only proposed because I was pregnant."

"If that were true, I would've backed out when you lost the baby."

"In my mind, it was the only truth I could see at the time. We wanted two different things. You were never going to leave here. I loved the horses, the land, but I didn't love the ranch. I wanted more."

He puts his hat back on. "And yet, here you are. Back to the place you couldn't run far enough away from...or the person," he adds.

"I'm so sorry I hurt you."

He starts fluffing the hay with the pitchfork.

84

"You weren't the only one that lost the baby. You wanted to keep it a secret from your family, and I've done that all these years out of respect for you. So, there's not been one soul I could talk to about it either. The person I needed was you." He throws the pitchfork on the ground and walks out of the horse's stall.

I march after him. "I've said I'm sorry. I don't know what else to do."

He stops and faces me. "I'm sorry too. I'm sorry that I made you feel like you were stuck."

"You didn't do that. I did." I reach up and lay the palm of my hand on his warm cheek. He closes his eyes and leans into it for the briefest second. When he opens his storm-filled eyes, his bottom lip quivers.

"I can't do this with you." He moves out of my reach, goes back into the Thoroughbred's stall, and leads him outside.

My sigh fills the space in the barn. I thought for a moment, I'd made a little ground on mending things between us. I hear my momma's voice in my head telling me to "try again tomorrow."

"I'm going to do better than that, Momma. I'm going to try every chance I get."

I finish cleaning up and rush back to the cottage

and grab the keys to Lizzy. Ethan's head is poking out of the tent when I open the door.

"Where are you going so early?" He scratches his head.

"To buy a goat." I crank the truck several times before she sputters to life. "Don't go far, I have boxes being delivered today, and I'm going to need help loading the tin in the bed of the truck."

"Where am I supposed to go? I don't have any wheels."

CHAPTER SEVEN
BOONE

"**D**amn woman." I touch my cheek where her hand had been only moments ago. "She still does something to me after all these years." I lead Whiskey to the track to get him ready to run. "She pisses me off, that's what she does."

Whiskey neighs at me.

"No one asked your opinion. Seems you and Margret are on the same side. She thinks I was giving Clem googly eyes across the table at her. I don't even know what the hell googly eyes are for Pete's sake. I felt like I was shooting burning flames in her direction. Margret said all she could feel was the heat bouncing between the two of us."

Whiskey's black main flops from side to side when he shakes his head.

"What do you know? You weren't there." I lead him to a trough of water. "So, now Margret is pissed at me because the fawn-eyed girl...woman, is back home, and she thinks I still have a thing for her. It doesn't help that the Calhouns don't like Margret."

Whiskey shakes his head again.

"Just a minute ago you were on her side, now you agree with the Calhouns?" His big round black eyeball stares at me. "Why? Margret's not so bad. I mean she's no Clem."

He shakes his head again.

"Wyatt thinks Margret is a gold digger, and Bear says she hates kids. If that were true, the joke's on her. I don't have any money, at least until you win me the Triple Crown. As far as kids go, I'm thinking I'm past the age of wanting any and I don't know that I'd risk the loss again." I walk him over to the shed that houses his saddle, blankets, reins, and brushes. I pull a plastic-bristled dandy brush from the shelf and start working on his coat, careful not to use it on his face.

"Why couldn't she come back here ugly or something? No, she has to be more beautiful than when she left." I stop brushing and gaze at my hands. "I want my hands on her so badly." I shake them out. "I always thought she'd come running back here to tell me she was miserable without me. Instead, she brings the man that she lays down with every night. I'm jealous of the air he breathes next to her skin." I roll my shoulders a few times. "Me. Jealous. Wow, maybe Margret was right."

I walk around to the other side and brush Whiskey's mane. "Clem never understood how much I loved her if she thinks I only asked her to marry me because she was pregnant at the time. I wanted nothing more than for her to be my wife. When I first came to work for the Calhouns, I kept my distance from her because she was only sixteen years old. But boy, did I fall hard for her. I couldn't stop myself once we started training the horses together. She'd look at me, or brush up against me and my body would be set on fire like a hot brand burnt into my flesh. Just like it did this morning with her hand on my face."

"Who you talking to, boss?" Jose's voice startles me.

"Are you ready to run him?" I pat the horse on his hindquarter.

"Why are we running him now? I was surprised when you sent me a text last night. I thought you wanted to keep the same routine racing in the late afternoon."

Jose is five feet two and has been riding Whiskey for six months. He and the horse move like they're one. He commands Whiskey as much as Whiskey commands him. He's got a good chance of winning with him if we can get him settled down. The horse is restless in his stable and the race gate. "I wanted to see if it would make any difference in his time." It's a flat-out lie, and he'll know it. I knew Clem would be in the stable this morning and I wanted to see her. I'm such a fucking idiot.

"If you say so, boss." He laughs and starts the saddling process. "You know the derbies are all ran late in the day," he adds.

I don't bother changing my story. "Let's see what he can do."

Once his saddle is in place, Jose places his foot in the stirrup and eases onto the horse. I grab the stopwatch that's hanging on a nail and walk over to the white fence that surrounds the track. I lean on it and observe him warm up Whiskey. When Jose indicates he's ready, I start the timer. I watch, but for the first time in a long time, I pay no attention. My mind is on the spunky little number that's back home. I have to stay away from her. My life is good. I have a woman that loves me and a job that I'd never give up. Horse racing and ranching are my life. Not Clementine Calhoun. She made it clear when she left, this wasn't the life she wanted with me, even though she never uttered the words. Her being a runaway bride spoke volumes. I had nothing different to offer her then, and nothing has changed. I think about my own words. Nothing has changed. "Damn, no wonder she left my sorry ass." She went off and grew up. I stayed the same.

I hit the stop button on the timer as Whiskey finishes his first lap. The jockey walks him around the second time.

Sure, I'm older, more mature, but nothing is really any different, including the fact that I still love Clementine Calhoun. I should've held her tighter after she lost the baby. I was in a tailspin myself, not knowing what to do for her. She started building layers of a wall that day around her. I should've seen it coming. That sparkle that was always in her eyes was dim. I saw her disinterest in this place grow almost overnight. I ignored it, thinking she needed space. It never dawned on me to ask her if she wanted to postpone the wedding. I loved her and didn't want to give her the opportunity to say yes.

I start the timer again when Whiskey is at the

starting point. I take my hat off and run my hand through my thick head of hair. "I've blamed you all this time, Clem. Maybe I should've pointed a finger in my direction rather than being pissed at you."

"How's his time?" Chet Calhoun's voice is behind me.

"He's running at two minutes, twenty-five seconds. If we can shave two seconds off his time, he'll win."

He leans his arms on the top rail of the fence. "You do that, and he'll beat Secretariat's record. Do you really think that's possible?"

"I do if he doesn't have that hesitation at the gate."

He looks down and digs his boot into the dirt. "You had every right to be pissed at Clem. The blame doesn't go on your shoulders. But now that she's back, what are you going to do about her?"

I click the timer again as Whiskey races by. "You're wrong. There are things between Clem and I that you don't know."

"Did you cheat on her?" He stands tall.

"God, no."

"Then there is nothing you could've done that caused her to leave as far as I'm concerned."

I want to tell him, but I promised Clem that if

her family ever knew, it'd come from her. "I think you should talk *to* her, not *at* her." I'm about the only one, other than his wife, that can stand up to him.

"You let me worry about my runaway daughter. But you avoided my question. What are you going to do?"

"Nothing. I'm going to do nothing. She's got a boyfriend, and I have no right to interfere with that."

"And you have Margret." He chuckles. "Or did you forget about that when you saw Clem?"

"I haven't forgotten."

"That boy, she claims is only a friend, and he's got his eyes, or at least I hope it's his eyes on my eldest daughter who seems to be a bit of a wild horse."

"I'm not sure Ellie would take too kindly to being compared to a horse." I chuckle.

"Do you want my advice?"

"Do I have a choice?" I laugh and face him.

"You get one chance at true love in life. Sometimes you have to wait on it. Sometimes it all gets screwed up, but if it's real...it's worth the wait, and the heartache."

"Wow! Is this you siding with Clem? She'd be shocked."

He gets off the fence and brushes the dust off his

jeans. "No, not siding with Clem, only stating some facts."

"Sounds like there's a story there between you and the missus that I've never heard."

"You mind your own business, Son." He adjusts his hat and walks toward the barn.

I watch Whiskey run for the next hour then help Jose cool the horse down. "He rode well. When are we going to try him in the gate again?"

"Yesterday we couldn't even get him in the gate stall. Let's give it a couple days. Work on shaving his time this afternoon."

"Whatever you say, boss man. Do you want me to take him back to the stable?"

"No, I'll lead him." Part of me hopes Clem is still there, part of me wants to run the other way. I brush him out again and head for the stable. I hear Clem's voice like she's talking to a small child.

"You're going to love it here."

When I open the stall door, she's sitting on the hay bale, patting the head of a goat.

"What the hell are you doing? And why is there a goat in my Thoroughbred's stall?"

"He's a pet goat."

"You can't keep your pet in here."

"He's not for me. He's for Whiskey River."

"Have you totally lost your mind?" I throw my hat off.

"When I first joined the army, I was stationed at a place that had horses. With my background, they had me training them. We had this one thoroughbred that was ornery and skittish. I did a lot of research on what I could do to calm him. The answer was a pet goat. Within two days of putting the goat in his pen, he was a different horse. The bond between them was incredible. If the horse got anxious at all, the goat would nuzzle next to him, and you'd see the horse relax."

"You're telling me that this goat is like how a human would use a dog to calm them?" I don't know why I'm yelling at her.

"I think you could use one of those comfort dogs right about now." She crosses her arms over her chest.

"This is one of the most absurd things I've ever heard."

"They thought so too. That's what led me to cybersecurity."

"You are one confusing woman." I scratch my head and pick up my hat.

"The research led me to more in-depth research for them, and I found I liked computers and digging into issues. I have the goat to thank for that."

Why does she have to have that sexy smile? I swallow hard. "I want that goat out of here."

"Please, just give it a try. What's it going to hurt?" She shrugs.

"If that goat messes with my horse's time, I'm going to run you out of town myself." I'm gruff.

"It'll work, I promise." She's awful pleased with herself and didn't back down from me being an ass. Not the Clem I remember at all. She used to cower when her dad laid into her. She could never stand up to him. I like this version of her. *Damn it.*

She walks up close enough I can see the tiny specks of green mixed in her eyes. They only stand out when her eyes are sparkling. "Thank you. I'll take care of Henry so that you don't have to."

"Henry?"

"The goat," she indicates with a turn of her head.

"Henry is your responsibility."

"I think that's what I just said." She gets on her tiptoes and places a quick kiss to my cheek, and it goes straight to my groin. I don't let her see any reaction other than me wiping it off with the back of my hand. The sparkle falls from her eyes, and the green is all gone. "I've got deliveries coming soon, and I need to go get the tin for the roof." She's backing away as she talks to me. "I'll catch you later."

"Aren't you going to stick around long enough to see if Whiskey and Henry are okay together?" I don't really need her for that, but I'm not ready for her to leave.

"They'll be fine. I'll check on them later." She rushes out the barn door.

I walk Whiskey into the stall, and he starts chomping on the hay. The goat bleats a few times before he walks up to Whiskey. I shut the gate to the stall and watch. Normally after a run, the Thoroughbred kicks around after his hay. He starts his prancing in a circle, and the goat talks to him. He spins slowly and stops when the goat stands under him.

"Well I'll be damned."

CHAPTER EIGHT
CLEM

"Jesus, it's hot out here." Ethan throws the last piece of tin in the bed of the truck.

"Hotter than the hinges on the gates of hell." I laugh at what my daddy used to say when he was working on the tractor.

"I've never heard it phrased like that before." He gingerly shuts Lizzy's tailgate.

"We have all kinds of sayings for how hot it is. Oh, my favorite was Momma's. She'd say, it's hotter'n a blister bug in a pepper patch."

"What the hell is a blister bug?" He tugs off his baseball cap and scratches his head.

"Never mind. By the end of the summer, you'll be speaking our language." I giggle and hop behind the wheel.

"God, I hope not." He gets in and shuts the door. "Unless it would help with Ellie. Has she ever dated a city boy?"

"Not that I know of. I really don't want you dating my sister." I start down the road.

"Why? What's wrong with me?"

"There ain't nothing wrong with you. It'd just be weird."

"It can't be any stranger than me banging her." He chuckles.

I reach over and slug him in the shoulder. "I told you to keep your sledgehammer away from her."

He grins a quirky smile. "Sledgehammer. I like that."

"Shut the hell up, Ethan. It wasn't meant to give you a big head about your manhood."

"Manhood? Fuck that! Sledgehammer it is." He snorts.

"Seriously. What are you doing with Ellie?"

"I thought I just made that perfectly clear." His Cheshire grin covers his face.

"You know what I mean. What if she falls for you? You plan on staying in Kentucky, being a ranch hand? You'll have to learn to shovel shit." I make my smile match his—before his falls.

"I hadn't thought that far ahead, but I get the

feeling that your sister takes what she wants and then moves along."

I reach over and take his hand. "Are you okay with that?"

"Sure. Why not? I've been with plenty of women and never fell for them. The bash-and-dash has always worked for me."

There is something in his eyes that makes me think he feels differently this time.

"We'll have some fun together, and then I'll go back home."

"I don't want to see either one of you get hurt."

"You're too damn serious, Clem. We only met yesterday."

I round the corner to the shack, and Bear is signing for the delivery of my furnishings. "Where do you want this stuff, Clem?"

"I already cleared out the space in the room. Have them carry the bed set upstairs." Bear directs them while Ethan and I start unloading the tin from the back of the truck. When the last box is out, he lends us a hand.

I stole the ladder from Dad's workshop and all the other supplies we're going to need to hold the tin in place."

"He'll be pissed." I snort.

"I've never let his ambivalent attitude stop me before." He chuckles. "I found a window to replace yours. It'll need a few adjustments, but it will work fine."

"That's great. Did it come from one of the other remodels?"

"You could say that." His smile is not innocent.

"Please tell me you didn't steal it? I thought you'd outgrown being a thief."

"Let's say, I borrowed it."

"From?"

"Missy and I were playing catch outside by Dad's office. I tossed it a little too hard, and it broke his window. So, I being the responsible son, ordered one to replace it."

"Let me guess? This is the replacement one."

"See, I knew you were a Calhoun. Such a smart girl." He winks.

"You know if he finds out, I'm going to have breeze replacing the opening in my cottage."

"Then let's not let him know." He shrugs.

We finish unloading. Bear runs off in my truck to bring back the window. He works on it while I instruct my city-boy friend on how to place the tin properly. When Bear is done, he joins us on the roof. We're about halfway finished when I see Boone's expensive truck stirring up dust, headed in our direction.

"I'm going to take a break." Ethan's t-shirt is soaking wet, and his face is the color of the sun. He climbs down the ladder, and I hear Ellie's voice coming from below.

"I brought some lemonade if anyone is thirsty."

Bear follows suit after Ethan. Boone's truck stops behind mine in a grassy patch. I swear to gawd, he swaggers out of his truck. Either that or the heat is getting to me, and I'm seeing things. Why do I find everything he does so damn sexy? When he was in the stable, running his hand down the horses back, all I could think about was those rough hands of his. It's his best feature...well, maybe not his best, but he sure knew how to use them to turn me on.

I keep my head low, so he doesn't see me gawking at him. He tosses his cowboy hat through the open window on his truck. The next thing he does has me drooling, and not just from my lips. He crosses his arms over his body and slings off his t-shirt.

Fuck me, he's ripped. Not the body of the man I once knew. His six-pack has a six-pack of its own. And shit, those guns of his have grown too. I wonder what other body part has matured with age. Not that he didn't have plenty to begin with, but a girl has to be curious, right? What stands out the most is the dark tattoo that runs over his shoulder and covers half his chest. I never knew Boone was into tats. I find his sexy as sin.

I wipe my forehead and continue working when he's no longer in sight. Boots stomp up the ladder, and I know it's him. Ethan doesn't know how to stomp in his tennis shoes, and Bear isn't heavy-footed. His head tops the ladder. "What are you doing here?" I ask him.

"I heard there was work to be done and I had some free time." He climbs to the top rung of the ladder and hoists up more tin. "You okay with that?"

"Yeah, just surprised you're helping me."

"I figure your father and I caused a lot of the damage to this place, so I feel responsible to help fix it up."

My heart feels heavy. I envision him losing his shit after I left. I'm such a bitch. I never thought about how much it would affect him until now. I bite my quivering lip and force back the sting in my eyes. "Thanks."

We work quietly and alone over the next hour. I think Bear and Ethan are afraid to come back up. We work well together, but every time his hand brushes any part of my skin, I'm a teenage girl again. All my body parts are soaking wet. I have to make conversation to steer away from what my body wants. It doesn't help that he's shirtless and little beads of sweat are dripping down his goody trail.

"How did Whiskey do with Henry?" He stops. Lifts his arm and wipes his head on his bicep. His fucking bicep that I want to nip with my teeth.

"It may have been my imagination, but he seemed not so restless."

"Good. I know it will help."

He half grins and goes back to work. Every now and then, when he thinks I'm not paying attention, I feel the heat of his gaze on my body. It doesn't help my current basement situation, nor the wetness of my skin. I don't understand why no other man has ever made me react the same way. It's wrong. I gave him up, and he has Margret. I picture the two of them together, and my sex-obsessed body simmers down.

"When are you and Margret tying the knot?" I regret the question the second it passes my lips.

"Margret and I are an off-limit topic for you and me." His hammer stops mid-swing.

"I'm sorry. I was only trying to make conversation."

"You don't need to make conversation with me," he snarls and beats the hammer down on his thumb. "Goddamn it!" he yells and holds his hand to his body.

I scurry over to him. "Here, let me see." I pry his hand from his chest. "That looks bad. You're going to need to ice it."

"I'll be fine. Not like I haven't done it before." He places the tip of his thumb in his mouth and bites down as to ward off the pain.

It doesn't ward off anything for me. Quite the opposite. I stifle a moan. "Let's take a break. I'll fix you an ice bag."

"I said I'm fine!" He shocks me with his snarl.

"I was just trying to help." I back away from him.

He shakes his injured hand, and the other runs through his wet mop of hair. "I didn't mean to snap at you."

"If it makes you feel better, then scream at me. Anything to break the tension between us."

"Look, I'm doing the best I can. I'm here, in the heat of the day, on top of this roof helping you." His jaw that was clenched loosens.

"Thank you," I say softly when all I want to do is kiss his boo-boo, among other things like his lips that are calling my name. "I really am sorry."

He grabs the hammer again. "My thumb will be fine, sore, but fine."

"I wasn't talking about your thumb. I'm sorry I left the way I did."

He stands and drops the hammer on the tin, making an awful sound. "I don't want to talk about it." He backs down the ladder.

I sit back on the hot tin and blow out a long breath and can't stop the sting of tears this time. After a few minutes, I see him peel out of the yard, and Bear climbs the ladder.

"What did you do to piss him off?" He sits next to me.

"I told him I was sorry," I sniff.

Bear wraps his arm around my shoulder and kisses the side of my head. "Give it time, Clem. It will get easier for the both of you. How about you take a break. You've been at this for hours. Go down and tell Ethan to quit trying to charm the pants off Ellie and get his city-boy ass back up here and help me finish."

I dry my tears and hug him. "Thanks, Bear."

"You're welcome. Fair warning, Ellie's been decorating while you've been up here working."

I move down the ladder and go inside the

cottage. "Ethan. Bear said to send you up to help him finish," I say before my eyes adjust to the light.

He scoots by me, and I peel off my sunglasses. The furniture I ordered is all in place. Dark denims with a white oak coffee table. There's a checkered navy rug on the floor that I don't recall ordering.

"It's been sitting in my garage, and when I saw the colors of your couch and loveseat, I knew it would match perfectly." Ellie sips on a glass of lemonade.

"Thanks for doing this."

"I called my handyman and ordered some paint to freshen up the walls. He'll be here tomorrow to slap it on. I think next on your list should be these awful floors. A nice gray laminate will look nice with these colors."

"I'm not sure that's in the budget."

"You may want to move it to the top of the list when you wake up to a raccoon in here." She points to a hole in the floor.

"Moving to the top of the list." I look down in it.

"I'll get the handyman to board it up for now. And you know, I think I have a spare curtain and a rod for your new window. It's bright yellow if that will work for you?"

"Yellow is fine. Thank you for helping me." She hands me a glass of lemonade.

"I've missed you."

"I've missed you, too. I wish now I would've come back sooner."

"You came back when you were ready." She shrugs and sits on the new sofa. I decide on the floor since I'm all sweaty.

"Why didn't you tell me Bear had a daughter?"

"I don't know. Maybe part of me felt as betrayed as the others, and I didn't think you deserved to know everything. Especially something as good as Missy."

I gulp down the sip I was taking. "Wow! That's blatantly honest."

"I don't know any other way to be. I've learned to be brutally honest and to take what I want, or as a Calhoun woman, you'll get run over by the men in this family."

"I see Momma has grown a pair of..." I stop, thinking about my choice of words.

"Balls!" Ellie laughs. "It only took her thirty years."

"You have changed. You used to scold me and rat me out anytime I used not-so-nice words."

"Fuck that shit! We're grown-ass women. I can

be the prim and proper lady when I have to be, I just don't choose to be when I'm not around the ladies with their fancy hats and dresses."

"What? You used to love to dress up and go to the derbies."

"That was a different Ellie. This is the new and improved balls-to-the-walls Ellie." She takes a sip of her drink. "You don't seem a lot different to me."

"Sure I am. I've grown up, gotten tougher, and more focused."

"Yeah, but you still have it bad for Boone."

"No, I don't. I don't know what you're talking about." *Well, shit.*

"Keep lying to yourself, Clementine. You were eye-fucking him all night at the table."

I spew out the lemonade. "Good gawd, Ellie, your mouth is worse than my thoughts."

"That's not a denial." She raises her eyebrow, and for the first time, I realize her brow is pierced with a small gold loop almost the color of her hair.

"Your eyebrow is pierced?" I get up on my knees and inch closer for a better look.

"That's not all that's pierced." She howls.

I stare at her for a moment. She gazes down at her lady parts and back up with a smile.

"No!" I gasp. "You pierced your Pink Panther?" I shriek.

"I was thinking cooch, but that works too." She snorts.

"I don't even know who you are. What did you do with my quiet, shy sister?" I say through rolls of laughter.

"She was a bore, but no more."

When our giggles die down, I ask her about Boone. "When did Boone get a tattoo?"

"He and Wyatt got drunk one night and decided a little ink would make them more manly."

"Maybe Wyatt, but Boone is all man. Wait, Wyatt has a tattoo?"

"Yeah, but he keeps his well-hidden under his staunchly ironed, stick up his ass, business attire."

"He is that, all right. Boone's is a lion's head? I didn't get a good look at it."

"He said that he should've been more of a lion when it came to you. Something about him letting you down."

Boone never let me down. He must've been talking about me losing the baby. "I didn't realize you and Boone were that close."

She stands. "Are you asking me if I fucked him after you left?"

"What? No." But now, I really want to know.

"If I was the Ellie I am now, I'd say yes, I'd of rode him like a horse, but the Ellie back then was too innocent."

"Right now, I'm thankful for that." I get off the ground.

She heads toward the door. "If I were you, I wouldn't wait too long."

"Wait for what?"

"Margret will put up a fight. She thinks she can get her hands on this property. Her daddy owns the adjacent hundred acres and would love nothing more than his daughter to get her claws into Calhoun land."

"If Boone knows that, then why? He loves this place and Daddy."

"She licked his wounds if you know what I mean."

"Gross! I don't want to know where her mouth has been."

"Then you better lick better." She winks.

CHAPTER NINE
BOONE

"**D**amn woman! Why did she have to come back here?" *Because it's her family, you idiot.* She had every right to return. I wash the grime off my face in the sink, then glance up into the mirror. The lion on my chest seems to take a breath of his own. I wasn't strong enough for her, that's why she left me. If I would've been the man she needed, her feet would've never left town, much less my bed. I thought I was a man at the time. I was only a kid trying to play the role. If I was a man, she would never have gotten pregnant. I convinced her to let me not use a condom. I wanted to feel what it was like to be completely naked inside her. She couldn't say no to me in the heat of passion, and I knew it. I was a selfish bastard and didn't care.

When she told me she was late, I assured her it'd be okay, but I was in a state of panic myself. I wasn't ready for a kid, and neither was she. Part of me thinks I got her pregnant on purpose. I knew she felt trapped on the ranch. She talked about it all the time. She wanted more, and I never wanted to leave this place. It's been the only home I've known, and I owe so much to the Calhouns. What I didn't owe, was getting Chet Calhoun's baby girl pregnant out of wedlock. Clem was right; I would've been thrown out on my ass. She knew how much they all meant to me. Mean to me. Still do.

My phone vibrates on my dresser. I grab it and throw on a clean shirt. "Hello."

"Hey, lover boy. Are we still on for dinner at my house tonight?"

Oh shit. I forgot all about meeting with Margret and her father. "Is there any way we can make it another evening?"

"You planned this with him weeks ago." Her voice is harsh.

He's been bugging me to meet with him about something. Some idea Margret says he has and I've been avoiding him like the plague. He caught me at a weak moment. "Why can't you just tell me what he wants?"

"Because he wants to tell you himself and I'm not going to spoil the surprise for him."

"Fine." I might as well get it over with. "I've got some things I need to do here. The weatherman says there's a big storm coming, and I need to help shore up the stables."

"You have ranch hands for that sort of thing."

"The Thoroughbred is my job, along with the other horses."

"Okay, but please don't be late."

"I'm not making any promises." I hang up. What the hell am I even doing with Margret? It's been a relationship of convenience. I care about her, but I'm not in love with her. She asked me to marry her, and I figured why not. It would be nice to not be so lonely all the time, and she helped me get over Clem. At least I thought I was over her. I've really got myself in a mess. I'll either have to man up and go through with my commitment to Margret or find a way out.

"What the hell am I even thinking? Clem doesn't want me and I sure as hell don't trust her. Margret is reliable."

I get in my truck and head over to the track to check on Jose and Whiskey. This is the usual time he runs him. I park by the fence and see Jose walking Whiskey and Henry on a leash behind him.

"Hey boss man," he yells when he sees me walking toward him.

"Why is the goat out here?"

"Whiskey wouldn't leave the stable without him."

"Just fucking great. Clem said the goat would help calm him, not make matters worse." I press my fingers to my temples.

"He's calm. He let me put him in the starting gate."

"Yeah, but even if it worked, I can't bring a goat to the tracks."

"We can keep him in the trailer outside the track. Whiskey can see him from there."

"Let me rephrase it. I'm not bringing a goat to the derby." I hang my hat on the fence post. Henry bleats. "I'll hold on to him. You get Whiskey in the gate and take him for a run." Instead of walking over to get the stopwatch, I pull my phone out of my pocket and find my timer.

"Who's this?" Chet walks up behind me.

"Clem's goat."

"What the hell is she doing with a goat on my property?"

"She has this wild idea that Whiskey needs a pet goat to settle him down."

He takes off his hat and props one boot on the lower rung of the fence. "I see the military did her a lot of good." He snickers.

We both watch as Jose loads Whiskey in the gate. It goes smoothly for the first time ever.

"Huh." I scratch my chin. "He's never been that easy before."

When Jose gives me the signal, I blow a whistle and start timing him. He lunges out of the gate in a quick stride, moving faster and easier than I've ever seen him. He's beautiful, all muscle and graceful. We stand and watch as he makes his way around the one and a half-mile dirt track. He's still flying when he crosses the finish line, and I hit the stop button.

"Well I'll be damned." I laugh.

"What was his time?"

"Two minutes twenty-three seconds."

"Don't go thinking that has anything to do with that goat." Chet's voice is gruff.

"I'm sorry I'm late. I had to return some tools," Clem says, moseying up beside us. I look back to see Bear driving off on the four-wheeler. He must have driven her.

"No excuses for being late. Try again tomorrow.

If you're late then too, consider yourself fired," Chet growls at her.

"Yes, sir," she says and stands on the fence. "What did I miss?"

I turn the timer in her direction. "Seriously?" Her eyes light up. She hops down and scratches the goat's chin. "I knew you two would get along."

"Don't you go taking credit for this. Jose and Boone have worked hard. That's what increased his time, not some damn voodoo goat." Chet marches off.

"I didn't mean it that way," she yells after him.

He turns and storms toward her. "You don't get to come back and be some type of hero." His finger is on her shoulder. "Now get that goat off my property." He snarls and turns back around.

I watch any pride that Clem has leave her face as her gaze follows him.

"I'll figure out a way to keep the goat," I say.

"It's okay. You don't have to do that."

"Whiskey bonded with him like you said. He went through the gate without any issues."

She chews at the inside of her cheek. "I'm glad it helped, but I'll never do anything right in his eyes."

"You need to give him more time."

"I've been hearing that a lot lately." She peers up at me from under her dark lashes.

I stick out my hand. "Let's call a truce. You've said you're sorry and I'll quit busting your chops over it."

"Really?" she all but squeals and plants her hand firmly in mine.

"We've both moved on, and there is no reason we can't be friends. Water under the bridge, so to speak."

"I'd like that. Are we friends enough that you'll let me help train Whiskey?"

"No," I answer quickly, and she frowns. "But, there's a young horse that's getting delivered tomorrow. He's all yours to train if you want him."

"I'd love it. I promise you won't regret it."

"Did your roof get finished? There's a storm headed in tonight."

"Yes. Bear and Ethan have it handled."

"What's the story with Ethan?"

"We're friends. He helped me get through boot camp, and we bonded."

"Was it difficult?"

Her brows draw together. "Was what difficult?"

"Boot camp? I mean you went from a sheltered life on the ranch to the military."

"I was scared shitless with what I'd done. I was heartbroken over what had happened, but I needed an out. I would've died on the inside if I stayed here." She takes my hand in hers. "I'm sorry—"

I stop her. "Don't apologize again. We are through that. Do you understand?"

She nods.

"Good." I glance at my watch. "I'd like to hear more, but I have a meeting I have to get to. Maybe we could catch up after you get the new horse settled tomorrow."

"I'd like that."

"Do you think you could help Jose cool off Whiskey and get him and Henry back to the stable?"

"Yes," she says enthusiastically.

"Okay then. I'll see you later. Tell Chet and your mom I won't be making it for dinner tonight. You'll want to get home before the storm hits."

I tie up loose ends in the stable and make sure all the horses are locked down tight to ride out the storm. I drive back home, shower, and change clothes. I don't know why I feel the need to put on a tie, but I do. I leave my dusty cowboy hat on the hook and head over to Margret's place.

"You're on time." She opens the door and kisses me on the cheek. "You look mighty handsome in that tie. You should wear one more often."

I tug at it, thinking how unnatural it feels around my neck.

"Daddy's in the study waiting for you. He wanted to meet with you before we sit down to eat."

"Mr. Maynard," I say, following Margret into his office.

"Please call me Tom. After all, you are marrying my daughter." He motions his hand for me to take a seat. His leather chair creaks as he rests back. "Margret, sweetheart, why don't you fix us men something to drink?"

"Yes, Daddy." She takes the hint and leaves the room, shutting the door behind her.

"I want to get straight to the point. I want to hire you to train my horses."

"I have a job."

"I'll pay you twice what the Calhouns are paying."

"I'm not interested in making a change, sir."

"I hear the youngest Calhoun is back in town. That wouldn't have anything to do with it, right?"

"No, sir. Not a thing. I'm happy where I am."

"Let me put it to you this way. You're marrying my only daughter, and I expect certain things."

My muscles in my face involuntarily flex a few

times. "You mean other than a husband financially supporting his wife and making her happy?"

"You will do both those things and so much more. As a member of *this* family, certain things will be expected of you. Namely, you'll work for me and bring that Thoroughbred with you. I'll pay top dollar for him."

"The horse is not for sale, and neither am I."

Tom leans forward, bracing himself on the desk. "I wasn't asking. While I'm at it, don't even think about ending things with my daughter. If you do, someone you love will pay the price."

"You're threatening me?" I stand.

"Call it what you want, but know that I keep my promises."

Margret comes through the door carrying two glasses. "Supper is ready. I don't want it getting cold." She hands us both our drinks. Tom comes from behind his desk and slaps a hand to my shoulder. "Perfect timing. Our meeting is done, and I believe we've come to a certain understanding."

Margret tucks into the crook of my arm. "I'm so happy my two favorite men can work together."

That tells me she knew all along what he wanted. Maybe she even insisted upon it. She and I will have a discussion about it, but not in front of her parents.

It's all I can do to sit and make small talk at dinner. Margret keeps pressing me for a date for our wedding, and Tom keeps talking about how my horse is going to win him a lot of money this year. He was even bold enough to make the comment that the Calhoun's would lose out and he'd be able to purchase up their land for pennies. Motherfucker was proud of himself thinking he'd best the Calhouns. No way in hell will I allow that to happen. I'll find a way to end this relationship so that it looks like Margret made the call, not me.

CHAPTER TEN
CLEM

Gawd, it felt good to work with Whiskey. I know I didn't get to train him, but the little I did reminded me of how much I loved working with the horses. Funny, something I wanted to run away from, turns out I love it after all. Time away did me good.

"I'll finish up in the stall, Jose. You need to get out of here before those storm clouds break loose.

"Are you sure, Ms. Calhoun?"

"Please call me Clem. Yes, I'm sure. Now shoo." I wave my hands at him to get him moving. The wind has picked up in the past five minutes, and the angry dark clouds are quickly headed our way. Whiskey settles down with Henry beneath him, but the goat is walking in circles.

"What's the matter, boy? You don't like storms?" A window that wasn't fastened down slams shut, spooking one of the other horses and Henry. I double-check all the latches and windows, making sure nothing else can fly open. I put the shovel and the pitchfork flat on the ground with the wheel barrel on top of them to weigh them down. A crack of lightning and a loud whistling sound rattles the stable. I peek outside, and there is no way I'm making it back to the cottage on foot. "Ethan," I say, pulling out my phone. I hit his speed dial number.

"Hey, Clem."

"Where are you? Please tell me you're not in the tent?"

"No, I'm at Ellie's. I couldn't find you so she told me I could ride out the storm at her place."

I bet she did. "Okay, stay put."

"Where are you?"

"I'm in the stable. I'm going to ride it out here with the horses. It's too late for me to make it back on foot."

"Do you want me to come get you?"

"No. I'll be fine." I hang up and try Bear. It goes straight to voicemail. "Looks like I'll be hanging out here for the night." I run my hand over Whiskey's mane. "I'll be right back."

I know we used to keep blankets in one of the storage cabinets. I scrounge around for them and take out a couple. Whiskey has lain down. Henry is nervous as a goat, as he should be, I giggle. Placing the blanket on the hay, I sit, and Henry crawls into my lap.

The wind has gotten so loud that it doesn't matter that the windows are battened down; they still shake and make an awful sound. Lightning flashes and thunder rattles the stable. I have to admit, I'm a little frightened. What if there's a tornado? I can't leave the horses alone.

A whirl of wind gushes through as a barn door flies open. "Clem! Are you in here?" Thank the heavens above it's Boone.

"I'm in Whiskey's stall!" I yell over the sound of the whipping wind.

I hear him pull the door shut, then his head pops up above Whiskey's gate. "Thank god you're okay. I drove down to your cottage. Ethan stuck his head out the window and told me you hadn't made it back."

"That must've been before I called him."

"There are trees down all over the property. I need to get you out of here."

"I'm not leaving them." I nuzzle Whiskey's nose.

He opens the gate and sits beside me on the blanket. "You're as stubborn as you used to be. I can't tell you how many times I found you in the barn sleeping with the animals when it stormed."

"I don't like the thought of them being scared." I rub the top of Henry's head.

"Fine. If you're staying, I'm staying."

"I thought you had a meeting?"

"I did." His facial expression changes from worry to almost anger.

"Did it not go well?"

"Not at all like I planned."

"Do you want to talk about it?"

"No, it's nothing for you to worry about."

His stormy eyes pierce through me. There's a look of concern in them. It's not something I ever recall seeing very often on his handsome face. He was always so strong and brave when I needed him to be. The pounding sound of the rain joins in with all the other noises.

"Damn, it's coming down hard." He gets up and checks the windows again.

"I think we're in for a long night." I pat the spot next to me, hoping he'll join me rather than finding another spot to sit.

"I'll get us a couple more blankets." He walks away, and I hear cabinets opening and shutting. He comes back with two more plaid blankets in hand. Spreading one out beside me, he sits, throwing the other one over the two of us. "You've got to be exhausted from working on the hot roof all day. Why don't you try to get some sleep?"

I lie down, and I feel him relax beside me. "Where's Margret?"

"She's at home, safe and sound." His voice sounds a little gritty.

"I'm glad you found someone." Not really. I'm such a liar. I hate her, and I don't even know her. I only know that Boone has had his hands on her. I have no right to feel this way, yet I can't seem to control the idea that he's still mine even after all this time.

"You're supposed to be trying to get some sleep."

His rough hand squeezes my shoulder, sending a wave of desire through me, and I have to press my thighs together. I decide in that moment, I want him back. He's not married yet, so he's still a free man. Of course, if anyone would've laid a hand on Boone when I was with him, I would've ripped their titties plumb off their chest. I slowly, full of lust, turn and face him. His dark eyes stare at me for a moment, then he closes them. I slip my eager hands under the hem of his t-shirt and run my fingertips over his muscles.

Without opening his eyes, he asks in a deep lull, "What are you doing?"

Holy mother of Mary his abs feel so good. "Nothing." I draw out the word with a southern charm.

"Roll back over and go to sleep." His tone is so sexy. I'm sure that's not what he was going for, but it tweaks my insides.

I do as I'm told, but not without an exaggerated sigh. "I'm not having sex with you if that's what you're thinking," I tease behind a smile.

"I wasn't thinking it." A hint of a chuckle comes from him.

I wiggle my ass closer. I don't even have to look; I know those stormy eyes of his popped open as wide as saucers.

"Whatever is pressed into my ass tends to disagree with you," I giggle.

"Quit squirming. It's a knife." His voice is strained.

I laugh. "A little big for a pocketknife." My nipples pucker, thinking about him pressing into my backend. My panties are soaking wet.

"You're playing a dangerous game, Clem." The

grinding of his teeth let me know he's struggling to brush me off.

"Seriously, Boone, I done told you, I wasn't having sex with you." Sweet Jesus, I want him to slide into my cupcake and spill my batter.

"Your mind is thinking something dirty, isn't it?" He scoots back, and I follow, grinding into his so-called knife.

He knows me so well. I reach back and grab his large hand I'm aching to have on me. I kiss the tips of his fingers, and I think he's going to give in when he drags mine to his mouth. I let out a chirp when he bites me. It does nothing but turn me on.

"You're a biter. I kinda like it." Damn, I don't remember him being a biter before. Maybe he's learned some new tricks.

He chuckles, then pushes my shoulders, laying me flat on the blanket. He hovers over me and for a minute, I think he's going to kiss me. His *lickable* lips are inches from mine. "Your eyes are beautiful," he whispers and swallows hard.

"You want to kiss me, don't you?" I'm not really asking, merely pointing out a fact that's given away in the way he's looking at me right now.

He falls back on the blanket. "No. I'm not

attracted to you at all." He groans as he adjusts the bulge in his jeans.

I lay my hand on his hand that's covering his cock, making sure my fingers brush over it. "I'm not attracted to you either, just so you know."

He's quiet. Moving our joined hands to his chest, I can feel the strumming of his heart. It matches mine.

"I'm wild about you, Boone."

"You just want the one that got away. I'm a taken man." His words aren't convincing.

"You're wild about me too. It's shameful, really. I'm embarrassed for you as to how much you like me."

He chuckles.

I roll over and face him.

"I can't, Clem," he whispers.

"Because of Margret?"

"No, because of you. You ripped my heart out." He moves to his side to face me. "I know you're sorry, but I don't trust you with my heart. I can't."

Well, that took the steam plumb out of me. "Do you honestly love her?"

"That's not what matters."

"You don't think love matters?" I raise my head to look in his eyes.

"I loved you, and you walked out, so I had to find something else that made sense. Margret is reliable, and she loves me even if I don't feel the same for her."

A tear slips down my face. "I get it, but it's sad that you've settled for something less than you deserve."

He runs his knuckles down my cheek, drying it. "I wish things were different. I won't deny that all the feelings I thought I'd left behind for you came crashing in that door when you did."

"Then why can't we try again?" I sniff.

"I've made a commitment, and I need to be with someone I trust."

I turn away from him and curl into a ball. He shifts and nuzzles into my neck. "Get some sleep, Clem."

Sleep is the last thing on my mind. My body doesn't seem to follow suit when exhaustion takes over.

"WELL, WELL, WHAT DO WE HAVE HERE?"

I jolt awake at the sound of Bear's voice. Boone is

on his feet in one solid movement, brushing the hay out of his hair.

"You've got a little something on your face." Bear is pointing at me, wearing a goofy smile.

I wipe off hay that was stuck to the side of my head.

"I guess Wyatt owes me a hundred bucks," he says, opening the stall gate, letting Boone out. He glances at me from the corner of his eye before he disappears.

"What are you rambling on about?" I snatch the blankets from the ground and Henry baas at me.

"I bet him that you'd have Boone in your bed by the end of the week."

"First of all, this isn't my bed, and secondly, nothing happened. Like it's any of your business." I snort. "Wait, you bet Wyatt?"

"Yeah, well, Ellie was in on it too."

Do I really want to know what her guess was? No. Yes. No. "What did she bet?"

"She bet day two, so she already lost her wager. Wyatt said it would never happen."

Good ole Wyatt, always betting against me. "Looks like you lost your money to our lawyer brother. Boone made it pretty clear that he's sticking with Magpie."

He laughs. "I'll have to remember that. Magpie. That will drive her crazy."

"You don't like her?"

"Missy doesn't, and she's a damn good judge of character. Matter a fact, my sweet little observant princess warrior said after dinner the other night, that Uncle Boone had hearts in his eyes when he saw you."

I love that kid. "I think she needs her vision checked. It was more like bear traps." I shake out the blankets and fold them. Whiskey stands and heads over to his watering trough.

"How did the ranch manage against the storm?"

"There are trees down on the property, and one of the houses took a lick on its roof."

"Oh my gawd, the cottage." I rush toward the door.

"I ran by there first to check on you. The cottage is fine. A few limbs down, but no damage."

I walk back over to where he's standing. "Thanks for coming back to get me, by the way. I blame this"—I glance over to where I spent the night with Boone—"whatever it was, on you."

He shuts the stall gate. "You can't blame me for any hanky-panky you two were up to." He chuckles.

"I've already told you, nothing happened." I let out a long-defeated sigh. "He doesn't trust me."

"Can you blame him?" He squares his shoulders toward me.

"Not helping."

"My six-year-old is really good at making voodoo dolls. Do you want her to make one of Margret for you?"

"What have you been teaching that girl?" My laughter rings out.

"Don't be blaming me. She's been hanging out with our mother."

"Momma doesn't know anything about voodoo."

He scratches his head. "Your guess is as good as mine. I know she's been learning how to make moonshine from Wyatt."

"Wyatt makes moonshine? And, why are you letting your six-year-old get anywhere near that stuff?"

"She's not drinking it, and she loves to hang out with Wyatt."

"Really?" My nose scrunches as my eyebrows flatten.

"I think Missy is the only person he's nice to other than Daddy."

I want to learn more about my niece, but I'm

itching to catch up with Boone. "I gotta go. I need to find out what time the new horse is arriving today." I take off for the barn door.

"That's code for you gotta go find Boone," he yells after me.

I flip him the finger.

"Charming as ever." He chuckles and climbs on his four-wheeler.

"Damn it, Boone. You're an idiot. Why did I go telling her anything about Margret?" *Because of those tempting fawn-colored eyes of hers.* She's got me wound tighter than a banjo string. It was all I could do to keep my hands off her when she said she was wild about me.

I know when we were together before, she loved me, but she was never wild about me, not like I see in her eyes now. I can't let that distract me. I'm not the cheating type. I've got to end things with Margret if I'm even going to consider any kind of relationship with Clem. There I go, being a moron again. She left me, and I don't trust her. I need to stay as far away from Clem Calhoun as I can.

"Boone! Wait up!"

She's not going to make this easy. I keep my eyes straight and my boots marching full steam ahead.

"Boone!"

Dang it, she's determined.

She's out of breath when she catches up with me. "Where are you going in such a hurry?"

I don't slow my pace. "I've got work to do. I'm late getting started as is, and now I've got cleanup of the property to manage."

"I thought maybe we could talk over breakfast."

She runs into me when I stop. "I don't have time for breakfast, and there's nothing for us to talk about. I made myself pretty clear last night. You and I are nothing more than friends. I'm marrying Margret."

"But you don't love her."

My feet start moving again. "Don't matter."

"It does matter."

I whirl around to face her. "You need to worry about getting your act together. That horse will be here by noon."

"But I thought you and I made some real progress last night."

"We did. We established that we're friends and that I'm a taken man. End of conversation." I'm lying to myself. I'd like nothing more than to strip her of her clothes right here in front of God and all these cows. I squeeze my eyes tight, trying to keep my dick from getting hard. When I look between my lashes, there are tears in the corners of eyes.

She opens her mouth to say something but snaps it shut and runs off. I hated doing that to her.

I should go after her.

I take one step.

Nope, don't do it. Leave well enough alone.

"Hey, handsome man of mine," I hear from behind me.

Margret. If I was prone to eye-rolling, mine would be stuck up to the sky. I can't deal with two women before I've had a strong cup of coffee.

"You have hay in your hair," she says, kissing my cheek.

"What are you doing here so early?" My words are gruffer than I mean them to be.

"Did someone wake up on the wrong side of the bed?" She ruffles her hand through my hair.

"I'm sorry. I've got a lot of clean up to do after yesterday's storm. I don't have time to visit with you."

She gazes around the area. "That brings me to one of the reasons why I'm here," she whispers.

I don't bother asking; she's going to tell me anyway.

"Daddy wanted me to come over and check on *his* horse." She's still whispering.

"I don't know anything about your dad's horse. The only animals on this ranch belong to the Calhouns."

"Don't be silly. After last night's conversation with him, you know exactly what I'm talking about."

"I told him last night, and I'm telling you right now, the Thoroughbred isn't for sale."

She pouts her painted-red lips. "You'll have to tell him yourself again. I don't want to get in between you and Daddy."

"I have no problem reminding him. I've got to get going."

She runs her hand down my arm. "You didn't let me get to the second reason I came here."

I have a feeling I don't want to know. "Spill it. I ain't got all day."

She steps on her tiptoes, and her lips are touching my ear. "You and I haven't had any alone time. I really could use a piece of my handsome cowboy." She grabs my crotch. Clem glares at me as she rushes by us.

I take her wrist and brush her hand off me. "You and I need to talk, but it ain't happening right now."

"Why you being so mean, Boone Methany?"

I grind my teeth together, reeling in my temper. "I'm sorry, I don't mean to be. You've caught me at a bad time. Please, we'll talk later."

"Okay, but I'll be expecting some Boone time." She glances down at my crotch.

I head out to the pasture where I see Chet and Bear swinging an ax on a tree that took out a section of the barbed wire fence. My boots sink in the spongy, wet ground underfoot as I make my way over to them. The smell of rain and manure hang in the air. Several cows are grazing, one looks up and moos loudly. His head swings to the right, and he starts walking sideways. Something has him spooked. I stand next to Chet.

"That cow sees something."

He and Bear stop chopping the limbs from the downed tree. "There, over the top of the hill." Bear points.

"That coyote is looking for food."

"Damn it. I was in such a hurry to fix the fence to keep the cattle from getting out, I forgot my rifle." Chet removes his hat.

He carries that thing everywhere. I take the ax out of his hand. "I'll keep him away from the herd. You two keep working on getting that tree out of here."

"I'll help too." Wyatt pulls up on a four-wheeler.

I step over the tree and avoid the barbed wire, heading straight for the cows. The coyote has inched closer, and he's brought a couple of friends with him. They spread out like they're on a hunt.

"Chet, I think we're going to need that rifle," I holler to him.

"I'll go get it." Wyatt hops on the four-wheeler and hauls tail toward the main house.

The pack is pretty brazen. I raise the ax when they move closer. "Get out of here!" I yell. I stomp my boots on the ground, trying to scare them away. One stops, but the other two pick up their pace toward a steer. One swings wide, the other straight on.

I take off, screaming at the cow to get him to move. He's like a deer in the headlights. I get to him just in time before the coyote can sink his teeth into him. I clip him with the ax, and he runs off. I look up to see the other one only feet from me, snarling, heading straight for me. Before I can swing back, the sound of a rifle blares out from behind me. The coyote falls lifeless to the ground.

Clem cocks the hammer of the rifle, waiting to take another shot. "I saw Daddy left his rifle by the door. I know storms bring out the coyotes looking for food. I thought I'd bring it to him."

"Good thing you did," I tell her.

"I'm thinking you'd have been his next meal had I not shown up."

"Thanks."

"Nice shot, Clem." Chet pats her on the shoulder.

"I had a good teacher."

He takes the rifle out of her hands. "Let's get back to work," he grumbles.

"Well, that was short-lived," I hear her mumble under her breath.

"I'm going to help get this fence back up. Why don't you go check out the chicken pen. Make sure they're still alive."

I watch her walk away. Damn she looked good holding that rifle. I love a woman that can take care of herself. I don't think Margret would know what to do with one.

"Boy, you're asking for trouble." Chet points at me.

"What?"

"I see the way you're watching her."

"Watching hell, I found them sleeping in the barn together." Bear chuckles.

"Is that why I couldn't find you this morning? Don't let that girl distract you from your work around here," Chet grumbles.

"You'd rather him be with Margret?" Wyatt's back, and walking in our direction. "That woman is after Calhoun money."

"Actually, her father is." They need to know what Tom is up to.

They all turn in my direction. "What are you talking about?" Chet tugs his work gloves off.

"I had a meeting with Tom Maynard yesterday. He'd been bugging Margret to get me to their house for dinner. He thinks that by me marrying his daughter, he owns me, and our prized Thoroughbred."

"What the fuck?" Bear yanks off his hat.

"Don't worry. I told him neither one of us were for sale."

"That man's been trying to buy our property for years. He tried to steal it from us when we were struggling." Wyatt steps in front of me. "You need to separate yourself from that gold digger."

"He threatened that someone I love would pay the price if I dumped his daughter."

"He did what?" Chet barks. "I'll kill that fucker if he steps one foot on this property."

"Let me worry about Tom. I'm not going to let

him anywhere near this family. I just need some time to come up with a plan."

Chet places his hand on my shoulder. "I trust you to take care of it, Son."

"Thanks, I will. In the meantime, don't treat Margret any differently than what you normally do."

"I'm good with ignoring her." Bear gets back to moving limbs off the fence.

"I'll be keeping a good eye on her and her family. He's a sneaky bastard. I'll do some snooping to find out what's up his sleeve." Wyatt climbs on the four-wheeler.

"I guess that means he's not helping," Bear fusses.

"I'll get some men over here to help us." I pull out my cell phone.

Within the hour, five ranch hands helped move the tree and mended the fence. I go back to the barn, get my truck, and they climb in the back. We inspect the property for further damage, stopping to fix it along the way.

On one pass by the barn, I see Mrs. Calhoun, Clem, and Missy working inside the chicken pen. I honk the horn and wave. Old lady Calhoun waves back, and Missy swings her arms over her head like she's calling for an SOS. Clem just glares.

CHAPTER TWELVE
CLEM

"**A**ren't those the same clothes you were wearing yesterday?" Momma asks as she reaches down to pick up an egg.

"Um...yeah, I got stuck in the barn last night when it stormed."

"You smell like horse poop." Missy pinches her nose shut.

I take a whiff of myself. She's right. I stink.

"Why don't you run to the house and get a nice long, hot shower. Bear keeps a clean pair of overalls folded in the linen closet. May be a little big, but they'll do the trick."

"Thanks, Momma."

"While Aunt Clem is in the shower, can we bake

cookies?" Missy has her hands pressed together like she's praying.

"Sure we can, sweetie. Let's finish up here first." Momma tweaks her nose.

I run to the house and take a quick shower. I've got too much to do to waste time scrubbing. I find a tank top in Ellie's old room and slip on Bear's overalls. Damn, now I really look like I belong here. The sound of Momma and Missy downstairs has me heading to the kitchen. Momma is pulling down supplies, and Missy is tying on my old apron.

"What kind are you making?" I slide up next to Missy.

"Chocolate chip. They're grandpa's favorite." Her smile is so sweet.

"I heard you make voodoo dolls." I lean my elbows on the chopping block island next to her.

She taps her finger to her chin. "You want one of Uncle Boone's girlfriend, don't ya?"

Smart girl. "No, I was just curious as to how you know how to make them."

"One of my friends at school says her momma is a witch. She brought one in for show-n-tell and taught us how to make them. They don't really work. If they did, Margret's hair would've turned the color of pumpkin when I dyed it."

I can't help but laugh with her. "You seriously don't like her, do you?"

"Not one little bit. I don't know what uncle Boone sees in her. You're much prettier than she is."

"Thank you, but..."

"I know you left him at the church. I've heard the stories. Why would you do that? Uncle Boone is so sweet." Her eyes look dreamy.

"Well, at the time, I had my reasons."

"You still love him?"

"You know, you're so grown up for a six-year-old. Why don't we talk about some things you like to do instead?" Thank goodness that distracts her. She goes on and on about Bear taking her to ride dirt bikes. I'm off the hook, at least for now.

The smell of cookies drags Daddy into the house. "Those cookies smell like they need to be in my belly." He places a kiss on top of Missy's head from behind her.

She tilts her head up to look at him. "You always say that."

"It's true. You and Grandma make the best cookies in the world."

I walk over to the sink and wash my hands. "I gotta get going. That horse will be here anytime."

"Would you like some company?" Daddy asks as he stuffs half a cookie in his mouth.

I'm stunned that he asked me. "I'd like that."

"I think I hear the horse trailer pulling up now." He grabs a handful of fresh out of the oven cookies.

"Can I come too?" Missy jumps off her stool.

"You have to help me clean up this mess first, then you can go see the horse." Momma waves a finger at her.

"Aw shucks." She pouts.

I squat in front of her. "It will give me time to get him settled. You can help me brush him out later if you want."

She flings her arms around my neck. "Thank you, Aunt Clem."

"You're welcome, sweetie." I stand, and Daddy holds the door open for me.

"Are you sure you're ready to train this horse?" he asks as he walks beside me.

"I am. It's been a long time, but I'm looking forward to it."

"I'm truly surprised that Wyatt agreed to let you be his trainer."

I stop walking. "Wyatt?"

"Yeah. He purchased the horse the day after you arrived."

"I thought Boone was letting me train him."

"He is. He's in charge of all the training around here, but Wyatt suggested it to him. He disagreed rather loudly, but something changed his mind. You wouldn't happen to know what it was, would you?" He's got a mischievous gleam in his eyes.

"I don't claim to know how Boone thinks. I'm more surprised that it was Wyatt's idea. He hates me." We start walking again.

"Those are some strong words. He doesn't hate you. He doesn't like what you did to this family. You should take the time to get to know him a little bit."

Maybe he's right.

The horse trailer parks and Wyatt is the first one to open the trailer. It's a beautiful chestnut-colored, hot-blooded six-month-old thoroughbred. His nose and front legs are pale white.

"He's stunning." I admire his beauty as Wyatt walks him down the metal ramp.

"He's from the same bloodline as Whiskey River," Daddy informs me. "He's already got some speed. Wyatt and I've had our eye on him since birth."

"What's his name?"

Wyatt turns in my direction. "You'll be training him, you name him."

"You're going to let me name your racehorse?" I'm shocked.

"You'll be spending more time with him than anyone. He'll talk to you and let you know what his name should be."

"We have Whiskey. He should be Moonshine," I tease.

Both men look at each other. "I like it." Wyatt smiles. "I like it a lot."

"I was only kidding."

"No, it's perfect. I can have a label made of the horse and put it on my homegrown moonshine."

He's right; it is the perfect name for him. I edge up to the horse and stroke his face. "Moonshine it is."

We get him settled into the barn, and Missy pays him a visit. It's been a long, hard day for everyone with the cleanup. I'm ready to go home and sleep for hours. I walk in my cottage, and Ethan is stretched out on the couch.

"Hey," he says when he sees me.

"Hey yourself. Where you been?"

"Bear found me, and I helped him chop up trees." He holds up his blistered hands.

"Ouch."

"These city-boy hands haven't ever seen hard labor."

"You'll live. Did you clean them up?"

"Ellie did, then she kicked me out."

"You mean for the night?"

"I'm not sure. She said something about needing to spread her oats. I have no idea what she meant."

I plop down on the couch next to him. "I think it's her way of saying she's done with you. I told you not to get attached to her."

He sits and runs his hand over his face. "I like her."

"I don't get the feeling that she's ready to be with one man."

"I'll give her some space, but I'm not throwing in the towel."

His words barely clear his mouth before Ellie walks through the door without even knocking. Ethan stands. "Did you change your mind?" He sounds so hopeful.

"Nope. Clem, get some decent clothes on. We're going out."

"I'm exhausted. Let's do it another night."

"Tonight is our night. Bear's band is playing at the Barn and Barrel."

"That place is still open?" It's been around as long as I can recall.

"Yep. Old man Tillie's son bought it a few years back and revived it."

"Scout Tillie owns it?"

"He sure does. Once he got his teeth fixed, he turned out to be one hot cowboy."

"All right, I'll go, but I'm not staying out all night. I have to start training Moonshine in the morning."

"What?" they say in unison.

"Moonshine. That's the name of Wyatt's new racehorse."

"He's letting you near his horse?" She laughs.

"I know, right? Do you think he has something up his sleeve?" I'm not very trusting of him.

"I think he remembers how good you were, that's all."

"Can I come to the bar too?" Ethan asks.

"No. It's just us girls." Ellie's voice is firm. Poor Ethan looks so disappointed. "I'll wait for you at the house." She turns and walks away.

"I'm sorry, Ethan. I'd let you come with, but I think you should give her some space. I can talk to her if you'd like?"

"No. I don't want you involved in my love life."

I want to mock him. I don't think love is even close to what Ellie is feeling, but he looks so upset, I decide better of it. "I'm going to go find something to wear."

Twenty minutes later, I'm walking over to Ellie's house dressed in a pair of tight jeans, a plaid shirt tied around my waist, cowgirl boots, and my hair is braided to the side.

"Now that's the Clem that used to live here." Ellie whistles at me. "Too bad Boone isn't coming along. He'd never be able to resist you."

"I heard you had a bet that he'd be in my bed in two days."

"Did I lose?" she asks, shutting the door to her truck.

"Not only did you lose, but he's made it perfectly clear that we are nothing more than friends."

She backs out of the driveway. I wave at Ethan who's standing in the cottage doorway, watching us leave.

"I won't count on that. He obviously wants that golden vagina of yours."

"Ellie!"

"What? You left the man at the altar, and he still wants you. There must be something magical about it." She howls in laughter.

"You leave my taco out of this." I try to sound

mad, but a giggle breaks free. "I want to know what you did to Ethan," I ask when we finally settle down.

"I let him dip his one-eyed monster into my pink taco a few times, and he liked it a little too much."

"You have such a way with words." I snort. "So you used him?"

"I don't want to be tied to one man. He got too clingy for my liking. Too bad, 'cause I kinda liked his city-boy ways." She waggles her colored-in eyebrows a few times.

"Please don't string him along. He likes you."

"I clipped those ties." She makes a scissor motion with her fingers.

She pulls in the dirt parking lot of the Barn and Barrel. The lot is full of pickup trucks and cowboys tailgating.

"I don't ever recall this place being this busy."

"It's been this way since Scout bought it."

"You and he ever hook up?"

"Every Saturday night." She applies a thick coat of red lipstick and hops out of the truck.

Why did I ask? I feel sorry for Ethan. I follow her inside, and all eyes are locked on her breasts that are protruding out of her low-cut top. She finds an empty table near the dance floor.

"I'll be right back." She winks and meanders over to the bar.

I sit and watch as Bear and his band come in from a side door and start picking up their instruments. Ellie walks back over with two oversized beers and hands me one.

"Ladies drink free." She tips her glass to mine and chugs half hers down in one swallow.

"Hi, Ellie. Well, as I live and breathe, please tell me that's not Clementine?" Scout, who was once homely but is now gorgeous, points at me.

"The one and only." I smile.

"Whoowee girl, you're a purdy thing." He scoops me into a hug, and I squirm free.

"It's good to see you too."

"Has Boone got a load of her yet?" He drapes his arm over Ellie's shoulder.

"That he has."

"Don't look now, but his snooty girlfriend just walked through the doors."

We all turn to see Margret. She's dressed in a bright red dress with expensive boots on. She appears too rich for this establishment.

"Does she always come to ladies' night?" I ask.

"First time I've seen her in here without Boone." He kisses Ellie on the cheek. "I've got to go help behind the bar. I'll see you later tonight." He slaps her on the ass, and she yelps.

We sit, and Bear's band starts to strum a few cords. "Welcome to the Barn and Barrel. Who's ready to get down and dirty tonight?" He's loud over the mic. The crowd responds with cheers and beer being spilled on the floor.

"Bear's Midnight Ranchers are going to keep you entertained tonight." The drummer hits the cymbals.

"Oh, I like the name of his band. Does he do this every weekend?"

"He plays here every other Saturday. Momma keeps Missy for the night. The money he makes playing, he's putting in a college fund for Missy."

"He really is a good dad, isn't he?"

"He's had a lot of help, but he's done good for a single dad."

The dance floor fills, and Ellie keeps ordering us drinks. I haven't had this much fun in a long time, and Bear's band is truly good.

"There's someone special back in town, and she plays a mean violin."

"Oh gawd, please tell me some other wayward sister has returned to town. I haven't picked up the violin since I left.

"Come on, Clem. Get your pretty little ass up here and play with us."

I shake my head.

"Go up there and play." Ellie's voice is blaring.

"I can't. I haven't touched the thing in years."

"It's like riding a bike." She pushes my shoulder.

"How would you know? Have you ever ridden a bike or played an instrument?"

"I've played many an instrument, but not ones with strings." She laughs and winks.

Bear moseys up to the table, pulling me and the chair from the table. "Help a guy out here. I've already told them how good you are."

He takes my hand and drags me on stage. One of his band members hands me a violin. I blow out a deep breath and take it from him, placing it on my shoulder. I take the bow to the strings, and Ellie was right—it all comes flooding back to me. I close my eyes and play like I haven't played in years. It's another thing that I'd forgotten how much I loved. The violin, the horses, and Boone. Not necessarily in that order. My life was good.

I play the next three songs with them and rejoin Ellie at the table. She's surrounded by hot cowboys.

"See I told you, like riding a bike."

I pick up my now warm beer and lift it to her.

"That was fun." I slosh it down. When I slam the empty mug on the table, I catch a glimpse of a red dress standing over me.

"You're a woman of many talents." Margret claps smugly. "The Calhouns never mentioned that you were musically inclined."

"She's inclined to a lot of things you don't know about." Ellie makes a jerking motion with her hand, and I nearly fall on the floor.

Margret narrows her eyes at her. "You're such the lady."

"Better I be me, than you," Ellie fires back.

"Did you need something?" I look up at her.

"I was wondering if we could have a chat?" She angles her head in the direction of the door.

"Go back to your lonely table in the corner," Ellie chimes in.

"No, it's okay. I'll be right back." I follow Margret out the door and over to her expensive car. A rather large man steps out from the driver's side. He walks up beside her and crosses his massive arms over his chest.

"I want the two of us to come to an understanding. Boone is my fiancé, and you will keep your claws away from him."

I brazenly step up close to her. "And, if I don't?"

"There's no question, you will. You'll also convince him to sell my daddy his Thoroughbred."

"I'll do no such thing."

She flips my braid over my shoulder. "Oh you will, or that pretty face of yours might not stay so pretty." Big guy uncrosses his arms.

"Is there a problem here?" Wyatt's voice comes from behind me.

"No. No problem at all." Margret bats her eyes.

"I believe I heard you threaten my baby sister" Wyatt doesn't back down.

Her bodyguard balls his fists. She touches his arm. "We were just coming to an understanding."

"When I tell Boone what you said, he'll never marry you," I spit out.

"You better hope he does or your family is going to be on the losing end."

"Why you..." Wyatt bolts forward. Big guy connects with his jaw and Wyatt falls backward.

I step between them. "That's enough."

"It's enough for now. Remember what I said." She gets in the car. Big guy eyes Wyatt until he's firmly behind the wheel.

"You okay?" I lay my hand on his chest.

"I'm fine." He moves his jaw back and forth.

"We should probably get some ice on that."

"I'll take care of it. Get in my truck, I'm taking you home."

"I need to go tell Ellie."

"I'll text her. We need to get you home where it's safe. I'll call a family meeting tomorrow."

CHAPTER THIRTEEN
BOONE

"She fucking said what?" Chet slams his fists on the dining room table where we're all gathered around. "I don't take kindly to anyone threatening my family. You better make sure she doesn't step foot on my property again!" His voice fills the room.

"This isn't Boone's fault." Clem tries to defend me.

"You stay out of this!" I swear his eyes burst with flames at her.

"I..."

"It's okay. I can defend myself." I rest my hand on her shoulder. "I'll deal with this."

"Damn straight you will!" Chet's still yelling. He straightens his spine and clasps Wyatt's shoulder.

"I'm glad you were there last night, Son. Things could've really gotten out of hand."

"I've filed a restraining order against Margret."

"Dang it, Wyatt. I wish you would've let me handle it. I created this problem, and I'll deal with it."

"We need to put twenty-four-hour security on Whiskey River until the race in two weeks. I don't trust that bastard to not try to pull something."

"What about Clem? The threat Margret made was against her."

"She'll stay in the main house with us until all this has blown over."

"I want to stay at the cottage," Clem interrupts.

"Goddamn it, Clem! For once in your life, would you do what you're told!" His fists make impact again, rattling the table.

"Why would I want to stay in this house with you. I don't even feel welcome here." Her face turns pink.

"She can stay at my place. I have security cameras set up. She'll be safe there." I know it's a dumb idea.

Clem's chair scraps the hardwood floor, and she storms out.

"Fine, but I want to be kept up to date with

anything that goes on around here. Two fucking weeks and that horse could bring in the money we need to save this place."

"Dad, we've already paid all the outstanding loans. You know we pooled our monies." Wyatt stands.

"I don't take handouts. I consider myself still balls-deep in debt."

"We're family. That's what we do. Look how many times you and Mom have helped me," Bear tells him.

"That's different. It's my job to help my children even when they don't deserve it."

"Are you ever going to let me live down my past?" Bear is on his feet. "Or Clem for that matter." He adds

Mrs. Calhoun, who's been quiet the entire time, taps her hand on the table. "We've all needed forgiveness at some point in our lives. Haven't we dear?" She speaks directly to Chet.

I can hear the gasps that are being held inside.

Chet locks his jaw and walks out.

"You boys do whatever you have to do to keep this family safe," she says, and everyone scatters from the table.

I make my way to the horse barn, knowing that's where I'll find Clem.

"I can take care of my own damn self. I don't need men to do that for me." She's saddling up Moonshine and muttering to herself.

"We only want you safe." She jumps at the sound of my voice.

"Don't be sneaking up on a girl like that." She grabs the horse's reins and starts walking him out.

"I'm sorry she threatened you. I won't let her hurt you or anyone else in this family."

"I'm not afraid of her."

I snag her arm before she can walk off. "You're more afraid you'll never be part of this family again."

Wetness fills her eyes. "He'll never forgive me."

"He's a hard man, but I know he loves you."

"Well, he's not any nicer to Bear."

"Bear's done a lot of things that tarnished the Calhoun name, and that's something your father has a hard time forgiving. Bear's changed, and he's a good guy. He'll eventually win him over."

"I don't know. I'm beginning to think it was a mistake coming back here."

"Ready to leave already?" Her words piss me off.

"What's the point? Daddy hates me, your fiancé

wants me dead, and you..." She doesn't finish her sentence.

"Me what, Clem?"

"You don't want me."

I jerk her body firm to mine and crash my lips on her mouth. She opens, and I sink inside her, tasting every corner of her sweetness. Our teeth clash, trying to crawl inside one another. When I draw back, we're gasping for air, our chests heaving. "Don't you ever think for one minute that I don't want you. That's never been our issue."

"But you don't trust me," her words blow across my cheek.

I release her. "No."

She licks her lips and then wipes her mouth with the back of her hand. She winds the reins tightly in them and leads Moonshine out of the barn.

Damn it to hell. Why did I kiss her? It's only going to make matters worse between us.

"Where is she?" Chet comes through the back door.

"She's headed to the track with Moonshine."

"I'll go find her."

"While you're out there, why don't you try telling your daughter that you love her?"

"She knows I love her," he growls.

"Really? How would she know that? You're constantly yelling at her and reminding her of all her sins."

He stops inches from me. "You've got a lot of room to talk."

"I told her I forgive her."

"Really?" He uses my words against me. "Then why do you watch her every move, yet keep her at arm's length?"

I stare at him.

"I'll tell you why. Because you don't trust her. You're terrified to let her in. You're afraid she'll crush you again."

"I'm not arguing with your logic, Chet."

"Then don't lecture me about my daughter. You'd be a lucky man to have her. She's fucking braver than all of us combined. It took lady balls for her to leave the way she did. Doesn't mean I condone it, but she did what she had to do. It took me a long time to realize it."

"Have you ever told her that?" I chuckle.

"She needs to earn my trust. I'm not going to cut her any slack. I wouldn't for the boys, and I won't do it for my daughter."

"Maybe she needs you to."

"Maybe you need to open your eyes as to the second chance you've been given."

We're at a standoff.

"I hate to interrupt this cockfight, but Margret is parked outside the main gate." Ellie sways toward us.

"I'll take care of it." I flex my jaw and keep my stare with Chet.

He doesn't give an inch. "You remember our conversation, and get that woman out of here."

I storm out of the barn and hop on one of the four-wheelers. Dust travels behind me as I speed to the gate. Margret is leaning against her car with her arms crossed over her chest wearing a smug smile.

I slide to a stop feet from her.

"You have some nerve coming here after last night's utter stupidity on your part."

She pulls a piece of paper from her purse. "This was served on my doorstep this morning. Wyatt works fast."

I rip it out of her hand. It's the restraining order. "What did you expect? You threatened Clem."

"I expected my fiancé to be on my side, not the bride that ran away from him." She steps up close to me and splays her hand on my cheek. "You and I were so good together until she showed up."

I move my face from her touch. "It's over, Margret."

She laughs. "It's over when I say it's over. You'll still marry me Boone, or I'll have this land stripped out from under the Calhouns."

"You're kidding yourself. You can't do that."

"I can't, but my daddy sure can. You see, your friend, the smart one," she says sarcastically, "borrowed money from a company to save this ranch. Guess who happens to own that company now. Daddy bought it when we got engaged. Call it a wedding gift if you will."

"So what. I'm sure he had paperwork drawn up and that he's been making the payments."

"Yes, but when Daddy bought the company, they agreed to let him handle all the outstanding loans. He holds all the cards, so to speak. He can call the note due at any time. He'd own this entire land and the cattle on it, including your horse."

"That horse is in my name, not the Calhoun's."

"Yes, and when we're married, half of whatever is yours will be mine."

"You bitch!"

"Now now, Boone. I think you might want to play nice with me. You'll do as my father has asked you or the Calhouns are finished."

"How have I not seen right through you?" My muscles strain in my neck.

"Oh, poor Boone. I picked up the pieces of your broken heart. Too bad the little whore came back."

"Don't you ever call her that again." I'm mere inches from her face.

"The sad part is, I really do love you, Boone."

"This is how you treat people you love?"

"Clem Calhoun walked out on your wedding day, and somehow you're still in love with her. Which by the way, you need to fix. I can't have my soon-to-be husband in love with the likes of her." She pats my cheek and gets back in her car.

"I'll be setting a wedding date for us and Daddy expects that horse to be on our property before the Kentucky Derby in two weeks."

I slam her door shut.

The four-wheeler tips on two wheels as I take off. I need to locate Wyatt to find out more details of the loan. His truck is parked outside his house. I don't bother knocking.

"Wyatt!"

"I'm in here!" he answers.

I throw my hat on his desk. "We're screwed."

"What are you talking about."

"The loan you signed to get your portion of the

money to save this place is owned by Margret's father. He bought the company out months ago. He will call the loan in if I don't marry his daughter."

He grabs a folder from a drawer and flips through the papers. "I didn't get any notice that the company had been bought out."

"How much money do you owe them?"

"I had to come up with the balance that we couldn't get together."

"How much!" I seethe.

"A quarter of a million dollars."

I drop down in a chair, feeling defeated.

"All my money was tied up. I had to borrow it. I don't want my siblings to go in debt to help keep this place, so they know nothing about it."

"How much can you scrounge together now?"

"Not near enough. I've been dumping funds into this place to keep it afloat. We didn't get near the money we needed for the cattle last year. My father was hoping we'd make up for it this year. We can't let this happen. He'll have another heart attack."

"So I'm royally fucked. I'll have to marry Margret."

"I'll try to find another way out of this."

"It won't be soon enough. He wants the horse

before the Derby. He knows we have a good chance of winning the pot this year."

"But you own Whiskey." After he says it, he has an understanding in his eyes. "You marry her and half the horse and its earnings are hers."

"Yep."

"Play along for now. I'll do some digging into his holdings. It sounds like he needs money. Maybe all his assets are tied up in something."

I stand to leave.

"I'm sorry, Boone. I didn't have any other choice at the time."

"It's not your fault. You did what you had to do to save your family. I'll have to do what I need to do now."

CHAPTER FOURTEEN
CLEM

"Are you going to be okay staying here by yourself?" Ethan is spread out on the couch.

"Yes." He's moping. "Your dad came by and installed security cameras on the outside. He was actually friendly to me and invited me to stay at the main house."

"You should take him up on his offer." I drag my overnight bag to the door.

"I'd rather stay here."

"I'm not staying at Boone's any longer than I need to. As soon as this crap is straightened out, I'll be back home. You're more than welcome to sleep in the loft."

"This new pull-out couch of yours is comfortable." He pats the seat cushion. "I'll be fine right here."

"Suit yourself."

"Do you think it's such a good idea to stay at Boone's?"

"My other option was the main house."

"You could stay at Ellie's."

"She didn't volunteer."

"You're still in love with him, aren't you?"

"Don't matter. He doesn't trust me, and if you don't have trust, you got nothing."

A horn blows in the driveway.

"Sounds like your ride is here."

"I didn't ask him to pick me up." I open the door and wave Boone off.

He swings open the truck door and stomps toward me. "I'm making sure you're getting your sassy ass to my house." He grabs my bag.

"I'm more than capable of getting there on my own." I jerk it back from him.

He snatches it from me and bends down, throwing me over his shoulder. "Damn it, Boone! Put me down." I swat at his backside.

He throws my bag in the bed of the truck and opens the door, placing me in the seat. "I swear you're pigheaded."

"And you're a pain in my ass!" He slams the door on me. Ethan is standing in the doorway of the cottage, laughing. Boone tips his hat at him.

"Have a nice time you two!" Ethan yells between his hands.

"I swear to baby Jesus that I hate both of you!" Boone chuckles as he puts the key in the ignition. His diesel roars. I cross my arms over my chest and don't say another word to him.

He drives down the dirt road and over a couple of hills, past several pastures. One fourteen sets directly across the horse track on the opposite side of the main house. He lived in one of the smaller houses before. We'd planned on living in it until we could build our own house on the back end of the property near the river.

He pulls in the driveway and parks. I stay inside the truck. He leans over the bed and carries out my bag, setting it in front of the door to the house.

"You coming or shall I carry you inside?" he hollers.

I kick open the heavy truck door. "I can walk on my own two feet. I don't need your help." I storm in his direction, and he opens the door for me to walk by him.

The place is nice, all decorated with wood and

leather accents. Very manly. He hangs his hat by the door and kicks off his boots. He strides by me, carrying my bag.

"You'll stay in this room." He opens a door to the left of the living area.

It's furnished with light colors of the same shades. There's a double bed, a nightstand, and a three-drawer dresser. The only real color in the room is a light blue comforter on the bed. He sets my bag on the dresser.

"Nothing fancy, but you'll be safe here."

"Thanks, I think." There is no warmth to my words.

"Are you hungry? I was going to make a pot of spaghetti."

"You cook?" I raise my brow.

"After you left, Ellie taught me."

What else did Ellie teach him? The biting thing? I squint my eyes at him.

"What?"

"Nothing. I can help you make dinner."

"I'd rather you not." He scrunches his nose.

"Why not? I know how to cook."

"Because you smell like Moonshine. I'd rather my food not stink like a horse."

I lift my arm to get a whiff. He's right. I smell bad.

"Showers through that door." He points and walks out.

I grab some things from my bag and make my way out of the bedroom. Boone's in the kitchen, whistling some tune with his back to me. I open the door to the bathroom, but a cracked door catches my eye. I quietly lay my things down on the counter and tiptoe to Boone's bedroom.

His bed sets in the center of the large master suite. The four-poster bed with hand carvings of horses on the wood is beautiful. All the furniture in the room looks specially made for him. I step closer and hear a crunch beneath my feet. A picture lays facedown on the floor with pieces of glass around it. Bending down, I carefully pick it up. It's a picture of Boone and Margret at a horse race. I lay it back down like I found it so that he doesn't know I was in here.

There's a drawer slightly ajar on this bedside table. "It's not nice to snoop, Clem," I whisper to myself. That doesn't stop me. I ease the drawer open, and there's a silver picture frame inside. It holds a picture of me. My long hair is blowing in the wind. I'm standing by my favorite black mare I used to ride all the time, dressed in my riding gear.

"He does still love me." I tuck the photo back inside and tiptoe to the bathroom. I wash and realize instead of smelling like a horse, now I smell like Boone. I'm not complaining; I love his scent. I brush out my wet hair and throw on a skirt and t-shirt.

The aroma of spaghetti sauce slaps me in the face when I open the door. "That sure does smell good. I guess I'm hungrier than what I thought."

"It's almost done. Can I pour you a glass of wine?"

"You drink wine?" I sit at the small-top table and tuck myself under it.

"Something else Ellie taught me." He puts the wineglass to his lips.

"Did you hook up with Ellie?"

He damn near chokes on his wine. "No! Hell no! She's your sister for Pete's sake. That would be wrong on so many levels."

"I think you're protesting a little too much." I can't help my glare. Boone's never been a good liar. If I'd looked at him funny, he'd rat himself out.

"You can cut those eyes somewhere else. I've never had sex with Ellie."

I evil-eye him for a few seconds longer. "Okay, I believe you. Now how about sharing that bottle."

He takes down a second glass and pours the red

liquid halfway full. I take it from him, and he serves up two plates of food and tosses on garlic bread.

"This looks so good." I place my napkin in my lap and dive in. "Oh my god. This is the best spaghetti I've ever had."

"Glad you like it." He bites off a piece of bread.

"Have you come up with a plan to take care of this mess?"

He lays his fork down. "The plan is to marry Margret."

"You can't marry her. You don't love her."

"I care about her."

"That ain't good enough. I don't understand the problem."

"No, you don't." He picks up his fork and shovels in a mouthful of food.

"You're still that angry at me that you'd choose to be with Margret out of convenience? Oh, what was it you said...she's reliable." I pick up my wine and take a few big sips.

"I can't tell you the details. Just know that I'm marrying her to keep every one of the Calhouns safe."

It's not only about me. There's something else going on. I'd lay money on the fact that Wyatt knows what it is. "It's not your job to keep us safe."

"No, it's not, but I love this family, and I won't see anything bad happen to them. Now I don't want to talk about it anymore. Eat your food." He points with his fork.

This is about as welcoming as my father's house. Maybe I should've taken him up on his offer. At least there, I wouldn't care if he doesn't pay attention to me. Boone and his darn good looks are distracting. I want to reach up and brush away the hair that's fallen on his forehead. He might stab me with his fork if I did. Even the way he chews his food is sexy. I need more wine.

I get up and take the bottle off the counter, refilling my glass then his. His heated stare burns my backside when I turn around. I sit, and we finish eating in silence. I wash the dishes while he pours himself a shot of whiskey.

"So when is the wedding?"

His glare is back. "I don't know. Soon, I assume."

"You don't even know when your wedding is?" I huff.

"I'm done talking to you about Margret. Why don't you tell me how it went with Moonshine today?"

"Fine."

"That's all you got to say?" He throws his hands in the air.

"You don't want to hear what I have to say!" I plant my hands firmly on my hips.

"Not if it's about Margret."

"How about I'm wild about you, and I'm right here. I'm not going anywhere."

He sighs and runs a hand through his hair. "We need to set some ground rules."

"I know you still love me. Tell me what I have to do to make you want me? I can strip down naked if that would help."

He almost laughs. "There will be no getting naked." He holds up one finger. "No mention of Margret." Another finger goes up. "No talk of how wild you are about me." His third finger rises. "And, absolutely no getting naked around me," I repeat.

I close the distance between us. "Why? You afraid you can't handle it?"

He swallows so hard his Adam's apple bounces. "Nothing is going to happen between us."

"Hmmm...if you say so." I storm off to my room. I sit in the middle of the bed with my arms wrapped around my knees. He slams things around for a bit, then I see the shadow of his feet under my door. I quietly climb off the bed and lean my head against the grain of the wood. I place my hand on it like I can feel him through it.

He breathes deeply, then blows out a long breath. He never utters a word. A tear slips down my cheek when I hear his feet pat away from the door. When his door shuts, I put a plan in motion to seduce Boone. I only hope he has what I need.

I silently move across the wood floor to his kitchen. "If I were Saran Wrap, where would I be?" Opening a drawer, I see it. "Good, it's a new box." I strip out of my clothes and start winding the clear plastic around my body a few times, covering my lady parts in several layers until the box is empty.

"That should do it." I'm naked, but I'm not. No rules broken. I open my mouth to call out Boone's name and the front door flies open at the same time Boone's bedroom door does.

I nearly pass out from embarrassment when I see Wyatt.

"Boone..." His words trail off when he gets a glimpse of me naked underneath the Saran Wrap.

Boone blinks several times as if he doesn't believe his eyes.

"What the hell kinda kinky shit did they teach you in the military?" Wyatt's mouth gapes.

Boone's face is covered in a smile.

Mine is probably the color of scarlet. "I...ummm..."

"You two will have to finish...this"—he points back and forth between the two of us—"hell, I don't even have words." He directs his voice to Boone. "The guard you hired said he saw someone snooping around outside the barn."

"Why didn't he call me?" Boone grabs his hat.

"I couldn't sleep so I was out double-checking all the locks. I told him I'd come get you." His gaze lands on me then he lifts his hand to his face, blocking his view of me. "I didn't realize I'd be interrupting something."

Why am I glued to this spot?

I could die of embarrassment.

I can see the headlines now. Woman dead on the floor. Her body was wrapped in plastic wrap. Momma used to say, *Remember, whatever you put on today might be your last day on this earth. Make sure it's something you'd want to die in.*

This is definitely not it.

"I'll just go to my room now." My body makes a swishing noise as I walk. Wyatt scrambles out the door. Boone takes one last, long look at me and chuckles before he leaves, shutting the door behind him.

"Well, my seduction of Boone didn't go as planned." I change my direction and find his stash of wine. I pop the cork and drink directly from the bottle. "I'm beginning to think the universe is against me and Boone getting back together."

I swallow down more wine.

"I'm sure if Wyatt wouldn't have come barging in, Boone would be ripping this wrap off me."

I drink some more.

"Hells bells, I'd be on my knees licking Richard and the twins by now." I've got to stop; I've got a puddle wetting my thighs.

"Another sip won't hurt me." I guzzle down half the bottle. There's no telling how long Boone will be gone, and this plastic wrap is making me sweat.

My head starts to spin when I put the bottle on the counter. "Maybe I shouldn't have drank that so fast." I'm starting to see double. I lean against the counter and try to find the end of the plastic wrap. "Hmmm...where did it go?" This shit is getting tighter. I bend over and try to find the end at the bottom.

No such luck. I try to tug it down, and the only thing I succeed in doing is getting it lodged in my dirty south. I wouldn't mind Boone exploring up there with his hidey ho, but this is seriously no good.

I try to pull it out, but somehow it gets sucked in further. This can't be happening. All I wanted to do was seduce Boone, and here I am smothering in plastic wrap that's tighter than a nun's rectum.

"Scissors!" Surely he has a pair. I rummage through all the drawers. "Nothing. Who doesn't have kitchen scissors? I know what I'll be buying him."

"Shit!" I've managed to pull it down enough that I have to waddle to walk and I'm dizzy on top of it. I look down, and I have one boob hanging out. "Real sexy, Clem." I stumble to my room and plop down on the bed. I eye my phone on the nightstand.

I could call Ethan.

No.

I could call Ellie.

She'd never let me live it down, or hell she may decide she wants a threesome.

Nope. Not happening.

CHAPTER FIFTEEN
BOONE

What the hell was she doing naked... wrapped in plastic? I've already asked myself this question a million times by the time we make it to the barn. I'm having a really hard time not wanting to turn around and go back to the house.

"What was that all about? Has Clem completely lost all her good senses?" Wyatt finally speaks.

"I have no idea what's going through her head." I intend on finding out as soon as I get home.

We walk the perimeter of the barn. There are a pair of footprints leading up to one of the windows. I compare it to mine. The markings of the boots are a size eleven, but there is no sign of whoever it was sticking around.

"It was probably one of Maynard's hired hands scoping out a way into the barn. I'm sure he ran off when he saw the guard inside."

"Yeah, well that means we're going to have to take turns monitoring all the entrances of the ranch. I'll make a schedule so we can each have a set time. I'll file a police report too." Wyatt scuffs his boots in the dirt.

"I don't think that will do any good. All we have is footprints. Any number of people could have left them here. You and I know they don't belong, but it will be difficult to convince the police of that."

"You're right. What do you suggest we do?"

"What are you ladies doing hanging out by the barn this time of night?" Chet walks up with his shotgun gripped in his hand.

"The guard saw someone snooping around. What are you doing out here?" I face him.

"I installed cameras around Clem's place. An alarm went off. I was going to grab one of the four-wheelers and go check it out. Want to come along?"

"I'll go. You finish searching around here." I follow Chet to the ATVs. We drive down to 102 and Ethan has all the lights on, and he's standing in the doorway.

"Did you see who was out here?" He acts nervous.

"No. I didn't get a good look on the screen." Chet calms Ethan as I walk the area. The same set of boot prints are on the ground. A branch makes a cracking noise, and I shine my flashlight. A raccoon's beady eyes light up. I scan the area with my light but don't see anything other than critters.

I make my way back to the front of the house. Ethan has a bag packed and is hopping on the back of Chet's four-wheeler. "I'm taking him back to the main house for tonight. I'll drop him off, then Wyatt and I will keep an eye on things. You get some sleep. You and Bear can take a shift tomorrow night."

"Will do." I jump on and ride back to my house. I'm anxious as to what I'll see when I walk inside. I unlock the door, and the lights are off. There's not even a beam of light coming out from any of the doors. For a moment, I'm terrified someone took her. My heart races as I make my way to her room.

"Clem, you in here?"

I hear a sniff followed by a soft yes. "I'm turning on the light." I do, and I see her curled up in the middle of the bed with the sheets drawn over her. "You okay?"

"No," she whimpers.

I sit on the edge of the bed. "What was all that about earlier?"

"I was going to try to seduce you. You laid down your stupid no naked rule, so I figured a way around it." Tears roll down her cheeks.

I chuckle. "You always were the creative one."

"Wyatt had to burst in and ruin everything."

"Is that why you're crying?"

"No!" she wails and pulls the sheet tighter with one hand.

"It wouldn't have worked anyway. I told you I'm marrying Margret."

"You don't love her," she cries harder.

"No, but you and I can't be together." *No matter how much I want you.*

"Just go away."

I see the shape of a bottle under her sheet. "What do you have under there?" I tug at the sheet and see plastic wrap. She pulls hard and tries to cover it. "Are you still covered in Saran Wrap?"

"Yes." Her cries get louder. "I can't get it off!"

I pull the sheets off her and pat the bed next to me. "Come here."

She wipes her nose on the pillowcase, then sits beside me. "I'm humiliated."

"If I were in your shoes—or should I say plastic

wrap—I would be too," I tease. The corner of her lip raises. I brush her hair over her shoulder, and my cock gets hard just from the feel of her. "Only you could be beautiful in this get up."

She blinks back her tears. "Don't say stuff like that to me if you don't mean it."

"I do mean it."

She leans in and brushes her soft lips against mine. I take both my hands and place them on either side of her face, drawing her deeper. She tastes like sweet red wine. "What the hell are you doing to me, Clem?" My voice is tight and low.

"I think it's called kissing? If you have to ask, I think you haven't been doing it right." She slides her hand to my thigh.

I squeeze my eyes tightly shut. I know I'm going to hate myself, but I can't do this with her. God knows I want to. I'd love nothing more than to bury myself inside her. I've missed her body, the taste of her skin, the cute noise she makes when she's trying to hold back her orgasm. My dick is protesting my decision-making right now.

"We can't do this. As much as I want to, we have to stop."

"Give me a reason other than Margret. I know

you want me as much as I'm dying to have you." She bites her lip.

"I can't deny that."

"We're back to the trust thing again." Her eyes tear over again.

"No. I don't want to be a man that cheats."

She hangs her head.

I run my hand over her back and feel for the end of the plastic wrap. I look over her shoulder, and I want to cup her breast that's outside the wrap. As if she could feel my thoughts, her nipple puckers like I've touched her, squeezed her, maybe even sucked her into my mouth. My dick is throbbing. I know she sees it when a small gasp escapes her.

"I found it," I all but groan. I slowly peel the plastic away. "Stand," I tell her, and she does as I ask. I do the same and move behind her. I circle her, unwrapping her like a present. A present that I desperately want. Every time I walk in front of her, her gaze is on me, etching into my skin. I know I've had her before, but not this version of her and I'm growing achingly harder, blinding me to the reasons as to why we can't do this. I never thought I'd want this woman again, but here I am, peeling off her layers in more ways than one, and wanting her more than I ever did before. Did I ever stop loving this woman? Am I an idiot or a man that sold his heart to Clem a long time ago? I hate her, yet I love her. It's a fine line I teeter on with her.

I keep unwrapping the layers until she's completely naked. She doesn't flinch or try to hide herself, which is an even bigger turn-on.

"Trust me when I tell you this is not what I want to do in this moment." I reach over to the bed, grab the sheet and drape it over her shoulders.

She bites her lower lip between her teeth. "What is it that you'd rather do?"

I swallow hard, not wanting to answer her, but not being able to stop the words from coming out. "I want to have my mouth on every inch of you."

She takes my hand and places it on the delicate skin of her neck. "Like here?" Her voice is sexy and raw.

I nod.

She lowers my hand to her shoulder. "How about here?"

I nod again.

My hand goes lower with hers, and I don't fight it. "And, here?"

I involuntarily toy with her nipple. "Yes," I hiss.

She licks her lips, causing another jerk from my lower body parts. She inches my hand down her body to between her legs. "And how about here?" Her fawn-colored eyes are luring me in further.

"Most especially here." I part her with my fingers and run them between her folds. Her head falls back, and she moans. I lose all control. Pushing her back on the bed, I kneel down and angle my head between her legs. She's wetter than a river. I can only imagine the dirty thoughts pooling in her head. She watches me as I ease my tongue inside her, rolling it all around her edges, not wanting to miss a drop of her. My mouth isn't the only thing that wants to explore her. I roll her nub between my fingers, and she purrs likes a kitten. I lap her up, sucking, dipping in and out like I would with my cock that's straining against my zipper. I know she's close when she drops from her elbows and her body crashes to the bed. Her hips sway and push harder against my mouth, needing more friction, which I willingly apply. Her body starts to shiver in small little waves. I suck harder and insert two fingers inside her. Her body rides them like she would ride me. I press my crotch into the side of the bed to stave off the pulses running through me. She makes the sweet sound that I remember, and her body lets go, totally submitting to me. I lap her up like a dog to water. My thirst for her only grows more with each pulsation against my tongue.

I want so much more of her, but I won't let myself go any further. I lick her off my lips and stand. Her head lifts to look at me. Her gaze can't help but land on the bulge in my pants. "Good night, Clem." It takes every ounce of my strength to walk out. I step over the pile of Saran Wrap on the floor and shut the door behind me. I go to my room and directly into the master bathroom, turning on the shower. I strip and stand under the spray of the water. I'm barely wet before I grasp my cock and start with punishing strokes. I muffle my groans and spill into the water beneath me.

"Damn her," I say under my breath. "Why does she have to make me want her so badly. She's broken my heart once. I refuse to let her break the man I am now. This family is counting on me to keep the wolves away. I need to become the Big Bad Wolf and keep little miss edible Red Riding Hood in her cottage made of wood, keeping her away from my *wood*.

I get in bed knowing darn good and well I'll either toss and turn all night or dream of Clem.

A door slamming startles me awake. I jump out of bed. "Clem!" She doesn't answer. I hear the motor start on the ATV. I peek beyond the curtain, and Clem is on it. I rush out the door and feel the warm air cling to my body.

"Clem! Where are you going!" I yell over the sound of the engine. She frowns at me as Bear pulls up alongside her. He chuckles and says something to her. It's then I realize, I'm stark naked. I reach inside the door and grab my hat off the hook, covering my junk.

"Momma's bringing breakfast over for you and Clem. You might want to put some clothes on before she gets here!" Bear is laughing.

I ignore him. "Clem. Come back inside. We need to talk!"

She gives me her evil eye and peels out of the driveway.

"Looks to me like she doesn't have anything to say to you. Maybe you should try some different moves on her next time." He points to my hat, snorting, then takes off after her. I see Mrs. Calhoun's car throwing up dust coming around the corner. I duck inside to find my clothes.

"What are you so all fired up about?" Bear asks as soon as we park in front of the barn.

"Nothin." I'm in no mood to discuss Boone. I can't believe he left my room. I kept expecting him to come back. How dare he! I'm dumber than a box of rocks. He's told me repeatedly he doesn't want me. He took pity on me last night, lapping up my lady flower and I melted right into it. His tongue is magical, turned my brains to mush.

I jerk open the barn door, startling the guard. I stomp past him straight into Moonshine's stall.

"You can go home now," I hear Bear tell him.

I give Moonshine a quick bite of oats and saddle him up.

"You training him this morning?" Bear leans his arms on the gate.

"I'm riding him."

"You sure got your panties in a wad."

"Don't talk about my panties," I snap.

He laughs. "Maybe you aren't wearing any... kinda like Boone." He snorts at his own joke.

"I'm not responsible for Boone's lack of clothing." I take Moonshines reins and lead him out. Bear follows me. "Don't you have something else you need to be doing?" I ask, over my shoulder.

"Right now, this is more fun."

"There's two cattle missing!" Daddy yells, marching in Bear's direction. "Whatever you're goofing off doing, you need to get your ass to the pasture and find them."

Bear does an about-face and runs to the four-wheeler.

"You got those stalls cleaned out already?" Daddy looks at his watch.

"I'll do them when I'm done riding." I walk Moonshine past him, not breaking stride. I fully expect a lecture, and I'm shocked when he doesn't say anything. He follows me, stopping outside the gate.

"You riding was always a thing of beauty." He puts his hat on the fence post.

Stepping in the stirrup, I swing my leg over the horse and plant my ass firmly in the saddle. I ride him around a few times.

Daddy's gaze is glued to me. "Take him for a run. I'll time you."

I start with a slow pace, getting a good feel for him and letting him learn me. I pick up the speed and make it once around the track. I stop at the gate and nod to Daddy to start the timer. "Let's go, boy." I dig my heels in, and he bolts forward. He's easy to ride with his lengthy, graceful stride. I round the first corner and push him harder. He responds nicely. He keeps up his pace until the mock finish line. I slow his speed and prance him around another time.

Daddy has made his way inside the racetrack and has his hat back on. "That was beautiful. Quick time for a young horse. With you working with him over the next two years, he'll be a winner for sure. Now, put him back in his stall and get your chores done."

I hop off the horse. "What is it with you men? One minute you're nice, the next you're acting like jackasses." I storm toward him.

"You watch your mouth, young lady." He points a long finger in my direction.

"You men are warm and fuzzy one minute, then colder than ice the next." I've made my way over to him. I should back down, I know I should, but I'm tired of being punished.

"You have a job to do around here like everyone else. Priority number one for you are the stalls."

"Why isn't training the horses my priority? Me mucking the stalls is you punishing me for leaving."

"That's where you're wrong. I'm treating you liked I'd treat any new hired hand. You have to start from the bottom and work your way up."

"That's just it, Daddy! I'm not a hired hand, I'm your daughter!" Wetness fills my eyes, and I try to will myself not to cry.

He tilts his head. "Is this about Boone?"

"No! Yes! It's about both of you. I've already apologized. I'm not doing it again. I'm your daughter Clementine Calhoun!"

"I know who you are." His voice is softer. "You're the one who forgot who you were when you left. Your family loved you, and you turned your back on us by not letting us in."

"Gawd, Daddy, please. I've told you a million times I wasn't ready and I was scared."

"I'm not talking about the wedding." At this moment, his eyes see straight through me, and there's a deep look of sadness floating through them.

"The baby," I whisper.

He nods.

"How did you know?" Tears are streaming.

"The night before the wedding, you and Boone left rehearsal and were sitting out back in the gazebo. Wyatt was out there. He overheard you and Boone talking."

My mind flashes back to the conversation. Boone and I were talking about why I didn't want to ride horses anymore. One of the horses I was training threw me off. It's what caused the miscarriage. I was angry, sad, and relieved all at the same time, but I wasn't ready to get back on.

"If you knew, why didn't you ever say anything?"

"Believe me, I wanted to. Your momma calmed me down. She said you didn't need us to make matters worse by crying over the baby. We both cried that night for you. I hated that you felt like you couldn't come to us. I'm sure you had your reasons."

I choke when I see a single tear slide down his weathered face. I've never seen him cry. "I'm so sorry. I was afraid and confused. I couldn't tell you that I was relieved. I was so ashamed at how I felt. I wasn't ready for a baby. Boone said he understood, but I couldn't live with it. I had to get away. I didn't want Boone to hate me for it if I was never ready again. He deserved more, and I wanted more for myself."

"You should have told us rather than run away."

I open my mouth to respond, and he holds his hand up.

"I'm sorry that you went through a miscarriage and that you felt lost. I get why you felt like you didn't have any other choice. Doesn't mean I agree with it, but I understand it. I love you, Clem. From here on out, promise me that you'll talk to me when you're feeling lost, afraid, or hurting. I'll always be here for you."

I run into his arms, almost knocking him over. "I love you too, Daddy. I promise." My heart aches that he's crying with me, but I feel like a weight's been lifted. The air between us is clear, and we can start over. "Thank you," I sniff.

He kisses the top of my head. "How about you clean those stalls one last time and we'll talk about your new job around here. Better yet, didn't you mention starting your own business?"

"Right now, I'd be happy to work here. The other can wait."

"Anything I can do to help with Boone?"

"He's going to marry Margret to keep this family safe."

"Do you still love him?"

"Yes."

"I'll go talk some sense into Maynard."

"You'll do no such thing." Wyatt is walking toward us. "Let Boone handle it."

"His way of taking care of it is marrying a woman he doesn't love," I snap.

"I don't want him with her any more than you do. Boone's a proud man and will do what he thinks is best in keeping their claws out of this family."

"I'll let him deal with it. In the meantime, we've got work to do to get ready for the Derby. Not only working with the horse but making sure our neighbors can't steal him or worse." He turns toward Wyatt. "I'll take a shift tonight on the main gate. Bear can take the rear entrance of the property."

"I want to help too." I frantically wipe the tears from my face.

"Come by the house later and pick up a rifle. Bear could use extra eyes. That property in the back is wide."

"Okay." I walk back over to Moonshine to take him back to the barn.

"You're late cleaning out those stalls," Daddy says and winks at me when I stride past him with the horse.

I get my job done and head to Boone's house. I saw him out riding with Bear trying to find the cattle, so I know the coast is clear. I'm not staying here again. I'd rather risk it at the cottage with Ethan. Daddy's given me a fresh start. I need to let Boone figure out what he's going to do. If he marries her, I'll have to accept it.

I hear loud voices coming from my cottage. Ellie opens the door and slams it as I'm walking up into the driveway.

"You can kiss my lily-white ass!" she yells.

"What's going on?" I drop my bag in the grass.

"Men!" She storms off.

I gingerly open the door, ducking when a pillow is thrown at me. "What the hell, Ethan?"

"Sorry. I thought you were Ellie."

"What in the world are you two fighting about?"

"She came over here telling me she wants to still...you know...screw around with me." He shrugs one shoulder.

"And that's a bad thing?"

"I told her only if we were exclusive."

"Ah, now I see the problem. Ellie doesn't want to be tied down to one man."

"That's what she said." He points in the direction of her house.

"I told you not to get involved with her." The look on his face shows the hurt. He really does like her. "I'm sorry, Ethan." I take his hand and drag him on the couch beside me. "I've never seen you like this before. You've told me of having women wherever you went, but you never mentioned liking them before."

"It's because I haven't. I don't know why, but she means something to me."

"You haven't known her very long."

He leans his head on my shoulder. "The same could be said for you. We've only been back a week, yet you know you love Boone."

"I think I've always loved Boone. I just lost sight of that. It doesn't matter now how I feel. I lost my chance. He's going to marry Margret."

"I'm sorry."

"Don't be. On a brighter note, Daddy and I've finally made amends."

"Does that mean I don't have to worry about him shooting me anymore?"

"I didn't say that." I giggle. "Why don't you stay

here. I don't mean just for the summer. I could teach you about horses."

"I've been hanging out with Bear. He's offered me a job in his garage."

"City boy wants to get his hands greasy?" I lift my shoulder, and his head raises.

"The first base I was stationed at I worked on Jeeps. I enjoyed fixing them."

"Daddy's not going to let you live here for free."

"Bears been teaching me about the cattle. He could use a hand so he can spend more time with Missy."

"Okay, but you can't keep living in that tent. It gets hotter than a hoochie coochie here."

"I'm not sure I want to know what that means." He chuckles.

"It means you're going to sweat your balls off."

"Note to self. Find a place to live."

"Seems Ellie's in charge of the housing on the property. I could ask her for you?"

He stands. "No. I'll man up and ask her myself. I'm not going to let her boss me around."

"That's the spirit." I fist-bump the air.

He heads out the door. "She's going to eat him alive."

CHAPTER SEVENTEEN
BOONE

"Looks like Maynard's henchmen came in through the gate here. The wires have been clipped."

"You think he took the cattle?" Bear squats next to me.

"I'd lay money on it."

He stands. "Then I'm going to get them back."

"You fix the fence. I'll take care of it."

I barrel over to my truck and skid down the dirt road, not stopping until I'm in front of Margret's house. Reaching over into the glovebox, I take my pistol and tuck it in the back of my pants. My boots ground into the gravel that leads up to the steps. "Tom!" I yell, pounding on the door.

Margret swings the door open. "Boone. What's wrong?"

I push past her. "Where is your father?"

"He's in the study. He's asked to not be disturbed."

"Well, I'm disturbing him."

She grabs my arm. "Why don't you tell me what happened?"

"I'm sure you already know. Someone was snooping around our barn last night, and two of our cattle are missing." I can't stop the tension in my jaw, causing it to flex.

"What did you expect? Daddy warned you." Her face is so damn smug.

"Then you need to tell your father if one of his men step onto Calhoun property without permission, my men have instructions to shoot to kill."

"Boone, calm down and be reasonable."

"Be reasonable? Your father is blackmailing me into marrying you!"

"Blackmailing is a strong word to use on your soon-to-be bride." She adds a southern slur to her words. I used to find it charming, now it pisses me off. I've been played by her the entire time. I close the gap between us. "When I'm finished, you won't want the likes of me. You'll end it yourself."

"My daughter will go through with marrying you regardless of what you do. She's a Maynard, and we don't back down." Her father comes out of nowhere.

"You need to return our cattle." I'm so angry my teeth nearly chip from gritting them together.

"I don't know what you're talking about." He stuffs his hands in his slacks and smiles.

"You know damn good and well your men were on Calhoun property."

"The cows are the least of your worries if you don't do as you're told."

I step up to him, towering over the little weasel. "I don't like being ordered around."

"Let me rephrase it for you." His chin juts in the air. "You will willingly marry my daughter and bring that horse to this property or that pretty daughter of Chet's will disappear for good this time. Do I make myself clear?"

"You won't go near Clem." My voice is so menacing I don't recognize it.

He chuckles. "You're right, I won't because you're a smart man and know what I'm capable of doing. You've heard the rumors." He walks over to his daughter. "They're all true."

I'd heard years ago that Margret had been dating some young cowboy that her daddy didn't like. He supposedly ended things with her and left town according to her, but the locals told a different story. They'd seen Maynard's men beat him up in a back alley, warning him off Margret. He didn't heed it. Rumor is, Maynard shot him. His body was never found. The local police filed a report saying the boy left town. He's a big contributor to the local police force, so I'm sure they covered his ass.

I glance at Margret, and her bottom lip quivers with a mist filling her eyes. *She loved him.* It's her Achilles' heel. I can use this against her when the time is right.

"The Derby is in two weeks. You and Margret will get married at Churchill Downs, in their reception hall before the race. Now, I don't want you to consider me an unreasonable man. You will be compensated for Whiskey River. I'll have a check with several zeros trailing the number waiting for you after you've married my daughter. Oh, and before I forget, you'll throw in that new horse that Clem Calhoun was riding."

"You sorry son of a..." I step toward him.

"That's no way to talk to your soon-to-be in-law." He drapes his arm around his daughter's shoulder, knowing damn good and well that I'm not the type of man who'd ever lay a hand on a woman. "Need I remind you that I'm holding all the cards on the Calhoun land?"

I feel the rush of blood in my mouth from biting my tongue. "I'll do as you want, but leave Clem and her family alone."

"That's more like it." He holds out his hand. "A man can't go back on his word."

I begrudgingly meet his hand with mine, sealing my fate, but securing the Calhoun ranch and Clem's life. "You need to stay clear of them. No more spying or breaking onto their property. Whiskey River stays safe."

"I'll see if I can locate your missing cattle and have them returned by morning." I nod, knowing I've made a deal with the devil and his daughter.

Margret moves from her father and places her hand on my elbow. "Now that we have that settled, we can talk wedding plans."

I jerk away from her. "In public, I'll play nice. In private, this marriage means nothing to me. So, plan your wedding however you'd like and tell me when I need to be there."

She brazenly runs her hand over my cheek. "Boone, you know I love you. This may not be how you want things, but I can promise you, you'll fall in love with me, and I'll make you a happy man."

"Don't fucking count on it." I angrily stomp toward the door, hearing the echo of my boots on the tile floor.

"Son..."

I turn a bitter glare toward her father. "I'm not your fucking son."

"If even one person thinks this marriage isn't real, all bets are off when it comes to the youngest Calhoun."

I want to strangle him with my bare hands and see the life leave his evil eyes.

He laughs. "My attorney has copies of the loan and instructions as to what to do if something should happen to me. Keep that in mind, boy."

The only thing I truly care about are the Calhouns. I'll sacrifice myself for them. It won't be easy because they won't understand, especially Clem. They'll all think me a traitor. The only person I can tell is Wyatt. Maybe by some dumb luck, he'll find a way out of this mess.

I nod and slam the door behind me, causing the big pane window in front to rattle.

Yanking the truck door open, I climb inside and see Margret running toward me.

"Don't be like that, Boone. Please don't leave angry. This will all work out for both of us. I promise to be a good and dutiful wife to you." Her hands are holding the truck door open.

"I will never love you, Margret."

"It's because of her, isn't it?" She lets loose of the truck and crosses her arms over her chest.

"No. It's because of you." I don't want to admit to her that it's because of Clem. There's no telling what she might try to do to her after the bar incident. "The guy your father killed. You loved him, didn't you?"

Her eyes glaze over. "That doesn't matter now does it. He wants us together."

"You know it's only for the Calhoun land. You could stop him if you wanted to."

"I don't want to stop him. I want to be Mrs. Boone Methany." She bats her thick, fake eyelashes.

I press my fingers firmly into my temples. "What about what I want?"

"You wanted me before little miss ray of sunshine showed up."

"Look." I hop down next to her. "I know that a big part of this is my fault. I was content with the thought of you being my wife until this mess. I would've followed through with my commitment to you, but now, with you and your father forcing my hand, I'd never be happy with you."

She wipes a tear away. "Content? Did you ever love me?"

"I loved you, but I wasn't in love with you. There's a big difference. I respected you enough that I would've given our marriage everything I had to make it work."

She runs her hand down my arm. "We can still do that."

"No, we can't."

She drops her hand. "Well, I'm afraid you're going to have to become a good actor because soon after we're married, I plan on getting pregnant. I want a tiny Boone running around."

Wyatt better pull a miracle out of his ass. "I've got to go." I climb back in the truck, and she blows me a kiss. Part of me feels bad for her in my part in this. She's right. If Clem hadn't come back, things would be different between us. It doesn't mean I'd be in love with her, but I would've made a life with her. What does that say about me? "Shit."

I aim my truck in the direction of Wyatt's house where I know he's working. I see Bear heading out in his Jeep. He stops beside my truck.

"Did you find the cattle?"

"They'll be back on the property by tonight."

"He admitted to taking them?"

"Not in so many words."

"I'll come by after I get off work and help keep watch. Missy can stay with Momma in the main house."

"Okay, but I don't think there will be any more issues."

"You must've given him an ear full."

No. I sold my soul to the devil himself. "I'll catch you later." I don't want to have any more conversations about the situation until I've spoken with Wyatt.

I park and stroll into his office. "I hope like hell you found a way out of this mess." I throw my hat on his desk and sit.

"I've been in contact with the board of the loan company, and they aren't willing to go up against Tom Maynard to override him."

"That means he has something on them."

"I offered them half as payout, and they rejected it."

"Do you have half?"

"I could liquidate some assets to get part of it and cash in my retirement. I'll take a big hit financially. It will still only total seventy-five thousand."

"How about a family meeting to see if we can make up the difference?"

"It's worth a try." He taps a pen on the desk. "They're going to be pissed at me."

I stand. "How would that be any different than any other day around here?"

"Fair enough." He laughs.

"I'll go gather the troops. Do me a favor and don't mention Margret. If we can't work this out, I'll have to cave into the Maynards."

"Let's hope that doesn't happen. Don't let my father see you rounding up the family. He'll want to know what's up."

I nod and step outside, calling each of them. I catch Bear before he's made it to the shop. He turns around and heads back to the ranch. Within an hour, we're all sitting in Wyatt's office. Clem brought Ethan along.

"What's this all about?" Ellie says as she prances through the office door.

Wyatt clears his throat. "Back when we all pitched in to help save this ranch, we came up short monies. I borrowed it from a loan company to make up the difference, and I've been making the payments."

"I didn't realize we were short. You never mentioned it," Bear replies.

"I knew each of you did what you could, so there was no sense asking for any more."

"Do you need money to help cover the payments?" Ellie sits on the edge of the desk.

"The company I borrowed the money from, Tom Maynard purchased not long ago. He's calling in the loan. If we don't pay him, he'll foreclose on this land."

"Can he do that?" Clem jumps up.

"It was a clause he had built into the purchase of the company. He's been planning this for a while."

"Bastard." Ellie slams her fist on the desk.

"How much money do we need?" Clem asks.

"Quarter of a million."

"Fuck," Bear groans. "I can sell my portion of the garage, but it won't bring in much. Maybe twenty-five thousand at the most."

"I've been saving every dime I could manage on the profits of the ranch, but if I move it, Daddy will know." Ellie starts pacing the floor. "I have ten thousand tucked away for a rainy day."

"Looks like it's raining," Bear adds.

"I saved some money while I was in the service, but it's not much. I was going to use in starting my company."

"How much?" Wyatt prods her.

"Twenty thousand."

He looks over at me. "Every dime I have is in Whiskey River. I've been paying the jockey, buying the feed, and paying the entry fees. Not to mention the recent purchase of Moonshine. I'm tapped out. I was planning on putting the winnings back in the ranch to get us through until cattle season. We should make enough off them this year to get us back on our feet."

Wyatt grips my shoulder. "You've done enough."

"I've got ten thousand saved, if that will help," Ethan chimes in.

"That still leaves us one hundred, ten thousand short." Ellie plucks away at her calculator.

"We could barter with some of the cattle?"

"Maynard won't take the deal. He wants this land and the horse."

"There has to be something we can do." Bear's on his feet.

"There is, but it doesn't involve a *we*." I blow out a long-defeated breath. "Keep your money. I've already made a deal with Maynard."

I can't look at Clem. "I'm going to marry his daughter and sell him Whiskey."

"No!" Clem gasps.

"It's a done deal, and I don't want any of you interfering."

"You can't marry her. That won't stop him in the long run. He'll still find a way to take this land." Ellie is chomping at the bit.

"I'll make sure I have an agreement drawn up that he'll try no such thing. I'll get my things and move off the ranch." I head for the door with my head down. I make it to my truck before Clem catches me.

"Please don't do this. We'll find another way."

I bend down and kiss her sweet lips. "I'm doing this to keep you safe."

"I can take care of myself."

"Not up against Maynard. He's made one too many threats against you. I love you and this family. I won't stand by and watch this land be taken away because of my choices. I want you to do me a favor." I run my hand along her soft cheek.

"What?"

"Forget about me. I'm going to make a life with Margret. If I'm marrying her, then I'm all in." I'm such a liar, but she has to believe me.

"You're really going to marry her?"

"Two weeks from today at Churchill downs before Whiskey races."

I kiss her one last time, hoping like hell it won't be the last time. I get in my truck and drive to my place, knowing darn good and well by the time it's all said and done, Clem is going to hate me for all the things I'll have to do. Before I leave, I'll have to break the news to Chet about Whiskey and my marriage to Margret. It might be harder than what I just did to Clem. The man has given me everything, and how do I repay him? By deserting him when he needs me the most around here. He'll keep his land, but the winnings from Whiskey would turn this place around. On top of it all, I break his baby girl's heart.

CHAPTER EIGHTEEN
CLEM

"I can't believe he's actually going through with this." My sister is fastening on my stupid hat for the Derby today, and it reminds me of my wedding day.

"He's really going to marry that hussy." Ellie pulls a bobby pin from between her teeth. "Have you tried to talk him out of it?"

"He won't talk to me. I tried when I saw Margret's father introducing them to the press. I couldn't stomach the way he was looking at her."

"Did you get to talk to him?"

"He told me to leave him alone, what's done is done. Margret was hanging all over him. It was sickening."

"You know he doesn't love her."

"You could've fooled me by the way he was eyeing her, and of course her hands were all over him." I slump down in my chair, feeling defeated and heartbroken.

"So what are you going to do?"

"Get over him."

"Pish! You left here for seven years and never got over him. You may have thought you did, but the moment you two saw one another, it was on."

"He'll be a married man after today. I don't have any other choice but to get over him."

"You mean to tell me, you came back here and figured out that you still love Boone Methany and you're just going to let him go? I'd like to kick your ass myself." She huffs.

"Oh, what would you do if you were in my shoes?" I'm up on my feet, holding my long gown off the ground.

"I wouldn't be going to his wedding. I'd scratch that hussy's eyes out and get my man back."

"You think I want to go see Boone marry that bitch? Daddy has insisted we all go. I don't understand that man. He was furious at Boone about Whiskey."

"Daddy is a strange one, that's for sure. But he

loves Boone like a son and maybe, just maybe, he knows something we don't."

"Like what?"

"I don't know, but there has to be some reason Daddy is asking us to support this marriage."

"Because he doesn't want me and Boone together. He thinks I'll break his heart again."

She punches me in the shoulder.

"Ouch! What was that for?"

"For being such an idiot. Daddy always thought you and Boone should be together. Even after you left him at the altar."

"That's news to me." My hands fly to my hips.

"Well, it's true. So you need to paint on some pretty pink lipstick and mess up Boone's collar before the wedding. Margret will see the lip prints and lose her shit."

"When did you get to be so conniving?"

"Stick around, and you'll learn a lot more about me." She laughs, slowly putting her hat on her head as to not mess up her hair.

We walk out into the formal living room where all our family is waiting on us. Daddy and Wyatt are in a corner whispering.

"Aunt Clem, you look so pretty. Pink is my

favorite color." Missy's little hand tugs at the hem of my silky dress.

"You look pretty too. Purple happens to be my favorite color."

She twirls around in her dress, and it flies out like a bell. "Can I sit by you at the races?"

"Sure you can." I take her hand, and we all go load up in the vehicles. I tuck in beside Momma, who's wearing a dress the color of a canary.

"You seem awful calm for a woman that is going to watch the man she loves get married."

"My insides aren't calm at all, but thanks to Ellie, I have a plan. Boone may not get married after all."

"I don't know what you're planning back there. You won't interfere with the wedding. Boone has made his choice, and we'll honor that." Daddy is glaring at me through the rearview mirror.

I go to say something and Momma puts her hand on my leg and makes a zipping motion at her lips. I pout, and Missy talks my ear off. "Where's Ethan? He's so handsome." Her eyes have stars in them talking about him.

"He rode with Ellie and Bear." He and Bear have become good friends in a short period of time. He still really likes Ellie. He follows her around like a lost puppy dog. She gives him morsels every now and then to keep him coming back.

SPECTATORS ARE POURING INTO CHURCHILL Downs. There is an array of colored floppy hats and men in suits. Flags are flapping in the wind around the oval-shaped track. Ads stand out bold on the track rails with a JumboTron lighting up for the races. The grassy infield is filling up with spectators. Water trucks and graders are finishing up their last-minute prep for the track.

As we walk through the grandstand area, the heat is already getting to the spectators. Some are fanning themselves with their programs to keep the heat at bay, others are snapping open a cold bottle of beer or sipping on some flavor of mint juleps. The indoor area has a glass wall that overlooks the track. We've had our own box seating section for years, so there's no waiting in line for tickets or to find our seats, other than to place our bets. I'm betting every dime I have on Whiskey and giving it to Daddy to help with the ranch. I was MIA before when he needed it, and this is my chance to make up for that.

I head for the betting line, and Wyatt takes me

by the arm. "We've got a wedding to attend to first. I've been instructed to make you behave."

"You mean to keep me away from Boone." I jerk my arm free.

"More like Margret." He chuckles.

"I don't want to watch him marry her." I told myself I wouldn't cry. Somehow, the tears win out. Wyatt pulls out his handkerchief, giving it to me.

"You have to accept the fact that he's marrying her."

"Fine," I sniff, knowing I'm only appeasing him. I walk with him into the reception area filled with the winners after the races. It's decorated in nauseating colors of orange and yellows. Who picks these colors for a wedding? The room is filled with guests, with no sign of Boone.

"I need to use the ladies' room," I whisper to Wyatt.

"Do I need to escort you, or are you going to behave?" He raises a thick eyebrow at me.

"I'll behave." I'm such a liar. If I get one second alone with Boone, my pretty little shade of lipstick is going to be in places that Margret will see. I should plant one on the zipper of his pants. That would rile her up. I giggle to myself.

I walk out, and there's a line to use the restroom.

I go to the end of the hall where it splits, and I wait my turn. A gruff hand snatches me by the arm and drags me around the corner.

"Boone."

He covers my mouth with his hand. "Do you have a dollar?"

I squint in confusion. His hand muffles my response.

"Don't say anything, just nod." He's keeping his voice low.

My head bobs up and down several times.

"Give it to me?" He leaves his hand in place.

I reach in my tiny purse and pull out some money. His hand falls from my mouth. "Why..."

"Not a word." He holds his hand out, and I place a single dollar bill in the palm of it. He tucks it in his pocket and pulls out a white envelope. "Don't open this until right before the race starts."

"Boone, I..."

He takes off in the opposite direction without another word. I hold up the envelope like I can see through it. No name, completely blank on the front. Is it a letter proclaiming his dying love for me? Does he want me to stop the wedding? It's flat, all but in one corner.

"A key?" I rip into it, and a tiny silver key falls to the floor. I pick it up and read the note.

I told you not to open it yet. This key will get you into a locker with a very important piece of paper in it. Please do as I ask and wait until they call out Whiskey River's name to open it.

He knows me too darn well. The key has the number 102 on it. I wonder if that was on purpose? I tuck it in my purse and head back to the reception hall. Boone is standing up front waiting for his Bridezilla. Gawd, he's so handsome in his tuxedo. I sit by Wyatt and Ellie leans over to look at me. She mouths the words, *did you do it?*

I scowl and shake my head.

The music starts to play and in prances Queen Froufrou with her hair teased high on her head. I don't know who told her that looked good. I turn back to face the front, and Boone is all smiles staring at her. My stomach turns in knots. A tear instantly spills down my cheek, and Wyatt squeezes my hand.

"I can't do this," I whisper.

"You can and you will," he says behind a fake smile.

She literally eye-fucks him all the way down the aisle, and his face is plastered with a grin. She says something to him, but I can't make out what it is. He

226

takes her hand and kisses her cheek. I sit frozen, watching the man I love say his vows to that wretched woman.

They're pronounced man and wife, and she throws her arms around his neck and sticks her tongue down his mouth far enough to touch his tonsils. I make a gagging noise, and Wyatt snatches me out of my chair and hauls me out of the room. Tears stream down my face, taking my mascara with it. I'm sure I look like some sort of crazed raccoon.

"Believe it or not, I'm sorry, Clem." He holds my head to his chest and lets me soak his jacket. "Boone did what he had to do, and one day you'll understand."

"Today's not that day," I sob loudly.

Ellie pulls me out of his arms. "Come on. Let's take you to the ladies' room to get cleaned up." I follow her with my head down. "What happened? I thought we had a plan?" she says as soon as we're out of earshot.

"We did, but Boone stopped me. He asked me for a dollar, and then he handed me this envelope." I dig it out of my purse.

"What's in it?"

"He told me not to open it until the race starts."

She takes it out of my hand and sees the ripped opening. "I see you did what I would've done."

"He knew I'd open it." I dump my purse upside down for the key to fall out. "I guess what he really wants me to read is in a locker."

Ellie glances at her watch. "Let's go place our bets and then we'll get to the locker and find out what's in it."

We walk out into the hall and Boone and Bunny Froufrou are coming out of the reception hall. She stops directly in front of me.

"I guess the best woman won his heart." She splays her hand on his chest. "No hard feelings, though. I want us all to be friends. Maybe you and that sweet boy you brought home could be our guests at dinner one night." Boone never looks at me.

Is she kidding? Surely she doesn't ever think we could be friends. I'd like to scratch her eyes out, and she wants to be friends? I can feel every ounce of my rage coming to the surface. I wish I had my daddy's shotgun. I'd sprinkle holes all through that gaudy gown of hers.

"Nice wedding," Daddy says, coming up behind them, slapping his hand on Boone's shoulder. "Congratulations, Margret."

Traitor.

"At least one of the Calhouns is supportive," she spats behind her fake-as-shit smile. She smacks a kiss on Boone's cheek then rubs her fingers over the lipstick smear. "Husband of *mine*, we better go place our bet on *our* horse to win." She emphasizes the word mine for my benefit.

I hope she gags on the sugar in her mouth.

She tucks her arm in his, and my heart sinks further when his hand goes to the small of her back. I watch the man I love walk away with his new monster of a wife.

"Do you want me to kill her. I've got a great place we can bury the body," Ellie whispers.

I release a snort. I'm not sure if it's a laugh or a cry. Maybe both. "No. He's made his bed with the she-devil." I'll get over it, eventually.

We all make our way to the betting booths. I study the electronic board that displays the odds for each horse. I can feel the anticipation in the air as people are placing their bets. When I'm done, I grab Ellie and slip off to find the locker. My hand trembles as I insert the key. There's another plain white envelope inside, except this one has my name handwritten on it by Boone. Ellie snatches it from me before I can open it.

"Hey!"

"We're going to our seats and waiting until we hear Whiskey's name called out on the loudspeaker."

"Since when do you follow the rules?" I try to get it back from her, but she tucks it into her bra.

"I'm not afraid to go after it," I challenge her.

"We don't know what's in here and it may be something that breaks your heart, and you'll need your family around you."

"He already broke my heart. I guess it was payback for what I did to him." I follow behind her, mumbling.

We make it to our seats, and Missy pats the place beside her. "You promised." Bear is standing, peering through binoculars out at the track.

I sit, and Ellie takes the seat next to me. I nervously bite my matching pink polish on my pointer finger.

"Grandma says that's nasty. She says it's like biting your hoo-ha. Whatever that means." She rolls her big green eyes, and it's the first time I realized they're the same exact color of Bears and Mommas.

I drop my hand from my mouth. The intercom comes on, and the announcement of the horses and the race begins as they make their way down the track to the gates. The starting gates clang open. Henry is tied alongside Whiskey, keeping him nice and calm. As soon as Whiskey's name is announced, Ellie hands me the letter. I rip it open and gasp at the contract inside.

"What's it say?" Ellie leans over my shoulder to read it. She lets out a laugh. "Well butter my butt and call me a biscuit."

Giggling, I tuck the letter in my purse. Looking around at my family, Wyatt winks at me. I bet he had something to do with this.

CHAPTER NINETEEN
BOONE

I can't believe she's here. I don't want her to watch me get married. Only seconds ago, I had my hand on her mouth. It's not what I wanted on her mouth. I had to fight myself from kissing her and getting her to run out the back door with me.

Instead, I'm standing here waiting for the woman I don't want to walk down the aisle. Why couldn't she be my runaway bride? No such luck.

My stomach rolls. I'm not sure I can do this, not with Clem here. I know I'm doing it to keep her safe. I figured out how to take care of one problem that will save the Calhouns, but not this one. I keep telling myself it's only a piece of paper. I would've never felt that way with Clem. Until death do us part. That's how it's supposed to be.

One of Maynard's hired hands slides in the seat behind Clem. He glares at me then focuses on her, patting something bulky underneath his jacket. I can only assume it's a gun, reminding me of why I have to do this. I straighten my shoulders and wait for my fate. I can't even look at Clem again.

The music starts and Margret appears at the entrance, holding orange and yellow flowers against her pristine white satin gown. What the hell is up with her hair? It looks like a rat crawled in it, dug around for days, and made itself comfortable under the pile of hair on top of her head. Oh god, she's smiling at me. Think of something nice. My mind goes to Clem in her Saran Wrapped attempt to seduce me. I can feel the smile covering my face as I picture her. She was so damn cute trying to get around the rules I had laid down. Another dumb move on my part. If I ever get out of this mess, I'm never refusing her to be naked around me again.

"I love that smile you have on your face just for me." Margret's standing in front of me. I kiss her cheek like she requested me to do in rehearsal. I have to refrain from wiping my lips with the back of my hand. God, this tux is suffocating. I go through the motions with a phony smile. As soon as the preacher announces we are man and wife, Margret sticks her tongue down my throat. That's not how we practiced it. I hear a gagging noise, and I know it's Clem. I almost laugh in Margret's mouth as she swirls her tongue with mine. When she finally frees me, I see Wyatt dragging Clem out by the hand.

"You're mine now," Margret purrs. "Don't even look at her." She spins around and meets the flashing cameras with a smile. I play the role, keeping an eye out on Maynard's man.

"It's almost time for the race. I can hardly wait to see our horse win." Tom shakes my hand.

He's in for a big surprise. "Me either."

"Why don't you two head to our seats. I've taken care of all the betting."

I stepped out and placed my bet while no one was monitoring me. I follow Margret out of the reception hall. She stops in front of Clem and Ellie. God, why couldn't she just let it go? I can't look at Clem and see the hurt in her eyes.

The sound of Margret's voice taunting Clem makes me want to choke her. What's she up to, inviting Clem and Ethan over for dinner? I'm sure she has something up her sleeve, or maybe she believes in that old saying about keeping your enemies close. If I were her, I'd be afraid of Clementine Calhoun.

Chet congratulates me. It damn near killed me when I had to tell him I was leaving and that I was taking the horse with me. At first, he was pissed and slammed his fists on his desk. Then a calm came over him, and he wished me the best in my marriage. It was the weirdest thing I'd ever seen from him. I expected Armageddon. Instead, I got a man that wished me good fortune.

I'm numb when Margret kisses my check. The touch of her fingers on my face makes me want to vomit. I smile instead. She says something, but I'm not really hearing her words at this point. I place my hand on her back to get her to move. I can't stand here anymore. Even if I can get out of this marriage, I'm not sure Clem will ever forgive me.

I usher her through the crowd in the indoor area until we make it to our box seats. The Calhouns' seats are a section down from ours. Wyatt salutes me when he sees me. Bear and Missy are already seated. Chet and his bride are taking a seat. He has tickets in his hand, and he's waving them at Wyatt.

If I know Clem, she's tried to read what's in the envelope. Putting it in the locker was only meant to slow her down. She tends to reveal her feelings on her face, and I didn't want her to show my hand. I put my sunglasses on so that I can stare in their direction without Margret making a fuss. Ellie walks in with Clem, who still appears upset. She sits next to Missy and straightens the little girl's purple hat.

I make small talk with Margret all the while watching Clem. The horses make their way down, and the announcements begin. Whiskey River is announced along with his owner, Tom Maynard, my name as the trainer, and Jose the jockey.

Ellie pulls the envelope out of the top of her dress and hands it to Clem. How did she get her hands on it? Ellie says something and Clem laughs. That's the best thing I've seen all day long.

I settle into my seat. I'm going to enjoy the outcome. Call it sweet revenge. I'm not sure what the repercussions will be, but at least the Calhoun land will remain theirs.

Henry is taken off to the side of the track when Whiskey River is loaded into gate number three. He enters meek as a newborn calf. Clem worked magic with that goat.

"It's time." Margret claps. "Aren't you excited? Our horse is going to win and go on to win the Triple Crown."

"Now, sweetie, don't get ahead of yourself," Tom tells her.

The bugle sounds Call to the Post. When the

race begins, Whiskey flies out of the gate, immediately taking the lead. Damn, he's a beautiful horse. He finishes the first turn with one horse on his heels, the other's he's left behind. The horse inches closer on the second curve. The running commentary over the loudspeaker has the crowd shrieking, swearing, and applauding. They are neck and neck. Whiskey is on the inside lane. With a quarter mile left, the other horse is a nose in front. Jose lowers himself closer to Whiskey. When he does, he picks up speed like I've never seen before. The thundering of horses' hooves get louder, and so do the spectators.

Whiskey crosses the finish line a full-body length in front of the other horse at a time of 1:59, beating the all-time record. The crowd cheers and the winner's hurried footsteps can be heard, racing to collect on their bets. Margret is on her feet, bouncing up and down. Tom looks like a proud man in this moment. The Calhouns are yelling and waving their tickets in the air. I gaze out over the crowd and see the distressed faces of those that lost a great deal of money. Tickets are crumpled in their hands, and loved ones are trying to console them.

"We won!" Margret grabs me in for a hug. "Our horse is going to make us so much money!" I don't contradict her. Her winnings from her bet will be substantial.

After all the final numbers come in, we head to the winner's circle so Tom can collect his prize. I brace myself for what is about to go down.

"Congratulations is in order," one of his old pals who hands out the winnings tells him.

"I'm one lucky man that I purchased this horse when I did from my new son-in-law." He slaps me on the back.

"All I need from you is the bill of sale on that beauty."

"Boone completed it all yesterday. Give him the paperwork, Son."

I pat my pockets like I'm searching for it, stalling for time. I placed the large check he gave me in a letter-sized envelope. I pull it out of my jacket pocket.

"Excuse me, but I'm the owner of this horse." Clem walks in right on time with Ellie and Wyatt by her side.

"The hell you are, young lady. I purchased Whiskey River from this fine gentleman." Tom grips my shoulder.

"I have the paperwork to prove it." She hands it

to the other man. He unfolds it and reads it. "You made a hell of a purchase, young lady."

"What are you talking about?" Toms snatches it out of his hand. "A dollar! You can't purchase Whiskey River for a dollar! He's worth millions from his bloodline alone."

"It appears legit to me." His friend shrugs.

"Let me see that!" He snatches the envelope from my hand. "This is the check I gave you to buy the racehorse!" He waves it in the air.

"Ms. Calhoun here had already made me an offer, so I felt obliged to take it."

Wyatt steps up to the table. "You'll find all the proper signatures are in order. The pot goes to Clementine."

"Why you!" Tom's face is redder than a bottle of ketchup. "You won't get away with this," he snarls.

"Seems like he already has." Wyatt chuckles.

"Did you do this?" Margret's lips are pursed together. "This was my horse."

"I'm sorry, Margret, but I had agreed to sell it to Clem." I rub my hand down her arm, trying to be the comforting husband. "You still won a bunch of money on your bid."

"You and I will have a discussion about this when

we get home," she says close to my cheek then puts on a fake smile. "He's right. My husband is a man of his word, and if he'd agreed to sell it to Ms. Calhoun, then so be it." She tucks her arm around my waist.

I'm no fool. This won't be the last of it. It's not her I'm afraid of; it's what Tom's revenge is going to be. When I met with Wyatt to have all the paper-work done up, he forged Clem's signature. I warned him at the time to keep a good eye on Clem, hire security to watch her but make sure they keep out of sight.

Tom storms out, and Margret follows him. I glance over at Wyatt and mouth the words, *thank you.*

"Are you coming?" Margret asks when she real-izes I'm not behind her. I take a quick look at Clem, who gazes up at me. There is no expression on her face. I gave her what I could. One horse back. I'll find a way to get Moonshine to her. I wish it was me going home with her rather than me going home with Margret.

We stop by the betting line and collect our winnings. From my calculations, between the bets the Calhouns placed to win, and the winning owner's jackpot, they made more than enough to clear the loan from Tom. I'll deposit my winnings and transfer the money to Wyatt to give them an extra cushion.

Tom has left with his barrage of men. Margret, still in her wedding gown, climbs in my truck.

"I'm so angry at you right now," she yells then calms herself. "But I'm not going to let it ruin our wedding night. I promised to be a good wife. I don't know why you did what you did, but I'll support you against Daddy."

"Thank you."

"But you better not pull anything like that ever again!" She points at me.

"You know your family doesn't need that money, right?"

"Daddy's got plenty of money." She pats down that wild hair of hers.

"Then why was it so important to him to own Whiskey River?"

"He's always dreamt of winning a derby. I think he saw it as his last chance."

I think there's a hell of a lot more to it than that, and I'm damn sure going to do some digging.

CHAPTER TWENTY
CLEM

As soon as we made it home and changed clothes, Ellie, Wyatt, Bear, Ethan, and I hit the bar. They're all happy and smiles, and I'm crying on the inside.

"Here's to Boone saving our land," Wyatt says, raising his glass. "He pulled off one hell of a stunt on old man Maynard." We all clink our glasses together.

"I'm worried about how Tom will repay him." Bear glances over at me.

"I've hired extra security for the ranch." Wyatt takes a sip of his beer, and I gulp mine down. "Boone will handle whatever is thrown at him. More than likely, Tom's anger is going to be torpedoed at this family."

"Has anyone warned our parents?" Ellie asks as I wave at the waitress to bring another round.

"I'll meet with Daddy in the morning and tell him about the loan and the threats from Tom. I don't want anything ruining his good mood after winning the race today." Wyatt downs a beer.

"Did Daddy know about the scheme to outfox Tom?" I grab Ethan's beer and finish it off.

"Whose idea do you think it was?" Wyatt chuckles. "When Boone went to him, he knew Maynard had something to do with it, so he came to me with some ideas. He called Boone, and they worked out the details. I only drew up the contract for him...and maybe forged your signature." He shrugs.

Our round of drinks land on the table, and I gulp another one down.

"You may want to slow down with the drinking, Sis." Bear puts his arm around my shoulder.

"Nope. Not happening. I'm drinking to forget that Boone is on his honeymoon tonight." The thought of him touching her has to be erased from my mind.

"I have a better way for you to forget him." Ellie is eyeing someone sitting at the bar. "That hot cowboy hasn't taken his eyes off you since we walked in the door."

I glance over at him. He smiles and tips his hat.

"He sure is purdy," she says, and Ethan frowns.

"I'm not interested." I continue with my drinking.

"Well, if you aren't, I am." She gets up, walks over, and starts flirting with him.

I push her beer in Ethan's direction. "Drink up, buttercup. Looks like we both need to drown our sorrows tonight."

"You know what would chap Ellie's ass?" Bear leans toward Ethan.

"What?"

"You hooking up with that pretty little blonde sitting at the end of the bar all by her lonesome." His gaze cuts in her direction.

Ethan's gaze follows Bear's, and he checks her out. "You think so?"

"I sure do. Turn the tables on her. I guarantee it will get Ellie's attention."

Ethan looks over at me.

"What do you have to lose?" I shrug.

He finishes Ellie's beer and smacks his hand on the table. "You're right." He smooths down his shirt and swaggers over to the blonde. It seems to work. Ellie notices right away.

"I'm sorry about Boone and Margret." Wyatt

seems so genuine. Maybe he's not the evil brother I thought him to be.

He scoots his chair out from under the table and heads over to a woman dressed in a skinny skirt and white blouse. He knows her by the way he's looking at her. She toys with a tendril of hair and smiles at him as she drinks him in.

"It's just you and me going home alone tonight." I raise my glass to Bear.

"Speak for yourself. Missy is staying with Momma, and there's a cackle of women who've been inviting me to their table all night."

"How do you know that." I laugh.

"Look at them." He gestures with his head.

Sure enough, all four of them are googling him like a piece of meat. "I thought you'd changed your ways since Missy came along?"

He stands. "I'm still a man, and when hot little numbers like that are eating me up with their eyes... well, a man's gotta answer."

"You're such a horn dog," I giggle. "Go get em, Tiger."

I'm all alone at the table. I haven't had enough to drink because I'm still thinking about Boone. I order another round for everyone, knowing they aren't coming back to the table. It should be enough to drown my sorrows.

I down another two glasses and feel the edge of pain lifting and my world is spinning just a tad. Someone puts a coin in the jukebox. "Stupid Boy," the Cassadee Pope version, fills the room. I get up and go to the empty dance floor. I lift my glass in the air and start swaying my hips to the music that speaks to me. I sing the chorus at the top of my lungs, screaming about the stupid boy losing the only girl that made him feel alive. "Stupid boy! You've lost the only thing that made you feel alive!" Maybe that line was meant for me. All the years I'd been gone, nothing made me feel more alive than Boone. I'm not sure I'll ever find someone that makes me feel the way he does.

"I'm invincible."

"I'm the Phoenix rising from the earth."

"I'm a warrior!"

"Screw you, Boone Methany. I hope your frank-n-beans rots off tonight!"

"I think it's time to take you home." Wyatt stills me with his hand. I look around the bar with all eyes on me. I didn't realize I said any of those things out loud, much less at a decimal that could be heard over the music blaring through the speakers.

"I'm not done yet." I finish off my beer and hand him the glass.

"He'll never taste from my juice box again!" I try to high-five Wyatt, but he doesn't raise his hand. "This is my fight song!" I stumble, and he catches me.

"I think your fight song, which truly isn't a song, is over for tonight." He scoops me in his arms and carries me out the door. One by one, my family and Ethan surround me in the truck. I lay my head on Ethan's shoulder. The world spins when the truck moves, and I close my eyes to suppress the motion.

"Oh, gawd! Why did you let me drink so much? You know I'm a horrible drunk." I retch in the bushes as Ethan holds back my hair.

"Evidently a dirty-mouthed one too." He laughs. "We need to get indoor plumbing in your cottage.

I straighten myself and wipe my mouth with the back of my hand. "Right now, that sounds like a good plan." I turn to walk in the house, and he follows me. "I'm not sure I can make it up into the loft." I look up the ladder.

"I'll help you."

He stands behind me and climbs the ladder as I do. I fall face-first into my soft mattress. "Get some sleep," he says and starts down a step.

I roll over. "Would you stay with me tonight? I don't want to be alone."

He climbs back up. Leaving his t-shirt and jeans on, he gets under the covers with me when I pull them back.

"You're a good friend, Ethan. Thank you for being here for me."

He kisses my forehead. "You're welcome."

"You didn't want to sleep with that blonde anyway." I tuck my head under his chin. "I saved you a lot of grief."

"No, I didn't." He chuckles. "Your crazy dancing antics saved me."

"Should I add, I'm a hero to my fight song?"

"You're a mess. Go to sleep, Clem."

"Damn." I press my hands to my temples. I swear my brain is trying to free itself from my head. Ethan is sound asleep with his head under the pillow. I creep out of bed without waking him. I softly pat down the ladder and go straight for the

248

coffee pot. I normally want it full of sugar and cream —this morning the blacker, the better.

My front door creaks open. "Clem, you awake?" Ellie's head pops in the door.

"Barely," I say, pulling down a coffee mug from the cabinet.

"You were pretty bad last night. I thought I'd come and check on you."

"Oh, please tell me I didn't do something completely embarrassing?"

"I'm hard to embarrass, but I think some of the patrons in the bar learned some new terms." She laughs, and my head vibrates.

"I guess I won't be able to go back there again."

"You're not the first person to make a fool of yourself in that bar." She sits at the small round table.

I take down another coffee mug. "Do tell," I say with a raised eyebrow, setting the cup in front of her and take a seat.

She opens her mouth to tell me, and her gaze goes upward. I turn to look, and Ethan's head pops up from the loft.

"It's not what you think." I sip my coffee. "I didn't want to be left alone last night, so he stayed with me. Fully clothed and a complete gentleman."

"I'm okay with that." She places her mug to her lips.

"Do you care about him?"

She nods so Ethan doesn't hear her.

"Maybe you should consider giving up your ways. He's a really good guy."

"I've had a so-called good guy before. He broke my heart," she whispers.

"Is that why you refuse to be with one guy?"

She nods again.

"That guy up there is crazy about you. I've never seen him fall for anyone before. You should risk that heart of yours."

"This coming from the woman who was wishing Boone's frank-n-beans fell off last night."

"Lord. Did I really say that?"

"At the top of your lungs," she snickers.

She watches with an appreciative look as Ethan climbs down the ladder.

"Good morning." He runs his hand through his bed head hair. "I...um..."

"Slept with my sister," she says, kicking me under the table. I hold back a laugh.

"That's not"—he points at me—"tell her that's not how it was." He's so flustered.

I crack up. "She's only teasing you, Ethan. She knows you and I are friends."

"Oh." He smiles.

"Was the blonde your friend too?"

"I..." Smile gone.

"My head hurts entirely too badly for this conversation. You need to take this back to your place."

Ellie stands, takes Ethan's hand, and leads him out the door.

"Great, now I can suffer in my own misery." I let my head fall to the table.

CHAPTER TWENTY ONE
BOONE

e being a gentleman is ingrained in me. Opening the truck door, I help Margret out. I've been living in a house on the Maynard property since I left the Calhouns.

I unlock the front door and push it open.

"Aren't you going to carry me across the threshold?" Margret holds her arms up.

"No," I say, and storm inside.

"But it's a tradition." She stands outside the door.

I flip on the lights. "There's nothing traditional about us being together."

"It's our honeymoon night." She gives up and walks inside.

"Let's get this straight right now." I'm in her face.

"I did what I promised I would do, and in the public eye, we look like the happy couple. But," I spit out the *T*, "in this house we sleep in separate rooms. We are not a couple."

She totally ignores my words and drapes her arms around my shoulder. "It's not like we haven't done it before." She slides her hand between us and places it on my crotch. "I promise to make you a happy man."

I yank her hand away and step back. "That was before I knew who you truly were."

"I'm the same person I've always been. You can't blame me for my father's actions. Besides, I defended you against him, and he was really pissed. So you owe me." She moves closer and kisses my neck.

I run my hands down her arms then push her back. "The two of you forced me into this marriage by threatening Clem. Why do you want a man that's not in love with you?"

"Clem was no good for you. She left you once, she'd do it again. I'd never leave you, and as long my daddy likes you, you'll be fine."

"Is that it?"

"What are you talking about? And, why are we still talking when I should be making love to my husband?" she purrs.

"He killed the man you loved because he didn't like him and you're afraid to love someone your daddy doesn't approve of."

"Don't be silly." That hurt in her eyes is back, and I know I'm right. "If that were true, after what you pulled tonight, I don't think my daddy is very fond of you."

She has a point. "But you think us being married, you can keep me safe. I don't need your protection."

"He'd never lay a hand on my husband."

I feel sorry for her. She really only loves me because I'm the only man her father approved of. It's sad. "Look, Margret, I don't want to hurt you. You deserve someone who's in love with you. Forcing my hand in marriage will not make me love you."

She steps back and loosens her hair. "You did at one time, and given time, you will again. I'm not the enemy. I'm your wife. Now, cut out all this nonsense and take me to bed." She grabs my hand. I walk her to the bedroom. "Peel your prize out of her dress," she says with a sexy drawl. She turns, holding up her hair. I unhook the eyelet and zip her dress down. Before she can turn around, I walk out and shut the bedroom door.

"Good night, Margret," I say from behind it. I go to my room, shut the door, and lock it.

"You open this door right now, Boone Methany!" Her angry fists pound on the door.

I ignore her and strip out of my clothes and get in the shower. I turn it on as hot as I can. I want her touch off my skin. As it rinses away, I close my eyes and see Clem's beautiful face. She's still wearing the pink dress from the derby. She's quirky in the flouncy hat, yet somehow still tough as nails.

I grab the bar of soap and lather my body. My cock is hard, thinking about her. I'd love to hear her dirty words in my ear right about now. Some men would be offended, but it would always turn me on. I love how she can be prim and proper one minute, and a dirty talker the next. She learned to only talk that way in front of me after her momma washed her mouth out with soap enough times. I'm glad it never really tamed her.

My cock is throbbing with thoughts of her. The night I unwrapped her from the plastic wrap replays over and over in my mind. She tasted so damn sweet on my tongue. I slide my hand down to my cock and grip it hard. She came so easily. I pump back and forth, almost a grueling punishing rhythm. "I love you, Clem Calhoun. Please don't give up on me." I watch as I explode on the tile wall and it runs down to the floor.

I press my forehead to the wall and let my tears mingle with the water and stay there until it turns cold. I wrap a towel around my waist and walk into the bedroom. Margret must've given up for the night, either that or her fist hurt from beating on the door. I pull on a pair of boxers and climb in bed, wishing I had a bottle of whiskey to knock me out. I don't dare unlock the door to get one. Punching my pillow a few times, I roll over. It's not long before my exhaustion takes over.

I WAKE UP TO SINGING COMING FROM THE kitchen and the smell of bacon. Throwing back the covers, I pull on a pair of blue jeans, a work shirt, and my cowboy boots. I open the door to see Margret standing in front of the stove, wearing an apron, but nothing on underneath it.

Running my hand through my hair, I force myself to start my day.

"Morning," she says, placing food on a plate.

"Why don't you have clothes on?" I pour myself a cup of coffee.

"I like to cook naked." She bats her eyes.

I glance at my watch, and it's seven in the morning. She's in full makeup, including bright red lipstick. "That could be a hazard cooking bacon."

"It's worth it to let my husband know that I'm ready for him anytime he wants." She slides the plate in front of me as I sit.

"Does that mean every time I'm home you're going to be floating around in your birthday suit?"

"If that's what it takes." She leans on the edge of the table next to me with her legs apart. She flips up the edge of her apron, making sure I have a good view of what's between her legs.

I push the plate of food away and stand. "I'm not hungry for either." I grab my hat off the hook by the door and get out as fast as I can. The door swings open behind me.

"Have a nice day, husband." She blows me a kiss.

I head out to the stable to check on Moonshine. Whiskey River was delivered back to the Calhoun's after the race. I had made all the arrangements the day I met with Wyatt. Clem will have to get him ready for his race in the Preakness.

"Hey, beautiful boy." Moonshine neighs at me when I open his gate. "One day that will be you running in the Kentucky Derby."

"I've sold him for a pretty penny." A voice comes

out of the shadows. I turn to see Tom with his arms crossed over his chest.

"You sold him?"

"I did." He steps closer. "And, I bought the one horse that will beat Whiskey River in the Preakness, stealing his chance of ever winning the Triple Crown."

That's what he did with his winnings. "There is no such horse."

"That's where you're wrong. The horse that came in second, Lucky Shot, with the right jockey, he'll win."

"We'll see about that."

"You got your kicks yesterday besting me, but don't think it will go unpunished."

I close the distance between us. "I don't know what it is you're really after, but I'm going to find out and expose you."

"There is nothing to disclose. You'll stay in line and keep my daughter happy."

"Why would a father want his daughter to be married to a man that doesn't love her?"

"She needs a man like you. She makes poor choices in men. You're the kind of man who can take care of my daughter and this ranch long after I'm gone."

Is he sick? Maybe that's why he needs money. But then again, why would he take his earnings and spend it on another racehorse? His winnings wouldn't have been enough to purchase the horse outright, even with the loan from the Calhoun's that will be paid in full. There has to be more to it.

"You don't give your daughter enough credit. She's more than capable of taking care of herself."

"You're already defending your wife. I like it."

"Now that you've sold Moonshine, what is it you expect me to do around here?"

"Lucky Shot will be delivered tomorrow. You have until the eighteenth to get him ready to win the Preakness. That should keep you pretty damn busy and away from the Calhouns."

"As long as you stay away from them, I will."

"I'm the only one with the bargaining chips around here. Do your job." He rushes out of the barn.

I open the truck door and pull out my cell phone, hitting speed dial for Wyatt.

"Hey, Boone."

"You need to do some digging on Maynard. See if there are medical bills piling up."

"You think he's sick?"

"I don't know, but there's something he's hiding,

and until I find out what it is, I have to do exactly as he says."

"I'll get right on it."

There's a lengthy pause. "How's Clem?"

"She got pretty messed up last night."

I blow out a long breath. "Work fast, man." I hang up. It takes everything in me to not jump in my truck and drive over there. She must hate me. I don't think I could've watched her marry another man. To think about her on her wedding night would've damn near killed me.

I decide to punish myself by chopping up a tree that's down on Maynard property from the storm. I peel out of my shirt and swing the ax for hours until I'm drenched in sweat. My hands are covered in blisters. I've let off steam, and I'm exhausted, but I have a meeting with Wyatt and Chet to make that Maynard can't find out about. I'll have to park in the wooded area on the west side of the property and hop the fence, so Maynard's men don't see me.

CHAPTER TWENTY TWO
CLEM

"What are you doing, Clem?" Bear asks as I climb on the four-wheeler next to him.

"I'm letting Whiskey River have a day of rest, and I need something to keep my mind busy, so I'm helping you with the cattle this morning."

"Suit yourself, but you better keep up." He peels out onto the ranch, only stopping to open the gate. I follow him through then hop off to shut it behind us. I follow him over the rolling hills, and the wind flips my long braid to the back, and it flies like a flag behind me. I haven't ridden in years.

Bear comes to a sudden halt and grabs the rifle that's attached to the back of his seat. I stop beside him and do the same.

"What do you see?"

"There." He points over the ridge of a hill. "I saw two men wearing bandanas over their faces headed this way. They ducked when they saw me."

"I thought we had extra security set up?"

"We do at night. Our men should be able to keep an eye out during the day."

We walk toward the hill with our rifles raised, watching for any sign of movement. When we make it to the top, two cattle lay dead on the ground. A shot comes out of nowhere, and we lay flat on the ground behind the cows.

"Do you seem them?" Bear has his weapon ready to fire.

"I can't see anything but the bright glare of the sun."

Bear takes out his radio that directly connects with all the hired hands that work for the Calhouns. "I need some men on the back forty of the property on the west side. Come armed."

Ten minutes later, a truck comes barreling in our direction. Five men get out with their weapons raised. "What is it, boss man?"

Bear points in the direction the shot rang out from. "Two men moved that way. They killed our cattle and took a shot at us."

They climb back in the truck and head the direction Bear pointed.

"Do you think it's Maynard's men?"

"No doubt." He takes his phone from his back pocket. "I'm calling the police. This is getting out of hand. First, they steal cattle, now they're killing them. What's next? Us?"

I listen as he makes the call. Our men come back in the truck. "We found their tracks, but they're long gone," one of them tells Bear.

"Police are on their way." He turns to me. "You don't need to be here for any of this. Go back to the house and check on Missy and Momma."

I don't hesitate. I climb on the four-wheeler and hightail it back to the main house. Missy is sitting at the table eating cereal, and Momma is washing the dishes.

"What are you two up to today?" I ask nonchalantly when I come through the screen door.

"I have my first riding lesson today," Missy says with a mouthful.

Momma turns in my direction. "It's Sunday. We're going to church before anything else is done around here. Do you want to come with us?"

"I'll pass. I need to catch up with Wyatt." I set up close to Momma so Missy can't hear me. "You need to keep a good eye out. Bear and I saw two men on the property. They killed a couple of cows and took a shot at us."

She holds in a gasp, covering her mouth with her hand.

I touch her arm. "No one got hurt, but I want you to be safe. Take a couple of men with you to church just in case."

"You think it's Tom?"

"Bear does."

"Maybe it's time I have a chat with him."

"Stay away from him. Let the men handle this."

She turns toward Missy. "Go upstairs and get your pretty new dress on." She climbs down from the stool and heads to her room.

"How are you doing?" she asks.

"I'm staying busy." I bite my bottom lip. "I hate that he married her."

"Boone is a good man. I'm sure he has his reasons."

"You mean like he loves her because that's what it looked like to me when he was standing up there at the altar, watching his bride walk down to meet him."

"I'd bet my life on the fact that he doesn't love

her." She dries her hand on the dishtowel. "He waited for you for years. You need to wait and see how all this is going to play out."

"Seems to me he's played his hand. He married her." I open the screen door.

"You need to have a little more faith. Men do things for their own reasons. Sometimes it's to protect us. Sometimes they're just being stupid."

I laugh and head back to the cottage to grab my winnings from the Derby. I crank up Lizzy and head to Wyatt's house. Daddy's truck is parked out front beside Wyatt's. I knock and walk through the door. I hear voices coming from Wyatt's office. The door is shut, and I stop mid-knock when I hear Boone talking.

"He's threatened repercussions on this family. Seems I'm in the clear because he wants me to keep his daughter happy."

"Why do I get the feeling you know more about what Tom is after than you've let on?" Wyatt asks, but I'm not sure who he's directing his question to until Daddy answers.

"Our fathers' feuded years ago over this land, but that was all settled when it was purchased. Maybe he holds a grudge."

"Enough to kill one of us?" Wyatt responds.

"I don't think he'd stoop that low. He's a resourceful man. If he wants this property, I'm sure he'll come up with a way to try and take it from us."

That's my cue to go inside. I don't want to see Boone, but the loan needs to be paid in full. "Knock, knock," I say, opening the door. All eyes are on me. Boone's eyes are round as saucers.

"I brought the winning check from the race." I skirt by Boone and hand it to Wyatt. "This should take care of paying the loan."

"It does, but there will be extra with all our winnings. Do you want me to set up an account for you?"

"No. Give it to Daddy."

"I don't want your money." Daddy's voice is gruff.

"I want you to have it. You can purchase another racehorse with it or cattle."

He stands. "Why, Clem?"

"Because I didn't get to help you before. Now it's my turn."

He faces Wyatt. "Set up a money market account for your sister." Then he turns toward me and pulls me in for a hug. "I'm proud of you Clem, but I don't want or need your money. Invest it in something you want for yourself." He lets go, and I stare at him like I'm in shock.

Wyatt's chair creaks as he rocks back. "I guess all is forgiven." He seems genuinely pleased. Not at all the Wyatt from just a few weeks ago. "I'll take care of this for you, Clem. Do you know what you want to use the money for?"

I glance at Boone, whose head has been down. "I want to buy Moonshine back."

"You can't," he says without peering up.

"Why not?"

"Because Moonshine's been sold by Tom."

"Then I'll buy him from whoever purchased him."

"I'll find out who that is for you, but they'll probably want more than you have."

"Then I'll take out a loan to get him back."

"Well, this is where all the handsome men are hiding on a Sunday morning." Margret prances through the door in her church dress.

"Who let you in?" Wyatt barks.

"The door was left open." Boone stands, kissing her on the cheek. "What are you doing here?"

"I need a lawyer to file some paperwork for me, and Daddy suggested I drop by and see Wyatt." She hands him a folder.

"I'm not your attorney." He shoves it back at her.

"I can assure you, you'll want to make sure this paperwork is filed properly, and you'll be handsomely paid." She hangs on Boone's arm. He's looking down at his boots.

Wyatt opens the file. "This is a life insurance policy on Boone."

Boone's gaze darts to Margret, who pats him on the arm. "Now that we're married, a woman has to protect her assets."

"Assets my ass," I snarl. "He's your husband, not your damn asset."

"You see"—she walks toward me—"that's where you're wrong. Whatever is Boone's is now half mine. That's how it works when you're married." She holds her hand to her mouth. "That's right, you've never been married so you wouldn't know such things."

"That's enough, Margret. Leave her alone." Boone's voice is terse.

"There you go, being all fake nice to her again. It wasn't that long ago you were cursing her name for leaving you." She walks back over to him and loops her hand with his.

I could launch flamethrowers with my eyes at her right now. Better yet, I'll go get Daddy's shotgun and see how many holes I can put through her Sunday best.

Boone purses his lips. "You're out of line, Margret."

"Silly me. You're right. Those were words whispered in the heat of passion, and I should've never disclosed anything you said. I'm sorry, please forgive me." She bats her fake lashes at him.

"Get the fuck out of here!" my dad barks. "You're not welcome on this property. See to it that you never come back."

Wyatt hands her the file. "Find someone else."

"If I'm not welcome, then neither is Boone." She pretend pouts.

"Boone will always be welcome here. Now get the hell out of here like I told you." Daddy's pointing toward the door.

Boone escorts her out.

"What do you think that was all about?" I ask.

"Claiming what she thinks is hers. I'm sure her father had some other motivation in mind." Wyatt runs his hands through his hair.

"Keep an eye on her. I don't trust her for one minute." Daddy's face is red with anger.

Boone steps back through the door. "I'm sorry

about that," he says, looking at Chet and Wyatt. "I'll make sure she doesn't come back."

"That was a substantial life insurance policy. I think you need to watch your back, especially with Tom's history." Wyatt paces behind the desk.

"I think it's a game he's playing. He's not really after me, or he would've buried me after the Derby."

"I can't listen to any more of this." I walk out of the office. Boone's boots can be heard running after me.

He snags my arm. "Clem, wait."

I blow out a breath and hold back my tears and turn to face him. "For what, Boone?"

"I'm sorry about everything. I wish you wouldn't have come to the wedding."

I want to step on my tiptoes and kiss his full lips. For a split second, I forget about Margret. I inch my way closer to him, and he steps back.

"I can't. I made a commitment, and I can't break it."

He wants to. I can see it in his eyes. But, he's right. "Please stay away from me. I can't be near you and not want you." I rush out the door with tears flooding my eyes. I start Lizzy up and see Boone filling the doorway, watching me leave. I'm done crying over him. He's made his bed with Margret, and I won't be the person to step in between them.

I've been working every day with Whiskey River and the jockey. They've shaved another two seconds off his time. The Preakness is only another week away, and I have no doubt that this horse is unbeatable.

I haven't seen Boone since the day I saw him and Daddy in Wyatt's office. Hell, I haven't even thought about him...much. I'm such a liar, but it's a lie that I need to keep telling myself.

I'm exhausted and want nothing more than to pass out in my bed. I turn on the AC window unit I bought and installed a few days ago. I can handle the heat during the day, but I want it ice-cold at night. Curling up in bed, I turn out the light and relax, focusing on nothing but breathing. My mind is hard to shut off, and it flashes to the information Wyatt found on Moonshine. He located the purchaser and made him an offer ten percent over what he bought the horse for from Tom. Surprisingly, he agreed to the terms. Wyatt arranged the additional monies to be paid out in a loan, of which I should be able to pay off once Whiskey wins the Preakness.

I go back to slow breathing to push out all the thoughts that keep popping up, finally drifting off to sleep.

A woofing sound wakes me, and the smell of smoke hits me. It almost smells like a campfire burning, but it's not outside. It's coming from inside the cottage. I scramble out of bed. Smoke is drifting to the ceiling. I turn on a light, and it flickers on and off. Billowing plumes darken to a sooty black as it takes hold of the paint on the walls. Ropes of fire are gnawing up the curtains, and the fire is spreading over the wood floor in a ripple. If I don't get down from this loft, the flames will find me soon. I scurry down the ladder, and my feet are hot when they hit the floor. I watch as my furniture transforms into a bed of fire. My throat and nose feel raw. I clutch my chest as I double over, coughing up the ash and smoke. Orange flames are spreading, only leaving a small path to the door.

It's now or never. I rush to the door, and as I do the window bursts. I instinctively cover my face as hot shards of glass land on my arm and leg. I fall backward from the slicing pain and feel faint, on the brink of losing consciousness. The door crashes inward, and two hands reach in and pull me out. I watch through hooded eyes as in slow motion, the roof beams cave downward, and the tin roof melts like it was plastic.

A siren can be heard in the distance, but it will be too late by the time they get here. My small cottage is fully engulfed in flames. I hear the voices around me. I'm in and out of consciousness. The sound of dosing out flames is loud, and I wake to a mask on my face and someone telling me I'll be okay.

CHAPTER TWENTY THREE
BOONE

"I'm sure glad you showed up when you did, but how in the hell did you know something was wrong?" Chet is inches from me trying not to let everyone in the hospital waiting room hear our conversation.

"I couldn't sleep, so I went to the barn to check on the horses. I heard a couple of Tom's men whispering. I couldn't make out what they were saying, but I knew they were up to no good. I had a bad feeling in my gut. I took off in my truck and headed straight for the ranch. The guard out front waved me by. I veered toward the cottage when I saw smoke and orange flames coming from Clem's direction. She'd almost made it out by the time I got there. Thank god she was laying not far from the door. I wouldn't have been able to get to her, but I'd have died trying."

"I know you would've, Son." Chet's large hand grasps my shoulder. I'm holding back a choke thinking about what could've happened to Clem. I blame myself.

Mrs. Calhoun walks out, holding Clem around the waist. "Our girl is going to be just fine."

Wyatt, Bear, Ellie, and Ethan surround her. I try to duck out, but Chet holds a tight grip on me. "Don't you want to make sure she's okay?"

I nod.

Clem makes her way toward me. "You pulled me out of the fire?" She glances down at my hand that's wrapped in white gauze.

"Yes." Her left arm and left thigh are bandaged, and there's a cut on her chin in the shape of a crescent moon with stitches poking out of it. "Are you okay?"

"Some minor cuts and burns. If you wouldn't have shown up when you did." She swallows back tears. "I don't think I would've gotten out of there alive." She nearly topples me over with a hug.

I want to hold her here forever. I'm terrified of letting her go. Her nose is nuzzled into my neck, and right at this very moment, I want her more than I ever have. Her heart is beating fast against my chest. Mine feels like it's going to explode.

Margret storms into the waiting room with her father. "There you are. I was so worried something had happened to you when I woke up and couldn't find you. I heard over one of the radios that there had been a fire at the Calhoun's." She literally says it all in one breathe while pushing Clem out of my arms, throwing herself around my neck.

"What the fuck are you doing here?" Chet bows up at Tom.

"My daughter was worried about her husband."

"You did this, didn't you?" Chet's inches from Tom's face.

"I've been at home in bed. How could I possibly have started a fire." His face is so smug I think Chet's going to beat him senseless.

"Your hired hands did it for you, and when I can prove it, I'm coming after you." Spit flies in Tom's face. He blinks and wipes it off.

Mrs. Calhoun steps between them. "I've had about enough of your nonsense. You're nothing but a bitter old man who can't let dead dogs lie."

I peel Margret from me. What the hell is she talking about?

"Amelia." Tom lifts her hand and kisses the back

of it. "Beautiful as ever and always defending your hot-headed husband."

"If you weren't such a mean old coot, you'd have a wife by your side."

"Go, Momma," Ellie cheers.

"I can assure you I had nothing to do with this little mishap and when I find the men that did, I'll make sure they're punished." He smiles at her.

"Mishap!" Bear has pushed between them. Wyatt is trying to pull him back, and Bear is shrugging him off. "That's what you call Clem's house burning down and almost dying?"

Tom looks over his shoulder at Clem. "You're being a tad bit dramatic, don't you think, Son? She's got a few bumps and bruises, nothing close to death."

"I'm not your fucking son!" Bear takes a swing, but Chet catches his arm before he can make impact.

"He's baiting you. Don't fall into his trap." Chet holds Bear back.

He gets him calmed down and out of nowhere, Wyatt decks Tom right in the face. His head falls back, and his hand flies to his bleeding nose. "I'll have you arrested for assault and battery," Tom seethes.

"It's was worth it." Wyatt shakes out his fist.

Margret runs over to her father. "Daddy, are you okay?"

"Call the police! I want him arrested!" He snaps at her.

I take Clem by the arm and escort her outside. "I'm so…"

"I know you're sorry, but that's not good enough anymore." She yanks free of my grip. "You can't keep coming around. Don't get me wrong. I'm thankful you showed up when you did, but look at what your wife and father-in-law are doing to this family."

"I just need more time. I promise I'll fix this."

"You may fix things with my family, but not me. You made your choice pretty clear."

Before her mouth is closed, I crash my mouth to hers. She doesn't resist at first. Our tongues are like wild horses that are thirsty trying to find water. We're desperate for a taste.

She pulls back, and her hand smacks firmly against my cheek. "We're done, Boone. I won't do this anymore with you."

I stand, holding my cheek as her mom rushes by me, following Clem into the car. Ellie and Bear come out shaking their heads. Ellie stops and hugs my neck. "Thank you for saving her." Bear shakes my hand.

Chet stays behind with Wyatt, waiting for the police. Margret has her arms crossed over her chest as she strolls in my direction. "Wyatt just told me you were the one that got Clem out of the fire." She stares at my hand. "What was my devoted husband doing at his ex-girlfriend's house at two in the morning?"

"I couldn't sleep. I had a bad feeling and saw smoke." It's a partial truth. I don't want her to know about the men I heard talking.

"So you decided to be the hero and rescue her. Didn't look like she showed much appreciation to me." She rubs my red face, and I jerk away from her touch. She tisks at me. "Maybe you've finally learned your lesson when it comes to that she-devil."

I step up close to her. "If you and your father don't back off of her, I'll walk away from you. I'll expose your father for attempted murder, and I'll dig up the case on your old boyfriend."

"And if you don't start acting like a man in our home"—she glances down at my crotch—"I won't back him down, and I'll cash in on that policy." She has the audacity to put her lips to mine.

I take a step back and wipe my mouth with my hand. "You can blackmail me all you want. I'll never love you like I do her."

"She doesn't love you anymore, didn't you hear her?"

"Doesn't matter if she loves me back or not."

"Kinda like you and me. I love you enough for the both of us." The cops pull up, and we follow them inside.

They cuff Wyatt, and I follow him to the station to post his bail. "Thanks, man."

"It's the least I could do. I wish it would've been me that knocked the shit out of him."

"Don't worry. I know a good attorney." He chuckles, getting into my truck. "You need to tell me everything you saw and heard tonight."

"I'll write it all down, but I'm thinking your mother needs to be someone you grill on Tom Maynard. There's a history there, and I have a feeling it's all coming to a head."

"I think you're right. She's a tight-lipped woman, but I'll try to get her to talk. In the meantime, you need to stay away from our family. Especially Clem. You know I love you like a brother, man. I have to keep them safe, and as long as you're married to Margret, things are going to get worse."

I know he's right. I could have lost Clem tonight. I don't want any more harm coming to this family. I'll have to keep digging on my own. "One thing about tonight."

"What's that?"

"Someone let his men on Calhoun property."

"You think we have a man working both sides?"

"I do. Have you hired anyone new recently?"

"Three new men. I'll check them out myself."

I drop him off at his house and detour slowly by Clem's cottage that's nothing but ashes. Little dots of orange are still glowing. At the main house, all the lights are on. I'm sure they have Clem safely tucked away. I fight the urge to stop and check on her. Instead, I make my way back home.

Home.

It feels nothing like home, more like a prison. I feel like I've been branded by the Maynard's and it's a burn that runs deep. I park in the driveway and turn off my truck. I can't bring myself to go inside. I lower my hat over my eyes and sleep in my truck.

Margret wakes me in the morning, tapping on my window. Her face looks as pissy as an old grumpy cat. Opening the door, stepping out, Margret's voice grates on my nerves. "I see you decided to not take my advice and act like a man."

I slam the door hard, and she jumps. "I've told you, whatever you think is going to happen between us, isn't it. I've got work to do." I storm into the house to change clothes.

She leans in the doorframe of my bedroom and watches me. "I did love him," she speaks. "I know Daddy did something dreadful to him. I don't want to see the same thing happen to you."

"Is that why you purchased a life insurance policy on me?" I say sarcastically.

"That was my father's idea, not mine."

"Is this all about money?"

"Not for him."

"Tell me, Margret." I sit on the edge of the bed.

"That would be betraying his trust, but if you were to act more like a husband, I'd shift my loyalty to you." She sits next to me.

"I can't do that, and you know it."

She stands. "What I can tell you is that it has something to do with my grandfather and Chet. Chet Calhoun wasn't always a good man."

"I'm sure we've all done things we're not proud of at some point in our life. It doesn't make us bad people."

"What have you done that you're not so proud of?"

"This marriage for one," I huff.

"Now here I was being all empathetic with you, and you have to go and be hurtful."

"That was your idea of empathy? If you want to show me any kind of compassion, you'll let me out of this marriage."

She walks over and lifts my chin with her fingers. "That's the one thing I have no desire to do."

CHAPTER TWENTY FOUR
CLEM

Lizzy rattles and jerks, sounding like she's dying as I roll up into the parking lot of Bear's garage. I leave a hue of black smoke behind me. He's in a blue uniform, standing outside talking on his cell phone. When he sees me, he holds a finger in the air and walks away. I push Lizzy's heavy door open, and it makes an awful racket. Almost as bad as the engine.

There is an assortment of cars in the parking lot. Some damaged and in dire need of repair, others appear brand new. The garage has three open bays, two of which have vehicles in them. One with a hood up, the other stripped of its tires. I walk inside the empty bay and take a look around. It appears like any other mechanic shop with hydraulic equipment, hoses dangling, stacks of tires and rims, spare auto parts, tool chests, and rolling bins. Complete with an oil-stained concrete floor. It smells of motor oil and sweat.

I'm very proud of Bear for having something of his own. I know he loves the ranch, but he loved the equipment better. This place suits him.

"May I help you?" a large man in grease-stained coveralls picking up and tossing down a huge tire like it was nothing, asks me.

"I'm Clem. Bear's sister."

He quickly washes his hands and crumples up a paper towel, throwing it in a bin. "Bear's told me a lot about you. I'm Falcon." He sticks out his hand that has grease caked under his nails.

"Is that your real name or a nickname?" I find myself smiling at the good-looking man in front of me who's larger than life.

"Sorry, I'm so used to people calling me by my last name. You can call me Jett."

"It's nice to meet you, Jett. I'm hoping my brother hasn't told you everything about me." For some reason, I'm blushing.

"Only that you were back in town and he's glad you're here. Oh, yeah, and that your horse won the Kentucky Derby. Congratulations are in order."

"Thanks."

I hear a clank. "Aw, shit!" An older man hits his head on the hood of a truck.

"How many times have you done that, old man?" Jett has a deep chuckle.

He slams the hood shut. "Enough you'd think I'd know better." He moseys toward me. He's sweating like a gorilla, and I think he has four teeth in his mouth. "I heard you say you're Bear's sister. I'm part owners in this garage with him." He wipes his hand down his coveralls. "I'm Gary."

I shake his hand. He turns back around to the car he was working on and sticks his hand through the open window, turning the ignition and letting the engine idle.

"Bear took a phone call. He should be right back. Can I get you anything while you wait?" Jett's voice is deep and kinda charming.

"No, I'm just going to wait over here by the oscillating fans." I wipe my forehead.

"Sorry, it does get kinda hot in here if you're not used to it." I move over by the fan to feel the cool air and admire Jett as he picks up another tire.

"You have a little drool on your chin," Bear says, handing me a paper towel.

"He is a fine-looking man."

"I could set you two up if you'd like." He raises an eyebrow.

"Admiring is one thing. Dating is an entire other." I turn to face him so I can quit staring at Jett's biceps.

"What brings you to my humble abode?" He laughs; I think at me.

"Lizzy needs a tune-up or something."

"She needs something all right. Driven to the junkyard would be my guess." He chuckles.

"As much as I hate to admit it, I think you're right."

"Why don't you buy a new one? Aren't you driving to Maryland next week for the Preakness?"

"Yeah. I want to be there ahead of time to work with Whiskey before the races."

"That piece of crap isn't going to make the seven-and-a-half-hour drive. I think it's time to put her out of her misery. You've had her since you were sixteen years old and she was used then."

We walk over to Lizzy, and he raises the hood of the rusty old truck. "Go crank the engine."

I know he's appeasing me. I get in and turn the key. She sputters and black smoke billows up in Bear's direction. He coughs and waves his hand in front of his face. "Turn it off, Clem!" he yells.

I get out and stand by him. "Looks like the same smoke from the fire."

"You okay?"

"Yeah. I miss my cottage and my privacy. Daddy walks through the house in his tighty-whities, and it scares me a bit." I shudder.

"That is something you can't erase from your mind." He laughs and shuts the hood. "How are you physically?" He tilts my chin up to check out my face.

"My arm and leg still hurt a little."

"When you're ready, I'll take those stitches out for you. No sense going back to the doc's to have them removed."

I take his hand and stare at his black nails. "Thanks, but no thanks. I'll get Ellie to do it."

"Have you seen Boone since the fire?"

"Boone and I are done. I'm staying out of his way and him mine."

He takes both my hands in his. "I know that's not what you really want."

"No, it's not"—I sigh—"but that's how it has to be. He's a married man."

"Let me know if you change your mind about Falcon. I'm sure he'd be thrilled to go out with you."

"Maybe drinks one night wouldn't hurt." I glance

over at him, and he smiles. "Not till after the race. I'm busy the next couple days, and I'm standing guard at night at the main house."

"Wyatt hired men to do that."

"Lotta good that did."

"He fired the man that betrayed us. Wyatt's filed a police report, but they haven't gotten the man to confess against Maynard."

"I'm sure he paid him a pretty penny for his loyalty."

"Wyatt's also going to rebuild 102. Ellie filed the insurance claim, and it should be enough to make it bigger and better, at least add indoor plumbing."

"Ethan would love that." I snort.

"What's the deal with him? Is he sticking around? I can't seem to get a straight answer out of him."

"He likes it here, but I think it depends on how things go with him and Ellie."

"I hate to break it to you, but she'll get bored with him and eat him alive. I've seen her do it over and over again."

"I hate that for him, but he's been warned. He's a grown man and can make his own decisions."

He pulls a green bandana out of his back pocket and ties it around his head. "I've got to get back to work, but let me give you a ride home on my bike first. Leave Lizzy here. I don't think she's salvageable and you should seriously think about buying a new truck."

I take him up on his offer and climb on the back of his motorcycle. It's a freeing feeling, kinda like racing on a horse.

Daddy's on the porch sipping on Momma's homemade lemonade when we pull up. I thank Bear, and he spins his back wheel, sending dirt in the air and takes off.

"What are you doing on the back of that boy's bike?" Daddy asks as I walk up the stairs and sit in the swinging bench that hangs from the porch ceiling.

"I think Lizzy has seen her better days. He gave me a ride home from his shop. He's done well for himself."

"That he has. What are you going to do about a set of wheels?"

"I'm guessing I need to go shopping."

"How about you and I head into town and see what we can find?"

I'm surprised he's offering. He made every one of us pick out our own vehicles and negotiate a deal. "If

I agree to let you go with me, will you quit walking around in your underwear?"

"Nope. My house my rules." He grins.

"Then I need to tell Wyatt he needs to hurry up with rebuilding the cottage." I laugh.

"Men will be here tomorrow to start removing what's left of it. We could rebuild somewhere else on the property. You've always had your eye on the piece of land by the river."

"Boone and I were going to build there," I say softly.

"I remember. There's no reason why you can't build it for yourself."

"You know what? I'd like that." I stand. "Do you still want to go truck shopping?"

"I do, but I'm still gonna walk around in my underwear." His face floods with a grin. "While we're out shopping, let's pick up a rifle for your new house."

"That's the cart before the horse, Daddy. Let's worry about building it first."

He sets down his glass of lemonade and gets up. "Come on, we'll go find you a sporty new Dodge truck."

"What if I want a Ford?" I say, teasing him. I know he's a Dodge man.

"Then I'd say you're not a Calhoun and run you off this property." He chuckles and puts his arm around my shoulder. So unlike Daddy. I like him like this. I still love him gruff and all, but I could use the sweet side of him after the past couple of weeks I've had.

❧

DADDY KNOWS EVERYONE IN TOWN AND GOT ME A sweet deal on a new truck. I kinda like the electric windows, leather seats, AC, big tires, and the drink holders. Ethan would be impressed.

We go back to the house for dinner, and after I've helped Momma with the dishes, I take roost in a rocker on the front porch with Daddy's rifle sitting beside me.

"There you are. I was wondering where you went." Momma sits in the other wooden rocker.

"I haven't slept well since the fire, so I figured I'd make myself useful and keep watch."

"Wyatt hired extra hands. There are men hidden all on this property. I don't think we'll have a repeat of a house burning."

I kick back in the rocker. "What is it you meant

when you told Tom that he couldn't let 'a dead dog lie?'"

"The Maynards and the Calhouns have a history, and Tom holds a grudge like no man I've ever seen."

"What's his grudge against this family?"

"That's between him and your daddy to work out."

"Don't seem like that's happening. Is it something we can talk about with him?"

"Only if you think your father would ever give up this land."

"If his issue is with Daddy, then why has Boone been dragged into it?"

"He knows how much Boone is worth to this family. He'd never have a Calhoun marry his daughter or live on his property."

"So Boone is a pawn in his game."

"I'm afraid so."

"Then why doesn't Daddy march over there and put an end to Tom's vendetta, so Boone doesn't have to pay the price?"

"Because he's a proud man, and he's not going to cave in to what Maynard wants."

"Haven't you always told me that pride cometh before the fall?"

"The pride of the Calhoun men is a different beast."

"What was Daddy like when he was younger?"

"He was wild. You remind me of him more than you know. He hated the thought of being a rancher."

"Seriously?" I raise an eyebrow. "I thought he loved it from the beginning."

"Nope, he loathed everything about it."

"What changed his mind?"

"The day I walked into his life."

The story is getting good. "Tell me more."

She stands and pats my uninjured leg. "That tale will have to wait for another day. I'm exhausted, and I've got an awful headache."

She looks more tired than usual. "Good night, Momma."

"Good night."

More than ever, I really want to know what the clash is between our families. It's more than about this land. When the dust settles, and I'm back from the race, maybe I'll ask Tom himself.

MY BRIGHT SHINY NEW RED DIESEL DODGE purred like a baby on the way to Baltimore. I have to admit, it is nice. Ethan didn't complain one time. He rode with me, but I dropped him off at the airport to fly home to New York and see his parents. It's a quick flight home for him. Whiskey's caravan left several days ago along with his jockey to become familiar with his surroundings before the race. Henry rode with Whiskey.

I stop before I pull through the gates. "Pimlico Race Course," I read the sign. I've dreamed about making it here ever since I fell in love with horses. After I left the ranch, I figured that dream was long gone. I got a little side-tracked, but I'm here now, and Whiskey has a real chance of winning the Preakness.

I drive in the gate and follow the signs to the stables. Don't you know, the first vehicle I see is Boone's. I shouldn't be surprised. I knew he'd be here for Lucky Shot. This will be the first time he and I've competed against one another with a horse. Boone is good, and if anyone can beat Whiskey, it will be his horse. Especially since he knows everything about Whiskey already.

Parking the truck, I grab my cowgirl hat and hop out. Boone comes out of one of the stables carrying a feed bag, looking sexy as ever. He drops it when he sees me and storms in my direction, stopping a few feet from me, pulling off his hat and wiping his brow.

"Hey."

"Hey." We stare at each other, neither one of us knowing what to say.

"Did you trade in Lizzy," he says, finally breaking the silence, looking at the Dodge.

"She didn't leave me any choice." I bite at my lip. He's so damn sexy in his faded blue jeans and cowboy boots. *Get your mind out of the gutter, Clem.* That's where it seems to go every time I'm around him. "I need to go find Whiskey."

"Okay." His dark eyes tell me he has a lot more to say, but he holds it in.

"I guess I'll see you around." I scuff my boots in the dirt, hightailing it away from him.

Damn, Clem looks sexy in that hat and red ribbon weaved in her braid. I'd like to wrap her cord of hair in my fist, drag her to the barn and screw her brains out. I'm sure it's the lack of getting laid that has me all worked up.

I don't want to be here under these circumstances, racing against her horse, yet at the same time, there's no place I'd rather be than close to her. I haven't seen her since the fire, and it's driven me crazy. Margret won't be here until race day to keep me away from her. She's still parading around the house naked, hoping I'll change my mind.

One night after dinner at her dad's house, I excused myself to the restroom and did some digging in Tom's office. I found an old photograph of what looked like his mom and dad, with him and another child in the picture. I didn't ever recall Margret mentioning having an aunt. I asked her about it, and she said her father was an only child. She told me about her mother, and she said she left them not long after she was born and she's never seen or heard from her. I let Wyatt know what I'd found, and he said he'd do some snooping into their family history.

When I went to put the picture back in its place, another one was sticking out from behind the frame. It was a picture of Tom, the same girl, and I could swear a younger version of Chet. I sneaked it out of the house, and I didn't tell Wyatt about it. I plan on asking Chet. It's in my glovebox. Maybe it would be a conversation starter with Clem.

I hike the feedbag up over my shoulder and take it to the trough in Lucky Shot's stable. He's a beautiful thoroughbred, and in any other race, I'd love to see him win. He has the speed and the spirit to beat Whiskey River. The jockey that Tom hired is cocky and hard to deal with, and he may be the horse's downfall.

I finish feeding and watering Lucky Shot and head over to find Clem. I've been keeping an eye out for Whiskey since he got here a few days ago, so I know exactly where I'll find her.

I amble over to the stable and damn near swallow my tongue. Clem has her khaki three-quarter length sleeve shirt tied up high on her waist and her jeans hugging low on her hips. I'm instantly hard at the sight of her. She bends over and talks to Henry, and I nearly come like a sixteen-year-old boy.

I move behind the gate to hide my erection, and she gazes up. "What are you doing here, Boone? Spying on me?"

"No, I came to show you something."

"Whatever it is, I'm not interested. I need to find Jose and get Whiskey on the track." She peers around the stable. "Is your wife lurking around somewhere?"

"No." I pull the picture out of my wallet. "Have you ever seen this before?" I try to hand it to her over the gate.

"I told you I don't have time."

"It will take you two seconds to look at it. Please."

She lets out a loud sigh and snatches the picture from my hand. She glances then does a double take. "Is that Daddy?"

"I believe so. The other young guy is Tom Maynard."

She squints hard at it. "Who's the girl that

Daddy has his arm around? It's not Momma. Where did you get this?"

"It was hidden behind another picture in Tom's office. The other picture may have been Tom's parents, and this same girl was in it. I asked Margret..." I pause for a second, regretting mentioning her name when Clem looks sad. "She said her father was an only child."

"Can I hold on to this?"

"What are you going to do?"

"Tom isn't going to give you information about it. Maybe Daddy will."

"Wyatt's trying to find out more on the Maynard family."

"Momma told me the Calhoun's and Maynard's go way back, and Tom is holding a grudge. This picture might tell the story." She tucks it into the back pocket of her jeans.

I should walk away, but I can't. "How're your burns?"

She puts the bridle on Whiskey. "Mostly healed."

"I see the stitches are out." I enter the stable moving closer to her.

Her hand rubs her chin. "Ellie took them out, and Ethan damn near fainted."

I laugh. "City boy." I inch toward her and lift her chin. "You'll have a scar."

She swallows hard. "You'd have to look close to see it."

"The crescent moon shape appears good on you."

She closes her eyes and swallows again. "Boone, I..."

I drop my hand. "I know." I turn my back to her and stop when she speaks.

"Would you come watch Whiskey River run the track? I know you're working with your horse, but you know Whiskey better than anyone."

I face her. "None of this is what I want, Clem. Whiskey deserves to win, and I'd be glad to help any way I can." I glance at my watch. "I have an hour before Lucky Shot's jockey shows up."

"Thank you," she says, leading the horse and Henry out of the stall.

There's silence between us as we make our way to the practice track. Jose is already suited up and waiting on her. She takes Henry to the side, and Jose leads Whiskey to the track and saddles him up. I step up onto the bottom rung of the white fencing to watch. Clem ties Henry to a post and joins me.

"I wish I'd have never left. I love this life. I was blinded by other things."

"Does that wishing you'd never left include me?"

She slowly nods. "You most definitely wouldn't be married to Margret." She half laughs.

"I'd bet we'd be living in the house on the river and had four or five younglings running around." I grin thinking about it.

The smile she was wearing fades, and she stays silent while we watch Whiskey and Jose warm-up, then take off around the track.

"Damn, he's a magnificent horse. I don't have any advice to give you. I think he's unstoppable."

"You did all the training. I hate that you're not the one to win with him."

I step off the rung and grip the rail. "If not me, then I'm glad it's you."

She jumps off. I see tears pooling behind her fawn eyes. She fights them off hard. Her lip quivers as she tries to form words and she gives up, untying Henry, and walking away.

I know how she feels, and there's so much more I want to say to her. When this is all over, I'm going to fight like a son of a bitch to win her back.

My phone vibrates in my pocket. I pull it out, and Wyatt's name lights up the screen. "Hey, man."

"Thomas Maynard, the first, was married to Hope Smith-Maynard. They had two children, a set of twins. Thomas Maynard the second, and a girl, Teresa."

"What happened to the girl?"

"I don't know. I only found one record of her. It's almost like she didn't exist after the age of twenty-one. There's nothing mentioned about her at all, not even a death certificate."

"That's strange." I take my hat off.

"I think it's time we question my father."

"I found a picture of Chet, Tom, and I believe his sister. I gave it to Clem. I think she's probably the best person to question your dad."

"You're probably right. He still has a soft spot for her after all these years."

"Let's let it play out and see what she'll come up with. In the meantime, she needs to concentrate on winning this race because there's a really good chance Lucky Shot is going to beat her out of a win."

"I hate to hear that."

"I can't throw the race." I put my hat back on. "I wish I could, but I can't."

"I know, and I'm not asking you to lose."

I walk toward the stables as I talk. "Have the men showed up to start rebuilding Clem's cottage?"

I've been putting money in an account that my wife knows nothing about to help build it. The money comes from Maynard, and it's my way of making him pay for having it burned down.

"She's having it built by the river." He hesitated, not wanting to tell me.

In our spot. "Build it wherever she wants. I gotta go. I'll keep you posted if I find out anything else."

"Before you hang up, do you want me to keep Margret from making it to the race?"

"Short of killing her, that would be great." I chuckle.

"Good. Bear came up with a plan. Let's just say his knowledge of vehicles will come in handy." He laughs.

I hang up and meet with the jockey and run Lucky. His time has improved since the Kentucky Derby. He's beat Whiskey by one second.

I drive to the hotel and Clem is checking in at the front desk. Stopping beside her, I wait for her to finish getting her keycard. "May I help you with your luggage?" I have my hand on the handle of her burnt-orange suitcase.

"Thanks."

"What's the room number?"

She hands me the card, and I laugh.

"What's so funny?" She follows me with her other two small bags in hand.

"Your room is right next to mine."

I hear her feet stop moving and turn around.

"I should see if they can change it."

"They're all booked. No rooms left." I don't dare tell her that I requested her room was next to mine, but I was told it wasn't possible. They must've had a last-minute cancellation.

She looks over her shoulder at the desk like she wants to turn around and ask anyway, but she doesn't. We hit the elevator to the third floor. I walk her down the long hall, rolling her luggage behind me. When we make it to her door, she places the keycard in, and the light goes green. She opens it, walking inside. I stay outside the door. I hold the door open with one hand, and she places her two pieces of luggage on the ground, turning around to face me.

"Thank you." I purposely don't move my hand when she takes the handle of the luggage. I can see the electricity light up her skin when she touches me.

"You can let go now," she whispers, with her gaze on my hand.

I release the handle. "I'm right next door if you want anything." My voice is husky with a need for her. I walk backward all the while she watches me. "Anything at all. I'm right here." I unlock my door.

Slowly with her eyes on me, she shuts the door. I softly pat back over to her room, and I hear her flop on the bed and cry. It takes everything in me to not bust down her door.

CHAPTER TWENTY SIX
CLEM

My sobs finally dry and I glare up at the ceiling. I can't believe he's right next door. A thin wall and a door are the only things between us. Well, not the only thing. He does have a wife.

I unpack my bag, tuck the picture in my purse, and take a much-needed long, hot shower. I turn on the air conditioning to make it ice-cold and grab the extra blanket and pillow that hotels always store in the closet. I'm not even in the mood for room service. All I want to do is make it through the next two days.

Turning out the lights, I lie in the dark and listen to every sound. People are walking in the hall, laughing. The ice machine makes an awful noise every time someone uses it. I swear I can hear Boone pacing around his room. I jab at the pillow covering my head, trying to muffle out the noises. I nearly jump out of my skin when the phone on the night-stand rings.

"Hello."

Quiet.

"Hello," I say louder.

"Is this Clem Calhoun?" a deep voice asks.

"Who is this?" I feel a chill run up my spine, unnerving me.

"Your horse better not win the race or you'll find more trouble, this time it won't be your house burning down." Click, the line goes dead.

I slam down the receiver and without thinking, run out of my room and pound on the door. "Boone!"

He opens immediately, and I run into his arms. "You're shaking. What's the matter?" He pushes me arm's length away to look at me.

"A man called me on the hotel phone and threat-ened me not to win the race. He said next time it wouldn't be my house that burnt down."

He walks me over to the bed. "Stay here. I'm going to go talk to whoever put the call through. Lock the door behind me." He rushes out.

I slow my breathing and look down. I'm in a skimpy nightshirt that barely covers my behind and a pair of panties. I find a long-sleeved button-down shirt of Boone's in the closet and slip into it. At least it covers me. Then fear slaps me in the face like a horse's whip. "Whiskey River." I frantically unlock the door and run smack into Boone's chest.

His gaze skims my attire. "Where are you going?"

"I have to check on Whiskey."

He pushes me back into the room. "Whiskey has security on him. I made sure of that when I got here. A guard is outside his stall all night. I was on the phone with him before you beat down my door."

"Thank god." I blow out a sigh of relief.

"The front desk couldn't tell me anything about the caller except that he asked for you by your full name. Did his voice sound familiar at all?"

"No, not that I recall. I mean, he hung up right after he threatened me."

He runs his hand down my sleeved arm. "You're safe here. I'm not going to let anything happen to you."

I go to move past him, and he snags my arm. "Whoa, where are you going?"

"Back to my room."

"You're staying here with me tonight. I'm not going to let you out of my sight."

"I can't stay in this room with you. Besides, my door locks just like yours."

"Then I'll stay in your room." He follows me to the door.

"Don't be ridiculous. I'll be fine."

"Just two minutes ago you came in here shaking like a leaf." His voice raises.

"I overreacted to the phone call."

"I'm either staying with you, or you're staying with me. Take your pick." His facial expression shows me he's dead serious.

"Fine." I huff by him and turn down his AC. "I like it cold when I sleep."

He walks over to the closet and pulls down a blanket. "You like it cold and then want to bundle under all the blankets."

He knows me so well. I take the pillows and line them down the middle of the bed.

"Now what are you doing?"

"This is my side, that's yours." I point.

He chuckles and starts undressing.

"What do you think you're doing?"

"I'm not sleeping in my clothes." He stops when he's down to his boxer briefs.

Good lord, his cock is much bigger than I remember. I can see the outline through his shorts. *Don't look, don't look.* I'm staring right at it. I want to look up...I need to look up.

"Clem." He says my name and laughs. "My eyes are up here." He's totally teasing me.

I squeeze my eyes closed to break the trance of his Dicktator. I crawl into my side of the bed and take his shirt off, tossing it on the floor. He turns off the light and the bed dips when he gets in beside me. Now there's no thin wall or door, just a pile of pillows between us. I press my thighs together to keep from wanting something I can't have.

"Good night, Boone."

"Night, Clem." He rolls in my direction. I can hear him breathing.

"Stop that." I swat one of the pillows between us.

"Stop what?"

"Breathing."

"You want me to stop breathing?" He snorts.

"Yes."

"My breathing bothers you that much?" The bed shifts and I know he's propped up on his side, staring at me.

"Yes."

His fingers trail over to my side. "How does it bother you?" He's drawing circles on my stomach. "Does it turn you on?"

"No," I protest loudly. "There you go embarrassing yourself again. We are not having sex."

His hand trails further down. "I'm betting if I stuck my hands in your panties, you'd be wet."

He moves lower. "Leave my sweetbriar alone." I slap his hand away, and he starts laughing.

"I knew if I messed with you long enough you'd say something dirty. I used to love when you'd make up names for body parts."

He's still laughing. A small giggle slips out, and soon we're both laughing uncontrollably. When we finally stop, I curl up on the pillows as close as I can get to him. He feels for my hand and holds it.

"I miss you, Clementine Calhoun."

"I miss you too, Boone Methany."

I don't know who drifted off first, but it felt good lying next to him...holding his hand.

When I wake up in the morning, my back is to him, and he has his arm over me, tucking me into his body. I squirm, and he rolls over on to his back. I stretch, sit on the side of the bed, and gaze over at him. His eyes are closed, and he's breathing softly through his mouth. My gaze then travels south until they pop open wide seeing the tent he's sporting in his boxer briefs.

My mouth waters just looking at him. It's not

only his pecker that makes me hungry for him. His body is perfectly sculpted from all the hard work he does around the ranch. His biceps bulge even when he's relaxed. His smooth chest is toned and is a byway down to his yummiest spot. His six-pack abs lead way to his dark trail of hair that blazes a path to his most prized possession. My fingers dance in my hands, wanting to touch him. I almost give in until I recall whose hands have been on him. I scoot off the bed and jump when he talks.

"I like that you were checking me out." He peers at me through half-hooded eyelids.

"What woman wouldn't check out a nearly naked man with a body like that, but it's wrong. I shouldn't be gawking."

"You're wrong about that. We should be waking up together every morning."

"We should be, but we're not. The wrong woman is in your bed."

He shifts his body to a sitting position, leaning against the headboard. "I haven't touched her," he says softly.

"Don't be making shit up. She's your wife for Pete's sake."

"I'm not lying. I haven't laid a hand on her since the night you came back to town."

"She's your wife," I say again, narrowing my eyes at him.

"Only on paper."

"I don't believe you. I've seen the way you look at her. You nearly ate her up when she walked down the aisle."

"You want to know what I was thinking about on my wedding day when Margret walked toward me."

"Her," I huff.

"You. I was thinking about you in that Saran Wrap dress. That's what I was picturing. The smile on my face was for you, not her. I swore to myself right then and there that if you ever wanted to be naked around me again, I wouldn't fight you."

"Little too late for that." I snicker and pull on his shirt, closing the gap in the front. "The point is that it doesn't matter if it's only on paper or not. We can't be together as long as you're married."

"I know." He lets out an exaggerated breath of air and runs his hands through his thick hair.

"Thanks for last night," I say and walk out. I change out of my nightshirt. I press Boone's shirt to my nose. God, I love his smell. I tuck it in my bag and order in a quick bite of breakfast and head for the stable. Just like Boone said, there's a guard standing outside Whiskey's stall.

"Anything out of the ordinary happen last night?" I ask him as I introduce myself as Whiskey's owner.

"It was a quiet night," he tells me and ends his shift.

All day while working with the horse and the jockey, I felt like someone was watching me. Boone was every time I saw him, but that's not what I was feeling. I took a break long enough to watch Lucky Shot make a run around the track. He's fast. It's the first time I've had any notion that Whiskey might lose. It makes me that much more determined to win, despite the threats against me.

CHAPTER TWENTY SEVEN
BOONE

I'm at the Preakness wanting to lose the race. As much as I'd have like to back off the training with Lucky Shot and his jockey, I gave it all I got. Now, it's up to the horses and the riders as to who wins.

Clem slept in my bed again last night with her makeshift wall between us. She fell asleep before her head even hit the pillow. I checked with the desk, and they said another call came through to her room last night, so I requested any future calls be sent to my phone. I haven't seen her since she left this morning. I'm sure she's in the stable talking to Whiskey and Henry, giving them a good pep talk.

I put on a pair of casual slacks and my dress boots, with a shirt and a loose-fitting bolo. I take my black Stetson out of the box and adjust it on my head until it feels comfortable. It only gets worn on special occasions.

Checking the time, the Calhouns' plane should be landing at any time. If I'm lucky, Bear was able to detain Margret and her father from making it to the airport on time. She's called my phone several times, but I've made a point of not answering it.

I spend my morning chatting with a few of the other owners and checking in with the jockey. Spectators are starting to gather on the infield of the track. Seats are starting to fill in, and the people are checking out the betting boards. Seats are reserved for the owners of the horses running in the race, so I can take my time. Whiskey and his jockey are trailing into the lineup, but there is no sign of Clem. I order a drink from the indoor bar and stand by the glass wall, looking out over the crowd. I feel someone walk up behind me and turn around.

Clem is dressed in a navy slim-fitting dress with white polka dots and a wide-brimmed khaki-colored hat with matching heels. She's damn sexy. "Are you ready for this?" she asks.

I nod and hold my arm out for her to place her hand in the crook of my elbow.

"Have you seen or heard from my family? It's

odd that they haven't called me to tell me they've landed."

She's right; it is strange.

"I tried Wyatt and Ellie's phone. They both went to voicemail."

"Let's get to our seats, and I'll try to find them."

She glances over my shoulder. "Where's your family?"

"The Calhouns are my family."

"I mean your wife and Tom."

I shrug and chuckle inwardly thinking about how mad Margret will be if she missed the plane.

We make it to our seats, and I dial Wyatt's phone, then I try Chet's. No answer on either one. Maybe their plane ran late, and they're still in the air.

The crowd cheers as the announcements are made, and the horses make their way to the gates. Whiskey got gate number one which is the hardest to win from. Lucky Shot is in gate number two.

"Did you place your bet?" I ask her.

"Yes. Whiskey to win. Lucky Shot to place." She flashes me her ticket.

I show her mine.

"You bet the same?" She laughs. "You're not supposed to bet against your own horse."

"Lucky Shot isn't my horse. He's Tom's."

"Margret will kill you when she finds out."

"Then I won't tell her." I chuckle.

All the horses are in their gates, waiting for the bugle to blow. It sounds, and the horses crash through their gates. Whiskey is hugging the inside, striding along in third. Lucky Shot is in the lead. The crowd goes wild as they round the first curve. The commentator is giving the positions of all the racehorses.

I glance at Clem, and she's biting her lip and has her ticket grasped in her fist. Her knee is bouncing up and down.

When they're on the backside of the track, we both take out our binoculars. Lucky Shot is still in the lead by a full body length, and Whiskey has moved into second. It seems like a long minute before they start into the final curve. The cheering is so loud you can barely hear the announcer.

I see the moment Jose makes his signature move, becoming one with Whiskey. The jockey on Lucky Shot sits taller with a show of confidence. Whiskey moves fast and inches closer.

"Go, baby, go!" Clem yells.

They cross the finish line, and from this angle, we have no idea who won. The crowd collectively holds their breath until the announcement is made.

"Whiskey River pulled it off! He won by a nose! This horse won the Kentucky Derby and now the Preakness. If he can win the Belmont in three weeks, he'll win the Triple Crown!"

Clem is jumping up and down and lands in my arms. She's so excited, she kisses me. I hold her head between my hands and delve in, mingling with her tongue. I lose myself in her and drown out the crowd. When she draws back her lips glisten, and she squeals, "We won!"

I don't care about the race; I won a kiss from her. It may have only been the heat of the moment from all the excitement, but I still won.

She stops moving and looks around the crowd. "My family still isn't here. Something must've happened." The joy immediately leaves her face and is replaced with worry. Other owners are congratulating her as I escort her through the crowd.

"Go to Whiskey, do your interview. I'll find them." As soon as she leaves, I locate a quiet spot and start calling them one by one. On the last ring before I hang up, Wyatt answers the phone.

"Are you with Clem?"

"Whiskey won. She's down giving an interview. She's been worried sick. Are you guys here?"

"No." I know the minute his voice cracks something is wrong.

"Where are you?"

"We never left. It's Momma. She wasn't feeling good, and Ellie called the ambulance. We're at the hospital."

My gut kicks into overdrive telling me it's not good. "Is she okay?"

Wyatt chokes. "The doctor said she had a major stroke. She's on life support."

"Damn. I'll get Clem on the next plane home."

"Do it quick. I'm not sure how much time she has."

"I will. Give everyone my love."

"Will do."

My heart races as much as I do to find Clem. She's in the middle of an interview when I make it down to the track. As soon as her gaze meets mine, she knows something is wrong. She cuts the interview short and marches toward me.

"What is it? What's wrong?"

I take her by the arm. "It's your mom. She's been taken to the hospital."

"Is she okay?"

I grab her into my arms. "No, she's not. She's on life support, and I need to get you home."

She gasps. "No!"

People surround us as they all want a piece of her. Tucking her into my side, I rush her through the crowd back to the hotel room. "Pack your things and mine. I'll go make sure the horses are taken care of, and the arrangements are made for them to be sent home. Leave your truck keys at the front desk, call Ethan and tell him to change his flight to land here and pick up your truck so he can drive it back to Kentucky. I'll call and get us a flight while I'm making my way to the stables. Be ready when I get back."

She nods as tears stream down her face. "I'm going to call Ellie while I'm packing."

"Get the front desk to call a cab to take us to the airport." I storm out, not wanting to leave her alone. I stop by the desk and ask that hotel security wait outside her door until I get back. Running down to the track while I call the airlines, I see Jose cooling off Whiskey. I congratulate him and update him on the Calhouns. Handing him my credit card, I tell him to make all the arrangement for Whiskey, Lucky Shot, Lucky Shot's jockey, and himself to get back to Kentucky.

I stop by the betting booth and collect my winnings. Then, I make my way to the winner's circle, explaining to them that there was a family emergency and they should mail the winnings to the address on the card I hand them.

I take off in a run back to the hotel and Clem is downstairs at the counter, escorted by security.

"The cab will be here any minute," she says through sniffs.

"The only flight I could get on the phone wasn't until this evening, but don't worry. When we get there, I'll get us an earlier one."

The cab pulls up, and I throw our bags in the trunk, Clem gets in the back seat, and I slide in beside her.

"Did you get ahold of Ellie?"

"Yes. She kept crying, telling me to get there as quickly as I could."

She lays her head on my shoulder, and her body trembles with her tears. The cab driver pulls into the departure's lane. I throw cash at him and grab our luggage. Clem stays glued to my side. I rush to the counter, not bothering with the line.

"There's a family medical emergency, and we need two tickets to Kentucky as soon as possible." I give the clerk my name, and she pulls up the flight. "I'm sorry, sir, but all the other flights are full."

"Then exchange someone else's tickets with ours."

"I'm sorry, sir, I can't do that."

Clem lets out a sob. I turn to the line of people. "Anyone here on the flight to Kentucky?" I yell.

Several hold up their hand. I walk over to a couple in their mid-twenties and tell them our story. They gladly change flights with us, and I hand them a wad of hundred-dollar bills. "Thank you." They walk to the ticket counter with us, and the attendant makes the adjustments. Within minutes, we are through security and getting on the airplane. Clem takes the seat by the window and buckles up.

"Thank you." She smiles, but her eyes don't.

I sit. Her head falls on my shoulder as her hand finds mine, tangling our fingers together. I kiss the top of her head. "We'll get there in time, I promise."

CHAPTER TWENTY EIGHT
CLEM

It's late when we make it to the hospital. The front entrance is closed, and we're told to go through the emergency room. Boone talks to the nurse manning her station and finds out which room to find Momma.

Outside the ICU doors, in the waiting room, Ellie, Wyatt, Bear, and Missy are huddled together. "Aunt Clem." Missy runs into my arms when she sees me.

"Hey, sweetie." I kiss both her tear-stained cheeks.

"Grandma is real sick."

"I know, baby."

My siblings surround me with Boone. "Thank the lord you made it." Ellie hugs me.

"Where's Daddy?"

"In with Momma."

"Have you guys seen her?"

"Yeah. We wanted to give Daddy some time alone with her."

"I need to see her."

"Come on. I'll get them to buzz you into the ICU." Wyatt directs me to the door.

I look over my shoulder at Boone. "Are you coming?"

"I thought maybe you'd want to go alone."

I hold my hand out to him. "You love her as much as the rest of us."

Wyatt pushes the intercom button on the wall, and we're let inside. I see Daddy through one of the glass doors at the end of the hall, standing at the foot of a bed. I see him wipe his face, and I damn near lose it. Boone seems to sense it and squeezes my hand, giving me the strength I need to hold it together.

"Daddy," I say softly outside the door.

His stance is tall as he brushes back his silver hair. He opens his arms, and I run into them. "I'm glad you're here." He kisses my forehead.

I turn my head in the direction of Momma. She's hooked up to a breathing machine. Her chest rises and falls just like she's sleeping. IV bags are hanging, one with a milky white mixture dripping into her arm.

"She looks so peaceful," I say, leaving his arms to stand by Momma's side. I touch her arm, and she doesn't move.

"What have the doctors said?" Boone steps up beside Daddy.

"The stroke was massive." He chokes on his words as he watches me. "There is no chance at recovery based on where the stroke happened."

I burst out in tears and drape my body over hers. "No. This can't be happening," I cry out. "I don't want to lose you." Right now I hate myself for all the years we weren't together. I never thought about my parents dying and losing Momma will gut me. She's loved me unconditionally.

Boone rubs his hand down my back, trying to comfort me. He touches her hand and tells her what a good woman she is and that he loves her. I cry harder and he leaves the room.

Daddy sits on the edge of the bed next to her. "Now that you're here, we have to make a decision." His voice is bathed in anguish.

"What do you mean?" I sniff.

"Your momma wouldn't want to be kept alive like this. She deserves to meet her maker in peace."

"I'm not ready to let her go." My tears are uncontrollable.

"None of us are, but it's not about us."

"Your momma loved Jesus, and we need to let her go to him. She's not here anymore, and we're holding her back. I've loved this woman almost my entire life, and it's hard to remember a minute without her in it." He brushes back her hair and kisses her forehead. "I love you enough to let you go, sweetheart."

That's it. I lose my shit. Tears fall so hard I find it hard to breathe. Gut-wrenching pain slices through me. I don't stop until I've convinced myself that if Daddy, who's loved this woman with all his heart can let her go, then I have to do the same. I wipe my tears and nod to him.

He steps out, giving me a minute while he gathers the family. "I love you, Momma. You've been the best mother, wife, and friend anyone could ask for."

Daddy comes back with everyone in tow except Missy and Boone. Wyatt pushes the call light, and the nurse comes in. "We're ready," he says. She steps out makes a few phone calls and comes back in with a respiratory therapist.

"Do you want to stay in the room while we remove the tube?" she asks. Collectively, we nod. They prepare everything as we stand out of their way. Once the tube is removed, we gather around her, holding hands. Each of us takes turns sharing a happy memory with Momma. We laugh through our tears, hoping she can hear our good memories and laughter, but most especially, the love we all have for her.

Her breathing slows along with her heart rate. She passes peacefully among her family, who all adore her.

❧

THE NEXT TWO DAYS ARE A BLUR. MY PHONE HAS rung nonstop either with condolences or congratulations on winning the Preakness from those that don't know my family. I've also had quite a few calls where there was no one on the other end, but I haven't had time to worry about it.

Today is Momma's memorial service. I've spent the morning with Missy, who's missing her grandma like crazy. Momma spent a lot of time with her, plus the fact that I think she basically helped raise her. I plan on filling in Momma's role with her. I've brushed her long hair out and picked out the perfect dress for her to wear today.

Wyatt's been stoic, with a stiff upper lip. Ellie hasn't left Daddy's side, and Bear looks lost. I haven't seen Boone since the hospital. It broke my heart seeing him cry for the first time. I wanted to comfort him so badly, but I was having a hard enough time with my own grief.

Friends and family have brought in enough food for the entire town of Salt Lick. The countertops and fridges are stuffed full to the brim.

When we're all ready, we head to the church. Flowers adorn the front surrounding Momma's coffin. Ellie had a picture board printed with our lives plastered all over them. Momma would've loved it.

The church pews are filled, and sniffles echo in the room. Missy sits next to me like a second skin. Wyatt gives a beautiful eulogy. I kept my eyes dry until his voice cracked, and he had to stop to regain his composure.

I glance over to Boone, who's sitting with his wife. Her hand is clasped with his, and she's dabbing her face with a tissue. My heart breaks a little more that she has him.

The service was beautiful, and there were so many kind words spoken about Momma. She was the kindest, fiercest lady who I was proud to call my mother. I have really big shoes to fill.

People fill our house, sharing their memories of Momma. I'm thankful Boone didn't bring Margret with him. I'm in the kitchen when he corners me.

"You okay?"

"I will be." I try to be convincing.

"I loved her too."

I rub my hand down his arm. "I know you did and she loved you like a son."

"I'm sorry Margret insisted upon coming to the church."

"It's okay, but I'm glad you had the good sense not to bring her here."

"It was a fight, believe me." He chuckles.

"Was she pissed that Lucky Shot lost to Whiskey?"

"To say the least. Tom fired the jockey on the spot."

"I hadn't had much time to think about it, but I've been getting a lot of calls with nothing but breathing on the other end."

"Give me your phone, so I can see where the number is coming from."

I walk over to my purse and hand him my phone. "Wyatt's kept Whiskey with security at night and has now extended it to twenty-four seven. Yesterday someone let Henry out of the stable and Bear found him in the pasture. We've been so unfocused that we didn't think about the stable."

"Good. I'm glad it will be around the clock until the Belmont race."

"About that, I'm going to pull Whiskey from the race."

"You'll do no such thing!" My father's voice bellows through the kitchen.

I square off with him. "There has been nothing but threats on this family, and it's just not worth it. Besides, I don't think now is a good time."

"I will not let you back out of this because of a few off-handed threats. And, as far as the timing goes, your mother would be angry if you let this interfere with your dreams. She'd be the first one telling you to not let anyone stop you."

"I don't think the threats are off-handed. They burnt down my house." I grab a tissue. "As far as Momma goes, I don't think I can do it without her."

Ellie, Wyatt, and Bear are all stationed behind

Daddy. "You'll have us," Bear steps up. "We'll all be there to support you."

"That's how Momma would want it," Ellie joins Bear.

"I'll be there every step of the way." Wyatt pushes between them.

"I think you don't have a choice," Daddy chimes in.

I can't believe my eyes and ears. The Calhoun family standing up for their little lost sheep. Momma's cheering from heaven. "Okay," I finally respond. "I'll keep Whiskey in the race." They all join for a family hug, including Boone.

After the food is served, one by one, the guests leave. Daddy relaxes on the couch, looking worn out and older than I've ever seen him. Bear takes Missy upstairs to read to her. Wyatt is on his phone and Boone is sitting in the recliner talking shop with Daddy. Ellie and I are in the kitchen cleaning when we hear someone come in the front door.

"What the fuck are you doing here?" Daddy's voice is gruff and loud.

We both run to the living room to see Tom Maynard in front of Daddy.

"I came to give my condolences on Amelia. She was a good woman. Too good for the likes of you."

Boone stands. "Get the hell out of here."

"You need to go home to your wife, boy." Tom is so indignant. He turns his attention on Daddy. "I've been waiting a lot of years for life to turn around and bite you in the ass. Seems it's finally caught up with you." He chuckles. "You deserve any misery that life throws at you, and I'm going to sit back and watch it all fall apart for you because as far as I'm concerned, Amelia was the only thing holding the pieces together."

I walk out the front door and grab the rifle. I cock it back and take aim at Tom. "You need to get the hell out of this house, right fucking now!" I seethe.

He holds his hands in the air. "I see this one is just like her daddy with that filthy mouth of hers."

Boone shoves Tom across the room. "You heard the lady, get the fuck out!"

Tom rights his jacket. "You best remember who you're dealing with, Son."

"I'm not your son!" Boone spats and I step in between them, pressing the end of the barrel into Tom's chest.

"You have until the count of five."

"You wouldn't dare."

"One."

He looks around the room.

"Two."

He curses under his breath.

"Three." My finger is itching to pull the trigger.

"This isn't over." He points at my daddy.

"Four."

He moves past me to the door. "You'll get what you deserve." He runs out the door.

I follow him. "You better never step foot on Calhoun property again!" I yell. I keep the rifle in place until he drives off.

"Wow, Sis. Remind me never to mess with you. You're pretty badass." Ellie high-fives me.

CHAPTER TWENTY NINE
BOONE

That had to be the sexiest thing I've ever seen, besides the plastic wrap dress. I wanted to stay at the Calhouns', but Lucky Shot arrived today, and I have work to do. I stop by the house first to change out of my dress clothes. I'm greeted at the door with what looks like an angry wife.

"My father called me and told me what happened. How dare you let Annie Oakley take aim at him. I knew I should've gone with you." She follows me in the house, snarling at me.

"Why so she could've shot you?" I bark over my shoulder.

"She had no right."

I whip around to face her. "Your father had no

right to be in their house, saying the things that he did."

"He only wanted to show his respect." She crosses her arms.

"I don't know what the hell he told you, but he went there for a fight, and that's what he got."

"You always defend them."

"I defend them when they are right, and they are my family," I seethe.

"You gave them up when you married me."

I run both my hands through my hair, wanting to pull it out. "You're right. I gave up my life, but they are still my family, not you and your bulldog of a father." I turn around and slam the bedroom door shut and it flies back open with her barreling through it.

"The only thing standing between you and my father is me, so you better learn to play nice."

"Are you threatening me?" I'm furious.

"Take it how you will." She defiantly shrugs.

"I don't have time for this argument with you. I've got work to do." I strip out of my dress attire and put on work clothes.

She watches me and cools down some. "Why do you have to be this pigheaded. Can't you see that I love you and want a real marriage?" She sits on the bed.

"And why can't you understand that I don't want to be married to you? You forced this on me." I squat in front of her. "You deserve a man that loves you. I'm begging you, let me out of this marriage." I search her eyes to see if there is any compassion in them. I think she's about to concede when she places her hands on either side of my face.

"You're my husband, Boone Methany, and I don't have any plans on that changing."

I hang my head in defeat then rise. "Then you'll be married to a man that will never love you." I walk out, not listening to any more of her nonsense.

I work until dusk, and my back is nearly broke. I'm drenched in sweat and smell like a horse. I'm loading tools in the back of my truck when I hear an explosion. I slam the tailgate and jump in, racing toward the Calhouns. I can see smoke and flames in the air. Speeding through the gate of the Calhoun ranch, the barn is ablaze. Bear is running the horses into the pasture. Wyatt has a hose, trying to douse out the flames heading for the main house. Ellie and Clem are shooing the chickens out of their pen. Chet has Whiskey and Henry tied off on a wooden post.

I skid to a stop and grab another hose, helping Wyatt. "What the hell happened?"

"We were sitting in the house when Missy came downstairs and said she smelled smoke. We rushed out and saw the beginnings of the barn burning. We were able to get all the animals out, but someone shot and killed the guard. They injured two of our men guarding the west side of the property."

"Shit! This has Tom written all over it. Has anyone called 9-1-1?"

"Yeah, they should be here any minute." As he says it, sirens can be heard in the distance.

"We have to put a stop to this before he has anyone else killed."

The fire truck parks and the men start wheeling out hoses. Wyatt and I step back and let them do their job.

"Unless we can find out what Tom's hiding, I'm afraid the only way to stop them is by me giving him everything thing he wants." He knows I haven't slept with Margret.

"You can't. If you do, you'll lose Clem forever."

"He wants more than me making his daughter happy. He wants this land, and he thinks I can get if for him."

"That's not happening."

"Is this land truly worth someone dying for?"

"It is to my dad."

"Then I'll do everything else he wants to keep this family safe."

IT'S MIDNIGHT BEFORE I MAKE IT HOME. Margret's fast sleep on the couch. I throw a blanket over her and get a shower, washing off the soot. I climb in bed, hoping to forget about the day, but my mind races on what I have to do. I end up getting up at four in the morning. Margret is where I found her with the blanket tucked under her chin.

I work all day, trying to avoid her. Tom strolls out to the racetrack where I'm brushing out Lucky.

"Seems you had a late night and an early morning."

"Someone blew up the Calhouns' barn, killed a security guard, and injured a few of his men. You wouldn't know anything about that, would you?" It's not really a question.

"I heard the explosion from my bedroom. It must've been a big one."

He's so fucking smug. "Why don't you tell me

what you want. At this point, I'll do whatever you want if you'll leave the Calhoun's alone."

"You can procure their property for me?" He raises one eyebrow.

"No. That's the one thing I can't do. But, there's more land around here for sale. Eight acres touching the far side of your property. The same river that's on Calhoun property runs through it."

"I want the Calhoun land."

I hang my head.

"But..." He closes the distance between us. "I love my daughter more, and she tells me you haven't consummated the marriage."

Of course she told him.

"You need to make my daughter happy."

"If I do, you'll back off the Calhouns?"

"For the time being. It's just a matter of time before that family collapses and I'll get what I want anyway. In the meantime, I suggest you go home to your wife. I better have a different report in the morning. A grandson would seal the deal." He slaps me on the back as he walks out. "And I better not hear you've spent any more nights with Clementine. If I do, she might keep getting those unpleasant phone calls."

Bastard. He's sealed my fate. I'll do anything,

KELLY MOORE

including playing nice with Margret. I'll hate every minute of it knowing I'll never get Clem back, but at least he'll leave her family alone.

I load up and head back for the house. Margret is in the kitchen, cooking in her usual attire. "Hey, sweetie. Dinner's almost done. You have time for a quick shower."

I don't acknowledge her. I stay in the shower until all the hot water is gone. I hate myself for what I'm about to do. I dry off and drop the towel on the bathroom floor. When I walk into my bedroom, Margret is sitting on the side of my bed.

"How was your day, dear?" She flips up the corner of the apron.

"Like any other around this place." I move toward her, stopping a few feet from her.

She stands, draping her arms around my shoulders. "You are one hot cowboy." She slowly rakes me in. "I've missed this fine body of yours." Her teeth graze my neck.

I inwardly cringe placing my hands on her hips.

"Mmmm...finally giving in to me." She kisses me, and I slowly open to her. Funny, I don't remember her tasting this sour before.

"You're such a good kisser." She slides her hand down my body and cups my cock. "I've missed this the most." She goes to her knees and draws me into her mouth.

I close my eyes, envisioning Clem. I grow hard, but I don't make a noise.

"I knew you missed me too," she purrs when I plop out of her mouth. I stand stock-still, and she sucks and licks me.

A single hot tear falls down my cheek and onto her face. She gazes up and stops. Standing, she wipes the wetness off. "These tears aren't for me, are they?" She tilts her head to look at me.

"I'm giving you what you want." I barely move my lips.

She sits on the bed. "I want my husband to want me, not someone else."

I sit next to her. "That's what you should have. I've made it no secret that I don't love you, but you keep thinking you'll change that."

She covers her face in her hands. "I'll never have that, will I?"

I brush her hair off her shoulder. "No."

"You'll always love her and not me."

"Yes."

"Why? She broke your heart."

"She did, but I love her."

"Why don't you love me?"

"You blackmail me into marrying you, and you have to ask?"

She actually laughs. "I just thought if she was out of the picture and I could be a good wife you'd forget about her."

"Have you ever truly forgotten about the man you loved?"

"No. But, he's gone."

"And why are you not angry at your father for that. Instead, you adore him."

"I guess that means there's something really wrong with me."

"I think he's brainwashed you and he's the only family you have."

She wipes her tears with her apron. "You're right."

"Am I right enough that you'll agree to an annulment?"

She shakes her head. "I'll give you back to her if you'll help me break away from my father."

"Deal. I'll make sure you're taken care of." I stand and start getting dressed.

"You leaving tonight?"

"I need to go to her before it's too late if it's not already." I storm to my truck. Once I put it into gear,

I drive like crazy over the dirt road and park outside the main house.

Chet is sitting in a rocker with a bottle of bourbon in his hand. I don't ask him if he's okay; I know he's not. I sit on the porch swing and wait for him to talk.

"I don't know what I'm going to do without her." His eyes are glassy as he tilts the bottle to his mouth. "She's been my life for so long, and she's the only one that could keep me in line. She whipped me into shape from the first day we met. I still remember her walking in with her daddy to come check on mine. My heart froze in my chest, and it was the first time in my life that I was at a loss for words. She smiled and said hello, and my voice sounded like one of those damn lovebirds when I spoke. She probably thought I'd not gone through puberty yet. I was skinny as a bean pole, had on a pair of tattered jeans, and a t-shirt that I could swim in. I didn't have the good sense that god gave a goose, but she saw something in me, and I'm sure glad she did." He wipes the corner of his eye with the back of his hand. "She was the prettiest little thing in her summer dress. I couldn't take my eyes off her. She's the kinda gal that makes you forget your own name."

"Did you ask her out that day?" I lean back on the swing and cross an ankle over a knee.

He tilts the bottle up again. "I followed her out of the room while her father did an exam. She batted her eyes, and my other head took over."

I laugh to myself thinking about how Clem might phrase that. "Purdy girls have a way of doing that to a man."

"I had other obligations to put to rest before she agreed to see me. I grew a pair of balls for the love of a good woman and straightened my pathetic ass out." He drinks again. "I took her to the town dance, held her in my arms, and never let go of her again. She made me a better man."

"You made Amelia very happy too."

"I don't know about that. There were plenty of days she wanted me out on my ear." He chuckles. "But she really did love me."

"You're a lucky man to have the love of a good woman."

He takes another swig. "Clem could do the same for you." The bottle sloshes as he points to me. "You need to get your shit together and win her back."

"That's the plan." I stand.

"The only difference is, she's more like me than she thinks. You'll have to keep her in line."

"There is one thing that's the same." I walk over to him.

"What's that?"

"She makes me a better man."

He grins through a tear falling. "You were a good man to start."

"Do you want me to stay here with you?"

"I'm suspecting you didn't come over here to listen to me cry."

"No, but I'll gladly stay with you."

He rises. "I'm afraid I'd be nothing but bad company. I plan on finishing this here bottle and dreaming about Amelia."

I grab him into a hug. "I'm here if you need me, just say the word."

He pulls away and opens the door. "My word for you is, Clem."

"Do you happen to know where she is?"

"She went to the bar that Bear plays at with his band. You might want to get there before they get too rowdy."

CHAPTER THIRTY
CLEM

"I can't believe I let you talk me into this," Bear has his arms over mine and Ellie's shoulders as we enter the bar.

"We all needed a night to blow off steam." He sits us at a table near the stage.

"Yeah, but why did you have to invite Jett. I'm not ready for dating."

"Chill out. It's only drinks, not a marriage proposal." He scurries off to the stage and picks up his guitar.

"I'll order us a couple drinks. Do you want anything special?" Ellie asks.

"I'll have water."

"Like hell you will. We're getting our drunk on tonight."

She's up for fun, and my heart's not in it. I hated leaving Daddy alone. Wyatt said he'd keep him company, but he can be a downer sometimes.

Bear steps up to the mic and starts singing a country song. Ellie returns to the table with two jumbo-sized margaritas. "Please tell me that's not your date. If it is, I'll have to kill you for him." I follow where her eat-him-alive glare is looking.

It's Jett. He has on a black t-shirt that shows off every muscle and a pair of loose-fitting blue jeans. He does look edible if I say so myself.

"That would be him. Please don't kill me." I giggle.

"Hi ladies," he says, pulling out Ellie's chair for her to sit down.

"Hi," she literally purrs.

"This is my sister Ellie." I introduce them as he takes his seat.

"Bear didn't tell me he had two gorgeous sisters." He's all smiles.

"I'm the sexy, hot one. She's the cute, adorable one." She messes up my hair.

"You're awful." I about spew my drink across the table laughing at her.

She cozies up to him and starts grilling him with questions. I only half listen. He's hot, but I'm not interested. All my heart sees is Boone. At some point, I'll have to move on.

The dance floor fills up as Bear's band joins him on stage. Ellie sends Jett to refill our drinks.

"You having fun?" I act like I'm pouting.

"I did totally take your date, didn't I?" She bats her long lashes. "I like him."

"Like you like Ethan?" I want to know what she's thinking about him.

"Ethan was a distraction. A fun one, but nothing permanent."

Poor Ethan. Good thing he's not here to watch her fawn all over him.

Jett returns with two drinks before he sits he asks me to dance.

"Me?" I look at Ellie.

"Yeah. I'd like that." He holds out his hand.

I stick out my tongue at Ellie like I did when we were children, and she shrugs as if him asking me to dance doesn't bother her a bit.

We hit the dance floor as the music slows. I place my hand on his shoulder, and his hands are on my hips.

"I know I came here to have drinks with you, but I'm really kinda liking your sister."

"Of course you are. Everyone falls for her

charms." I snicker. "Be careful, I'm told she's a man-eater." I playfully warn him.

"You aren't mad?"

"No. Not at all. My heart belongs to a man I can never have."

"I'm sorry to hear that."

"It's okay. I have plenty of other things to focus on."

"You truly are a beautiful woman."

I lay my head on his chest. "I just can't compete with my sister."

"It's not that."

"What is it then?"

"I guess it's chemistry. And your sister has tons of it." He smiles over at her.

"That she does." I lay my head back down, and we sway to the music. I glance back up and see Boone enter the bar. "Ah, shit!"

"What?"

"That man I can never have just a walked in the bar."

"Do you want me to kick his ass?" He looks around.

"No. But do you mind playing along?"

"Anything. What do you want me to do?"

"Kiss me like you mean it. I'll fix things with my sister later."

He dips his head down and slowly kisses me.

"What the fuck are you doing?" Boone's voice barks out over the music.

I untangle my tongue with Jett's. "What's it look like? I'm kissing the hot cowboy."

"Looks to me like he wants more than a kiss." He throws daggers with his glare.

"So what if he does? You're a married man." I know I shouldn't taunt him.

He turns around, and I think he's going to walk away. There's fire in his eyes when he turns back around and grabs my hand, dragging me from the dance floor.

"What do you think you're doing?" I fight him to let go of my wrist.

"Taking what's mine!" he says without turning around.

"I'm not yours." I give up the struggle because his words have me wetter than a mermaid's tail. He drags me outside. "Where are we going?"

"To my truck."

"Is your wife in there?"

"No," he growls and opens the door. "Get inside."

352

"Why should I?"

It throws him off that I won't do as he's told me even though I'm dying to. He rolls his shoulders a few times. "Please get in the truck. We need to talk."

"I'm done talking to you, Boone." I try to walk around him, and he throws his body in front of me.

"You are the most stubborn woman I've ever met." His teeth crash harshly on mine as he savagely kisses me. It's so lusty I hardly know my own name when we pull apart. "Get in the truck."

I leap inside, wanting more of him. I'm a needy little puddle at this point. He runs over to the driver's side and climbs in. The key is barely in the ignition when he peels out of the parking lot. He doesn't stop until he's on the backside of our property where my house will be built. He parks the truck in front of the river and gets out. He opens the back door and grabs a blanket then comes over to my side, holding the door open.

I don't say a word. He spreads the blanket on the ground. Our only light is the moon reflecting off the water. He sits and pats the ground next to him.

Sitting, I cross my legs and wait for him to break the silence. He starts to speak as he looks out over the water.

"I've loved you as long as I can remember, even

when you were a young girl and I wasn't supposed to notice you. The day you left me at the altar broke my heart, but somehow I knew you'd find your way back to me. Then I fucking blew it. I waited for you all those years. Margret was a distraction. I had settled myself into thinking I wanted to be with her because she loved me, not because I loved her.

"Then this whole thing with your family and the Maynards exploded, and I did what I thought I had to do to keep you safe. Every move I made was with this family in mind."

"You made your choice, and I get that."

"No, you don't. It killed me to marry Margret in front of you. I hurt both of you, and I'm ashamed of that."

"It's my fault for running away in the first place. You don't have to worry about me anymore. I'll be okay. I mean, I hate seeing the two of you together, but it's my punishment for leaving the way I did."

"Do you think it's fun for me to see you with your tongue lodged down some guy's throat?"

"I'd say by you dragging me out of that bar the way you did, the answer is not so much."

He stands. "It took everything in me not to punch him in the throat." His voice is strained and angry.

I get off the blanket. "And how do you think I felt laying in bed the night of your honeymoon? I mean besides the fact that I got drunk and wished for your frank and beans to rot off." I wave my hand. "So I've been told. I don't remember it."

He chuckles. "That's pretty harsh."

"Well, all I could picture was you on top of her."

"I meant calling my junk frank and beans." He looks down at his crotch. "Bushwhacker would've been better."

I roar out in laughter. It's so unlike Boone to name is body parts. "I like that one."

All the stress leaves his face, and I'm staring at a man that loves me, despite my dirty names. "I got rumors of a fight song too."

"I have no idea what you're talking about." I snicker.

He steps up real close. "Something about the Phoenix rising from the earth, and being a warrior, then came the part about wishing something really bad on me."

"I don't know who told you such things." My heart picks up its pitter-patter.

"Small town, you know. Word gets around."

I place my hands on his chest and shove him

away. "At least I had a fight song. I didn't stick my head in the sand like the proverbial ostrich."

"You want a fight song? I'll give you a fight song."

He clears his throat. "Something, something... a man and his will to live."

"Um.. excuse me, but you can't have that one. It's from *The Eye of the Tiger*. At least I think. You brutalized it. You have to make up your own."

He starts over. "And the last known survivor does something I don't know the words to the song," he sings.

"Nope, same song." I giggle.

"Hell, Clem, it's all I got. At least I wasn't singing for your..." He steps back and points to my lady parts.

"My what? Be creative." I cross my arms and tap my foot on the ground.

"Your...your..." He's flustered. He snaps. "Your lady toupee to rot off."

I howl, bending over in laughter. I catch my breath and stand. He's looking at me lustfully. "You really suck at this," I whisper.

He closes the gap between us and crushes his mouth to mine again. It's longing, frustration, anger, and love mixed together in what he's giving me. I give him the same back.

His fingers are knotted in my hair, and I'm gripping his chest like it's a lifeline. Our lips and tongues are a brutal lashing, taking from each other and giving at the same time. I've never wanted him as badly as I do right now. His rough hands jet under my blouse and rip it off over my head.

"Wait," I pant. "We can't."

He stops my words with another kiss, convincing me that we can. Then he places his hands on my face. "Margret's agreed to an annulment."

"Well, why didn't you lead with that," I rasp.

"Then you would've missed me serenading you."

I make a snorting noise. "I could've lived another day without that."

He chuckles and continues stripping me naked, then wastes no time removing his clothes. "I love you, Clem. Let me show you how much."

He nips at my lips, then my jaw, and moves gently down my neck to that little spot behind my ear that turns me on. My shoulder doesn't get missed as he casually makes his way down to my nipple that's already twisting with a need to be in his sweet mouth.

My moan falls in the night air, and I can feel his smile on my delicate skin. He shows both the girls lots of love before he lowers me to the ground with

KELLY MOORE

him. His rough hands massage my stomach, and his kisses heal me. He leans back on his knees and spreads my legs.

"You are mine, Clem Calhoun, and you'll never forget it after tonight," he says.

"Now that's a fight song I want to hear." I bite my lip, and he lowers his head between my legs. My head falls back, and my eyes damn near roll out of my head when his tongue spreads me apart. His mouth is magically making me all tingly inside. He grasps my hips firmly and applies more pressure. The man has skills he didn't have a few years ago.

He laps me up until I squirm for my release. He inserts two fingers inside me and makes me come like water from an elephant's trunk.

He lifts his head and licks his lips like a thirsty man needing to hydrate. He rises to his knees, and I get to see him in all his glory, and boy his glory is large. He's right; franks and beans weren't even close. I'm thinking more along the words to my song. His phoenix has risen, and I'm climbing aboard for the ride.

He reaches over to his jeans lying on the ground and digs a condom out of his pocket.

"Were you planning this?" I draw my brows together.

He digs deeper in his pocket and pulls out a row of four condoms. "You bet I was." He smiles and opens a foil packet, rolling the love glove down his heat-seeking missile. He stops midway and stares at me. "You're calling my manhood something in your head, aren't you?"

"Think something large and in charge, and that's what I was thinking." A sexy grin plays on his face as he finishes rolling down the condom.

He kisses me again, and I lie down. His muscles strain as he hovers over me. "Tell me you love me, Clem.

I rake my fingers through his hair, then grip the curls at the back of his neck. "I love you, Boone. Always have, always will."

He thrusts inside me and shifts his hips at the same time. In one single move, the man has found my magic box, and he's tickling it. His mouth surrounds my nipple, and he tugs. I hiss, and he does it again. He moves in and out of me lazily, savoring the feeling. I want him deeper and faster. I shove him off me, and he lies flat on the ground. Straddling him, I lower myself onto him. One of his hands grips my ass, trying to calm my rhythm. The other squeezes my breast hard. I rock my hips, giving in to my need to ride him.

His eyes are darker than the night, and his moans are heated, making me wetter. He fills every inch of me, and I stretch to accommodate his girth. The pressure it creates makes me throb around him.

"I need to move," I rasp.

He lets go of my tit and both his hands leave prints on my hips as he lifts me up and down his length. I reach behind me and lightly grasp his balls. He bucks upward, and I push downward.

"You like that." I smile.

"Fuck yeah," he grits out. "Do it again, and I'm going to load you with my shotgun."

I hold back my laughter at his attempt to talk dirty and put both my hands on his chest, riding him past the finish line. We both come muffling each other's sexy noises with our lips and tongues warring with each other. It's the most sensual thing I've ever felt. Heat, raw desire, greed for one another, a downright dirty thirst that's yet to be quenched.

I lay my head on his chest to catch my breath and rein in the need to already go again. He grabs my hair and pulls my head up, making me look into his eyes.

"You're mine. I love you, Clem."

CHAPTER THIRTY ONE
CLEM

Some would call it the walk of shame, me...I scored with the man I love tonight. I tiptoe inside the house, hoping not to wake Daddy or Missy. I darn near pee my pants when Daddy's voice comes out of the darkness.

"You're gettin' home late." He flips on a lamplight.

"Shit, you scared me. What are you doing still up?"

"I can't sleep in that bed without your momma."

He sits and runs his hand through his messy hair. I take the cushion next to him. "I know that has to be hard."

"Forty years and we never slept apart."

"Really? You've been in the doghouse a lot, and she never made you sleep on the couch?"

"Not one time. She had a rule to never to go to bed angry, and we honored that. Course I said my fair share of apologies." He chuckles.

"I miss her too." I curl my legs underneath me and lay my arm on the back of the couch. "Tell me about when you met Momma."

"You've heard the story a million times. When you were a kid, you used to ask her every night to tell you the story of us like it was some goddamn fairy tale."

"I did, but I always knew she left something out. That's the part I want to hear."

He stares at me hard. "I don't think now's the time." His voice deepens like he does when he's mad at me or any one of his kids for that matter.

"I disagree. I think now is the perfect time. This mess with the Maynards has gotten out of hand, and we need to deal with it." I reach in my purse and pull out the picture. "Boone found this." I hand it to him.

He leans forward, looking like he's lost in a memory. "This is something that needs to be left alone."

I touch the picture. "Who is the young girl?"

He's quiet for such a long time, I don't think he's

going to answer me. "Her name was Teresa. She was Tom Maynard's twin sister."

"How old were you in that picture?"

"I was eighteen, they were twenty."

"Wyatt could be your twin."

He gives me the picture and rests back on the couch. "Actually, I see you."

I squint to look harder. "Maybe around the eyes a little bit."

"That's not what I'm talking about. I left home shortly after that picture. I ran as far away from cattle ranching as I could."

"Where'd you go?"

"To the tracks. I loved betting on the horses. I'd spend every dime I made working nights at a grocery store so that I could be at the track the next day. I even stole money out to be able to bet. Not something I'm very proud to admit. I chose the wrong path."

"I'm betting Papa didn't like that at all."

"Not one lick. He wanted me to come back home and run the ranch, and I hated this place. I felt trapped into a life I didn't want like you did."

I hold the picture toward him. "What does any of that have to do with them?"

"I wanted to marry Teresa and take her away

from this life. I was a young, stupid boy who didn't know a damn thing about love or ranching until I met your momma."

"My father wasn't in good health, and he put the ranch up for sale. He begged me so many times to come home. He wanted to keep the land in the family. Your great grandfather bought the land for next to nothing and labored over this property. Started out as farming, then decided to get into the cattle business. He wasn't very good at it, but my daddy was, so he took over and grew the ranch."

"But what does that have to do with Teresa and Tom."

He holds his hand up. "I'm gettin' there."

"Sorry."

"When I left, I told Teresa I'd come back for her when I'd made enough money to make her my wife. I sucked at gambling on the horses. I barely kept enough money in my pocket to eat most days. I tucked my tail between my legs and crawled back home. By then, my dad could hardly get out of bed anymore. My mom took care of him. The property had a contract on it with Tom's dad. He'd owned the adjacent property and wanted to extend his land for cattle grazing. I was all for it until the doctor paid a house visit to my dad. He brought along his pretty daughter."

"Momma." I smile, remembering how she told me she fell in love with him at first sight.

"God, she was beautiful. She had chestnut curls and the prettiest set of eyes I'd ever seen. She smiled, and I became a man that day. I don't know why she fell in love with the likes of me. I was a skinny kid with nothing in my pocket but trouble. She loved this property and the river that flows through it. She'd wanted nothing more than to be a rancher's wife. Problem was, I was still promised to Teresa, and her daddy was buying the land. I didn't have a plug nickel to offer Amelia, but I knew I'd do anything for her. I had to be a man for once in my life and end it with Teresa. Your mother insisted that I be a free man before she'd give me the time of day. I took my ass over to Teresa's house and broke things off with her. She was devastated, and Tom was furious that I had broken his sister's heart. I didn't realize how upset she was until they found her body floating in the river."

I gasp. "No!"

"Back then, people didn't talk about depression, but looking back, she had all the classic signs. Tom blamed me. He thought I had killed her at first and had me arrested for murder."

"Damn, Daddy."

"They had to let me go when they found a note she had written, telling them all goodbye."

"But Tom still blamed you."

"I blamed myself for the longest time. Amelia's dad being a doctor, helped me see that Teresa was sick, and it wasn't my fault."

"What happened to selling the land?"

"That's where the real feud came into play. The day the land was to be sold, my father begged me one more time to keep the land. I agreed, but his attorney said the sale was underway and the only way they could get out of it, is if I purchased it. Now, I don't know if any of that was true or not, the rules were different back then."

"You didn't have any money."

"I had a dollar in my pocket."

My eyes grow wide. "You didn't?"

"I did. I told you my great grandfather bought the land for next to nothing. He purchased it for a dollar. So, I offered what my grandfather bought it for, and my daddy took the deal to keep the ranch in the family, and Tom's dad was furious."

"So that's why he feels you stole it from him.

Then you turned around and gave the idea to Boone for Whiskey River to be purchased by me. It all makes sense now. He wants what he thinks is his, plus a good man like Boone to be married to his only daughter."

He stands. "I want you to understand something. As much as I hated this ranch and life in the beginning, it became mine and your momma's entire life. When I fell in love with her, I fell for all of it. I regret my actions as a teenager, but I've put my heart and soul into this land. There are a few things in my life I got right. Amelia, my children, and this ranch. I'm not selling it or losing it to Tom because he feels I owe him something. I will leave this land to my children."

"Have you tried to talk to him since this nonsense started with Boone?"

"We've had many a conversation. Your momma spoke to him a few weeks ago. She begged him to leave Boone and this family alone. She even offered to pay him monthly the amount of money he thought he was owed for the land. He turned her down flat. He said the only thing he wanted was to see me lose everything I'd worked for all these years, including hurting my children."

"Bastard," I snarl.

"Watch your mouth, young lady." He raises an eyebrow.

If he only knew, he'd have me over his knee. "Margret's agreed to an annulment."

"That means there's going to be more trouble once Tom gets wind of it. Tell Boone to watch his back."

"I will."

"That goes for you too. It's late. Try to get some sleep."

I kiss his cheek and head upstairs. My body is exhausted, but my mind is on the time I spent with Boone tonight and the story my daddy told me. I'm lucky to have both these men in my life and a strong family. It's the first time I've truly felt sorry for Margret.

Wyatt comes rushing through the front door before I hit the first step. "He's dying!" he yells, with a paper clenched in his hand.

"Who's dying?" I ask.

"Tom Maynard. I accessed his medical records. He has stage four colon cancer. He received treatments last year, but they didn't work. That's his motivation."

"Come sit." Daddy points Wyatt to a chair. I

head to bed as he starts filling Wyatt in on the history of our families.

CHAPTER THIRTY TWO
BOONE

"W"here the hell do you think you're going, cowboy?" Tom Maynard jumps out of his truck, toting a rifle, gripped in one hand.

"Margret and I have come to an agreement, and I'm moving back to the Calhoun ranch." I throw my luggage in the bed of my truck.

"Like hell you are." He lifts the rifle, aiming it at me.

I raise my hands. "Don't do anything stupid."

The rifle goes off, and he cocks the lever. A loud pop and my tire blows. "You aren't going anywhere. We made a deal."

"The deal has changed."

The rifle goes off again, blowing out my other

tire. Margret comes running out of the house. "Daddy. Stop! Leave Boone alone."

"If you know what's good for you, you'll get back in the house and keep your mouth shut."

"This has gone on long enough! Whatever beef you have with the Calhouns needs to end. I've lived with your hatred of them my entire life. Never understood it or why you even encouraged me to be with Boone. He may not be a Calhoun by name, but he's as much of one them as Wyatt and Bear."

"That made him my target. I'd never have my only daughter marry a Calhoun boy." He directs me with his rifle. "Get in the house."

Margret steps between me and his aim. "Don't do this. Boone doesn't love me. The only man that did love me, you made disappear."

"That was for your own good. He wasn't the right man for you."

"Neither is Boone. You're using him to get what you want. Don't you care about me at all or is your grudge against the Calhouns more important than your only daughter?"

"I'm doing this for you."

"Stop lying to yourself, Daddy. I'm done being told what to do by you and how to do it. You've been scheming this for years. Ever since Clem left him at the altar."

He lifts the rifle and shoots it. The sound can be heard for miles. "Shut the fuck up and get back in the house!"

I run over to Margret and shove her behind me. "For god's sake, Tom. Have you lost your mind?" I keep my hands out in front of me.

"You're not going anywhere. You'll win the Belmont with Lucky Shot. That family doesn't deserve to win the Triple Crown. The only way you get out of any of this is after I get the Calhoun property. Then I couldn't care less what you do."

He starts coughing, trying to keep his aim on me. Blood splatters from his mouth.

"Daddy!" Margret runs by me to his side.

He wipes his mouth on his plaid shirt and moves out of her reach. "This doesn't change a thing," he snarls.

"You're sick." I state the obvious. "Is that why you're doing this? You want Margret to be taken care of after you're gone?"

"That's only part of it. I want to see justice done before I'm six feet under. Chet killed my sister and stole his land from underneath my family."

"Daddy, what are you talking about?"

"I had a twin sister that was in love with that bastard. He broke her heart, killed her, and never paid for his crime."

"Chet Calhoun isn't capable of murder." I take a step toward him, and he cocks the rifle, squeezing the trigger. I'm jolted back when I'm hit in the shoulder. Pain rips through my chest, and I fall to the ground.

Margret screams and runs to me. "What the hell have you done?" she cries out and holds pressure on my shoulder.

He coughs again and falls in the grass.

"Go," I tell her. "Help him."

"What about you?" she sobs.

"I'll be okay. It'll be quicker for you to take him to the hospital than it will for the ambulance to get here."

"I'm not going to the hospital," he groans.

"Get him to the house," I tell her, making it to my feet. Blood drips down my arm and spills off my fingers into the dirt.

"I can't leave you like this." She's frantic.

"Yes, you can. Go take care of him."

She helps him off the ground and gets him in the backseat of his truck. Feeling light-headed and unsteady, I make my way to my truck and hit the garage door opener. I climb on the four-wheeler and back it out. Waves of nausea are rolling through me, and I can barely keep my eyes open. I ride slowly down the road that leads to the Calhoun property. Blood is soaking through my shirt, down to my jeans. My eyelids are heavy with darkness fading in and out. I make a sharp turn at the entrance of the ranch and hit something. "I just need a minute to shut my eyes." I lean over the steering wheel.

"Boone! Boone!"

My eyes flutter open, but everything is blurry. Someone drags me off the ATV. "I've got you."

I think it's Bear's voice. He picks me up and sets me on his four-wheeler. "Can you hold on?" I fall against his back. He grabs my uninjured arm, holding on to me, and drives with the other. My eyes close again, but I feel every dip and bump jarring my shoulder. The pain keeps me awake.

"Clem!" Bear yells when we finally quit moving. "Daddy!"

I hear stomping of feet coming down the porch. Bear clenches an arm and pulls me off the four-wheeler.

"What happened?" Chet asks, helping him get me inside.

"Boone!" Clem cries. "Is he alive?"

"Looks like he took a bullet to the shoulder. He's lost a lot of blood."

"I'll call for an ambulance." Clem walks behind us.

"No," I mumble.

"Let's get him inside first and get a good look. If the bullet cleared him, we can take care of him," Chet barks.

Clem runs in front of us and holds the door open. "Put him on the table."

My eyes roll back as I sit on the edge, and Bear lifts my feet. "Get some water and clean cloths. I need to clean this up to see the bullet wound."

Clem runs off, and Chet cuts me out of my shirt. Bear turns me. "It went clean through. Lay him flat," Chet orders as Clem returns with a stack of white towels and a bowl of water. Chet takes a towel from her and places it on my shoulder and leans his body weight into me.

"Shit!" I yell from the pain.

"Sorry, Son. I have to stop the bleeding first."

Black spots fill my vision, lulling me in and out of consciousness.

Voices and a sharp tug on my skin bring me to.

"Who did this?" Chet's voice is loud.

"I don't know. I found him by the ranch sign. He

ran into it with the four-wheeler and was out cold when I found him. I'd heard shots in the distance and was out patrolling the property."

I roll my head to the side to see what's sticking me.

"You're awake," Clem says, running her hand through my hair, then she sets back to work, stitching me up.

"Where'd you learn to do that?" My voice is gravelly.

"In the army. They made us all learn how to do some basic medical things, like suturing."

Chet angles over me. "Who shot you?"

My throat is so dry, and I have to swallow hard to speak. "Maynard."

"I'll fucking kill him." He takes a step, and I grab his hand.

"No. He's sick."

"I know he's dying, but he damn near killed you."

"He needs help." Clem tugs hard at a stitch. "Ouch!"

"All done," she says, stands and washes her hands in the sink.

"We can't let him get away with this." Bear's boots sound heavy as he paces the floor.

"I'm not sending a dying man to prison." I slowly sit and waver. Chet's large hand steadies me.

Clem storms by all of us. "I'll send him to an early grave." She unlocks the gun cabinet and takes out a pistol and bullets.

I stand, and Chet walks me over to her. "Please don't. Margret needs help."

I see her jaw clench, and she bites her bottom lip. "I'm not making any promises." She slams the door shut behind her.

"Bear, go with her," Chet orders. "And, for god's sake, make sure she doesn't kill him. Leave that for me." He drops his arm from around me. "Let's get you cleaned up. Are you steady enough to make the stairs?"

"I can manage." I hold on to the railing, and he directs me to the master bathroom.

Chet turns on the shower, and I gaze into the mirror. My shoulder is red and angry. Six black stitches hold me together. I turn my shoulder inward, and the same goes for the other side.

"You're lucky it was a clean shot, or you'd be waking up in the hospital."

"He told me about Teresa," I say, glaring at him in the mirror.

"I'm sure it was only his version of what happened." He rubs his hand over his mustache.

"He said you killed her."

"Teresa was sick. She killed herself. That doesn't mean I don't feel some guilt in my part that pushed her over the edge. That's something I will take to my grave, but I did not kill her."

I nod, knowing he's telling the truth.

"I'll be outside the door if you need any help."

I get under the spray of the water and hold myself up with one hand on the tile. The water turns red as it runs down my body and pools on the shower floor.

I want to hate Tom for the things he's done, coming after this family, using his daughter, but I can't help but feel sorry for the man living a life full of hate and fueled by revenge. Margret is the one who will have to live with his sins.

After I've washed, I step out and towel off, wrapping it around my waist. My jeans are too bloody to put back on. Opening the bathroom door that steps into Chet's room, he's standing by the window, peering out, and Wyatt's walking through the door with clothes in his hand. "You look like shit."

"Thanks." I chuckle. "Those for me?" I point.

"Yeah, Dad called and told me what happened. I thought these would work." He holds out the clothes.

I dress while they talk.

"Have the police been called?" Wyatt moves toward Chet.

"That's not how Boone wants this handled."

"I didn't see Clem when I walked through the house."

"She and Bear went to Maynard's."

"I think he'd have been better off with the police than in the hands of Clem."

CHAPTER THIRTY THREE
CLEM

"Slow down, Clem." Bear is tugging at my arm.

"Either get in the truck or stay here, but quit trying to talk me out of going to Tom's house to put a bullet in his ass." I swing open the truck door and jump inside. Bear barely gets in before I shift into drive.

"You need to calm your ass down."

"Calm down? He shot Boone!"

"Yes, but I don't want you to end up in jail right along with him."

"You heard Boone. He's not going to report him." I glare at him.

"Why don't you let me handle things when we get there?"

"He could've killed him, Bear!"

"Yes, but he didn't. If Tom would've wanted him dead, he'd be gone, and we'd never have found his body."

"Fine! If he threatens one of us, I'm shooting him."

I fly over the dirt road like my truck has wings and park outside Tom's house. The front door is wide open.

"Margret! You in here?"

"In the family room," she answers back.

Bear races in front of me. Margret is kneeling on the floor, and Tom is lying on the couch with a washrag over his eyes.

"You fucking shot Boone." I push past Bear.

"He's sick." Margret has black streaks of mascara smeared down her cheeks.

Bear reaches down and touches his forehead. "He's burning up. We need to get him to the hospital."

"Jail is more like it," I snarl, then feel bad when Margret bursts into tears.

"I'm not going to the hospital to die. If it's my time, I'll do it right here in my own home."

"Daddy, please," Margret sobs.

I roll up my sleeves. "Let me take a look at him." Margret stands and moves to the end of the couch.

I feel his pulse. "Your heart is strong. I don't think today is your day unless Bear lets me shoot you for what you did to Boone. So, I suggest we get you to the hospital."

"I'm sorry for shooting Boone," he says.

"You're telling the wrong person you're sorry." I help him to a sitting position. "Bear, get him to the truck." He throws one of Tom's arms around his shoulder and puts his arm around his waist.

Margret takes me off guard by hugging me. "Thank you for helping him. I know he's been awful and to shoot Boone"—she lets out a whimper—"I know he doesn't love me, but I love him, and I thought when that rifle went off that Daddy had killed him."

I peel her off me and hold her head, so she has to look me in the eyes. "Boone is going to be okay. The bullet went straight through him. He's already been doctored up and resting." I can see in her eyes that she truly does love him.

Her hair is a wild mess as she nods. "Okay."

"Go wash your face and meet us in the truck." She appears like a rabid animal.

Bear has Tom lying in the back seat. His face is beet red, and he's shivering into a little ball. I climb in the middle, and a few seconds later, Margret is beside me.

❧

"THE DOCTOR SAID HIS FEVER IS FROM AN infection, but he'll have a hard time fighting it with the cancer eating up his body." Margret sits beside me in the waiting room.

"Did you know he was sick?"

"I knew every now and then he'd cough, and he'd look weak, but when I asked him about it, he'd tell me he was fine. I didn't know he had cancer. I'm such an awful daughter."

"You're not. He hid it well and how can you say you're awful when you've done everything he asked or ordered you to do?"

"I feel so bad that I listened to him. I was willing to do anything he asked of me to get Boone. I wanted him to love me so much that I missed all of Daddy's motivations. I knew he didn't like Chet, but I had no idea why until today. I've been such a selfish bitch."

I want to tell her no she hasn't to make her feel better, but that's exactly what's she's been. "You can fix this."

"I've already agreed to an annulment."

"That's a start."

"I want you to know, Boone never touched me. As much as I tried to entice him, he never gave into me. I knew the first night you came back that our relationship was over. I could see it in the way he looked at you."

"You knew more than I did then because all I could feel were flaming arrows coming from his eyes when he was near me."

She shifts her weight in her chair. "Do you think when this is all said and done, you and I might be friends?"

"Why don't we just start by calling a truce and we'll go from there?"

"Deal." She half smiles.

My phone starts ringing in my purse. The only picture I still have of Boone when we first started dating, lights up my phone. I walk away from Margret to answer it.

"You okay?"

"Where are you? Please tell me you didn't kill Tom."

"No. Bear, Margret, and I loaded him in my truck. We're at the hospital right now. He's really a sick man."

"How's Margret?"

I want to be irritated for him asking about her, but he's a good man with a big heart and I know he cares about her regardless of what she's put him through. "She'll be okay. She hates what he's done to this family."

"I don't think he was much better to her from the things she said."

"Sadly, I don't believe so either. How's your shoulder?"

"Pretty damn sore. When you come home, you could kiss it and make it better." He deepens his voice.

"You take a bullet to the shoulder and still, all you can think about is sex." I laugh.

"I said a kiss, nobody mentioned sex, but now that you have, I'll sacrifice through the pain to make you happy."

I can't see him, but I can envision him waggling his eyebrows. "How about you get some rest, and when I'm done here, I'll meet you back at your place."

"Sounds good."

"Bye." I hear his voice before I hang up.

"Clem."

"Yeah."

"I love you."

"I love you too, Boone." I glance over at Margret, and her tears start falling again. I put my phone away and sit beside her, holding her hand until the nurse comes to get her to take her back to see her father.

"Will you be okay if we head home?"

Bear stands. "I'll come get you when you're ready to go."

"It's okay. I think I'm going to stay the night."

"Call us in the morning or if you need anything." I know in my heart, it's the right thing to do.

She hugs my neck again. "Thank you. I don't deserve your kindness."

I park out front of 114. It feels so good that Boone is back home where he belongs. There's a lamp on inside, and he's sound asleep on the couch. I take the blanket off the back of it and softly put it over him.

"Hey." His voice is scratchy.

I sit on the floor beside him and run my hand along his cheek. "You okay?"

"Chet found some pain pills from when he hurt his back and gave me two of them."

"Good. You need to rest. I'll go stay at the main house and check on you tomorrow."

"I want you here with me where you belong." He sits, and his body wavers.

"Okay, cowboy. Let's get you to bed."

"Now we're talking," he slurs.

I seize him around his waist, helping him to stand. We make it to the bedroom before he collapses on the bed.

Unbuttoning his shirt, he has a lopsided grin. "I like you undressing me." His smile disappears when I inch his injured shoulder out of it. His eyes are heavy, and he can hardly help me.

I finagle his shirt off and work on pulling off his boots and undoing his belt buckle. He falls back on the bed, and I try to take his jeans off, but he's dead weight and too heavy for me to move. I lift his legs, and he's catawampus in the bed. After I cover him, I rummage through his drawer and find a t-shirt of his to wear. I slip it on and snuggle in beside him, careful not to touch his shoulder. He lets out a loud snore, and I know the pain pills have fully kicked in. It's been a long and very strange day. Who would've thought I'd be feeling sorry for Margret or helping get Tom to the hospital.

Boone and I have a do-over now, and I'm not

going to blow it this time. I make a promise to myself to adopt Momma and Daddy's rule about never going to bed angry or run away from him again. I was a foolish girl once, and I'm lucky to have a second chance. I close my eyes and drift off to sleep next to the man I thought I'd lost for good.

CHAPTER THIRTY FOUR
BOONE

Damn, she looks good in my "This ain't My First Rodeo" t-shirt. I sit cross-legged on my side of the bed to watch her sleep. It's amazing what I feel for her. Seven years ago if someone had told me she'd be back in my bed, I'd have told them they were lying like a no-legged dog, and yet, here she is. I reach over and brush a strand of hair from her cheek, and her eyes flutter open.

"Mornin', how you feeling?" She scoots lower in the bed and rests her head in my lap.

"Better than I should be." I tug at the hem of her shirt. "I like this on you."

Her hand rubs up and down my thigh, making me achingly hard. "I like me on you." She grins.

"We need to talk."

"Doesn't look like talking is what you really meant." She licks her lips and reaches for the fly of my boxers. I stupidly stop her.

"I'm serious, Clem."

She gets up and sits with her back against the headboard. "All right, I'm listening."

"I don't want to marry you." I know I shouldn't have led with that by the gawk on her face. This is one of those moments where if brains were leather, I wouldn't have enough to ride a June bug. She tries to scurry out of bed, but I stop her. "Please, let me rephrase that."

"I'm going to assume those drugs my daddy gave you were tainted and affecting your good sense." She sits facing me.

"I do want to marry you..."

"So the opposite of what you just said." Her brows furrow into a straight line.

I take her hands in mine. "I don't want to marry you..."

"For Pete's sake, Boone, make up your mind!"

"Let me finish." I inhale, trying to find the right words. "You weren't ready last time, and I was. I've had years to think about that. I shouldn't have proposed because of the baby. That wasn't my reasoning. I was crazy about you and wanted to spend the rest of my life with you, but that's not how you saw it. I've grown up, yet my life hasn't changed much. I love this ranch and this family. I have no desire to go anywhere else or live a different life. This is who I am." She starts to say something, and I press my fingers to her lips.

"I know you want more out of life. You want to go places and see things. Being trapped here scares you. I don't want to be the man that holds you back. I love you enough to let you go, but know that I'll always be here waiting for you. There is no other woman in the world I want but you." There's a long pause between us.

"Are you finished?" Her fawn-colored eyes do what they always do to a man like me; they draw me into her. "I ran away once. I saw the world. It's both beautiful and ugly at the same time. I met plenty of good-looking, charming men that could have swept me off my feet. They didn't. As much as I loved what I did and the things I learned, my heart was always back here. I needed to get away to see this place for what it is. It's family, hard work, a love for this land, a place to belong, and damn well something worth fighting for. I love the horses, the cattle, and even those darn chickens of Momma's." Her voice cracks, mentioning her.

"I'm not scared anymore, nor do I feel the need to run. I want roots, and I want them here with you. My biggest regret is losing our baby. I would've never left this place, and it wouldn't have taken me so long to realize how much I belong here. There were times I'd be resting in my cot and picture a little boy the spitting image of you, learning to ride a horse. Or a little girl holding her daddy's hand as they watched the horses run." She releases my hands and places them on either side of my face.

"There is no other place I want to be than right by your side. I want to convince you of that. I want you to know that when the day comes for me to walk down that aisle, I'll be there. I won't run unless it's into your arms. And, when the time is right, if you're too gun-shy to ask me, then I'll get down on my knees and beg you to be my husband."

I wrap one arm around her, dragging her into my lap. "I love you, Clem."

"I love you too. Do you think you're up to a little fooling around?" She looks at my shoulder.

"Depends what your definition of 'a little' is?" I grin and kiss the soft skin of her neck.

"A *little* kissing wouldn't hurt."

"I think I could manage more." I brush her hair back and nip at her collarbone.

"Could you round second base?" Her voice grows raspier.

I slide my hand under her shirt and squeeze her breast. "Is this second?" A low chuckle rumbles through me.

"I'm really needing third base, but if you're in too much pain, I could give you a home run." Her gaze travels to my cock. "I wouldn't mind a *little* tonsil tickling."

I roar out in laughter. "You are one dirty-mouthed woman. How many names do you have for my member?"

"Well, not member. That's a boring one." She giggles. "But, I promise to stick around and come up with a few more for you."

I trap her mouth with mine so she'll quit talking. I push her back on the bed and with one hand, rip my t-shirt off over her head. Her hands push down my boxers at the same time, freeing me. I kneel between her legs and lean over her, putting all my weight on one hand. She grasps me and cups my balls, leading me into the glory land. She's hot and drenched as she inches me inside, creating an instant tingle down my spine.

Once she has me right where she wants me, I shift my hips, rocking into her. She arches, grabs my hips, pushes back and then yanks me back into her harder. It starts a frenzy that I can't stop, nor do I want to. Pain rips through my shoulder when she loses control and forgets about my wound. I pull out of her and stand by the side of the bed.

"I'm so sorry. I got carried away." She sits on the side of the bed and splays her hand on my chest.

"Get up."

She does.

"Turn around."

She does.

I kiss her between her shoulder blades. "Bend over."

She does.

I widened her legs, pressing between her. Guiding myself into her from behind makes me hard as hell. She pushes her hips back, and our skin slaps together. I place my hand in the center of her back to brace myself for better traction. It drives her wild, and she keeps moving her hips. Sliding my hand down to the dip of her back, over her ass, stopping on her nub, she gasps when I apply a "little" pressure.

"Yes!" she hisses, and there is no stopping her movement. She's so wet I slide in and out of her with ease. I know the minute she can't take anymore when her hands grasp the sheets. She throws her head back, riding out her pleasure and it's so fucking beautiful I can't help but join her. I lower myself over her body and wait for us both to calm our breathing.

"If that was a little, I can't wait until you're a hundred percent better." She laughs.

***

"WHAT ARE YOUR PLANS FOR THE DAY?" I ASK AS we both get dressed.

"I'm going to go check on Daddy. Make sure he's had something to eat, and then I'm going to go spend some time with Missy. She's got to be missing Momma. What about you?"

"I'm going to go check on Margret."

She turns around to look at me.

I hold up my hand. "Before you go getting upset..."

"I'm not upset. I was going to ask if you wanted me to go with you?" She walks toward me. "You're a good man, Boone. I know she put you through a lot, and yet, you want to help her."

"I hurt her when you came back to town. She didn't deserve it. Her father was the one scheming, and yes she played along, but I think she really loved me. She and I spent a lot of time together over the last year. She isn't all bad, but she was never you."

"You don't have to explain. Do what you need to do, and I'll support you."

"Thanks." I place a tender kiss to her lips. "Let me know what I can do for Chet."

"I think we all need to spend a few extra moments with him every day. Time is the only thing that's going to help him." She sniffs. "I miss her like crazy, I can only imagine the hole left in his heart. Daddy depended on her, and she kept him in line."

"I think, for now, we need to keep him away from Maynard."

"I agree. At some point, he'll need to talk to him without wanting to kill him, but now is not the time."

"Agreed."

We walk to our trucks. She heads toward the main house, and I go straight to the hospital. I find Margret sitting in the waiting room with her head tilted, and her eyes closed. I sit quietly in the chair beside her.

A voice comes over the paging system, and she wakes up. "Boone," she says, wiping the drool from the corner of her mouth. "How long have you been here?"

"Only a few moments. How's Tom?"

"It's been a long night, but he looks better. The doctor says he'll be here for a bit, but that I need to make some arrangements for him at home. They say he'll be weak and may not regain the strength he had."

"Is there anything I can do for you?"

She leans her head on my shoulder. "You're sweet, and I don't deserve it."

I move, and she lifts her head. "You do deserve kindness, Margret. We all do, and forgiveness. I'm sorry that I hurt you, and I'm sorry that your father coerced you into helping him with his vendetta against the Calhouns."

"You're an easy man to love, so it wasn't a sacrifice on my part. I just wished you loved me like you do Clem. If she wouldn't have come back, we'd be married for real."

I kiss the top of her head. "Yes, and I would've kept my word to you, but I would've never given you my heart like I should've. It belonged to someone else, and it wasn't mine to give away."

"I only hope that one day I'll find a man that loves me like you do her."

"You will, I'm sure of it."

"Will you do me a favor?"

"Sure. What is it you need?"

"For you to stay on as trainer for Lucky Shot and run him in the Belmont."

"Why?"

"Because he's got a chance to win or place."

"He'll be competing against Whiskey River."

"I know, and I realize it's a lot to ask, but I could use something good to happen in my life. I won't be able to make the race with Daddy being sick."

I don't know why I agree other than maybe it will make amends for my part in hurting her. "Okay, I will."

A man walks by us in a suit and stops at the nurse's desk. "I'm here to see Tom Maynard." He hands her a business card.

"Do you know him?" I whisper to Margret.

She shakes her head.

"I'm sorry, Mr. Maynard is only allowed family for visitors."

"Tell him I'm here. He called me."

The nurse makes a phone call.

"Excuse me, but I'm his daughter. I don't think he needs to be handling any business right now." Margret gets up and walks toward him.

"I'm here at his request."

"Do you mind telling me what this is all about?"

"I'm not at liberty to say, ma'am." The nurse hangs up and escorts him back.

Margret tries to follow him. "I'm sorry, but Mr. Maynard specifically requested that you not be let in right now."

"What the hell is he up to?" She marches over to me.

"I don't know. I'm assuming that's his attorney and it has something to do with his will."

"I hope you're right."

CHAPTER THIRTY FIVE
CLEM

"I can't believe we're finally here." I grab our luggage from the baggage carousel, with Boone by my side. "We really have a chance to win the Belmont race and the Triple Crown."

"This is what I've been working for since the day I bought Whiskey River." He hails a cab with one arm, keeping his other arm pressed tightly against him in his sling.

"What about Lucky Shot?" I load the luggage in the trunk and get in the back seat with him, sitting as close as I can. We haven't been able to keep our hands off each other over the past two weeks. Boone hasn't let his injury slow him down when it comes to me. I swear he has the horniness of a teenage boy. Then again, he's one big walking aphrodisiac that I could eat up every time I'm near him.

"He'll be his biggest challenge."

I slide my hand to his crotch and whisper, "Have you ever had sex in a cab before?" I run my tongue along the rim of his ear.

He swallows hard. "No." He picks up my hand and kisses my fingertips. "I'm at a disadvantage with one arm."

"It wasn't an issue with you last night when you had two fingers buried in my love box and the other hand massaging my airbags."

He snorts and places a quick kiss on my lips. "You need to behave."

"You're no fun." I giggle and peer out the window. "Oh my gawd, look at the size of those buildings. Have you ever been to New York before?"

"Nope, first time for me."

"Daddy's gonna hate this."

"So will Ellie and Bear."

"None of them are the city type."

"Speaking of the city, is Ethan meeting you here?"

"He'll be at the race. He's going to pick up my family from the airport."

"Is he coming back with us?"

"No. He and Bear are going to take a road trip in my truck before they head back Kentucky."

"That should be an interesting trip. Who's going to take care of Missy?"

"Daddy and I are going to take turns. She's having a hard time with Momma gone."

"Why don't you just have her stay with us?"

"I'd like that, but I think Daddy needs to have her around too."

"I need to tell you something, Clem."

"No good conversation ever starts with those six words." She scoots over and faces me.

"I'm running Lucky Shot. Margret asked me as a favor."

"So, you're going against my horse?" Her voice raises.

"Both horses are good. Would you want to win simply because Margret's horse was pulled out of the race?"

"Maybe." She shrugs.

"I know you. You want Whiskey to win because he's the best, not because he didn't have any competition."

She rights herself in the seat. "I'm not liking you much right now. Why do you have to know me so well?"

I chuckle. "You love a good race as much as I do."

"Well, I have something to tell you too."

I squint. "What?"

"The Belmont board won't let Henry near the gates. They say he has to stay in the stables."

"Damn."

"There's no telling how Whiskey's going to behave."

"Hopefully Henry can work his magic by being there whether he can see him or not."

Thirty minutes later, the cab driver pulls through the green wrought iron gates of Belmont Park. "Home of the Belmont Stakes." I read the sign. We drive to the main entrance of the building and he parks. We get out and get our luggage.

The building's arched windows have greenery growing up the walls. I can feel the excitement the building holds. I walk over to the bronze statue of Secretariat and read the tribute to the horse, the owner, the trainer, and the rider. I run my hands across the year 1973. "This could be us soon, winning the Triple Crown and breaking this horse's legend. I'd like a statue of Whiskey right alongside of him."

"Right after I bought Whiskey River, I went to

Lexington, Kentucky where Secretariat is buried. I wanted inspiration."

"Really? I didn't know that."

He grabs my hand. "I'm a man of many surprises."

I can't help but laugh at him. We drop off our luggage in a holding area and locate the stables. Boone checks on Whiskey before he finds Lucky Shot. We both spend the rest of our day with the riders and the horses. We meet back up at the end of a long day to check into a hotel room not far from the park. Even though I'm filled with excitement for the race, I fall asleep in Boone's arms in no time at all.

❧

As soon as our eyes open in the morning, it's a race for us to get everything done. Ethan's called and is already headed to the airport to pick up my family. Boone takes off one direction and I another. I fill out last-minute paperwork and go over all the rules of the race. I meet with Jose and tell him about Henry. He didn't seem overly concerned at all. I run back to the hotel to change for the race. As an owner, I don't have to wear one of those silly fancy hats, but I honor the tradition. My black-and-white polka-dot dress is knee-length. I fasten a wide red belt around my waist and slip on a pair of two-inch black heels. I pair it with a wide-brimmed black hat trimmed in white and braid my hair down the side.

As I'm rushing out the door, I run into Boone's hard chest. "Damn, you are hot." His voice oozes with sexiness.

I walk back into the room with him. "I've got like five minutes before I'm supposed to meet my family at the gate."

"Don't wait on me. I'll meet you there," he says, taking his suit off the hanger.

My mouth waters thinking about him being all sexy in it.

He chuckles like he's read my mind. "You're staying to watch me dress, aren't you?"

"I'd like to stay and get in a world of trouble with you, but there's no time, so I'll have to settle for watching you put that suit on your sexy body." I admire his every movement. I think he taunts me with his grin.

His jeans fall to the floor, and so does my jaw.

His boxers are next, and I lick my lips.

He does a sexy sway, pulling his shirt over his head. I know he's enjoying it because his Rodger Dodger is saluting.

He pulls on a pair of boxers and groans as he tucks himself inside. His slacks fit him snuggly with that bulge in the front. He tugs on a white t-shirt, then his white button-down.

I grab his silver tie from the hanger and drape it around his neck, while purposely pushing my lady parts against the tent in his slacks.

"If you don't stop that we'll never make the race in time." He groans.

"I guess that wouldn't look good if the owners didn't show up"—I grin—"but it would sure be fun."

He places a quick kiss to my lips. "You've had your fun, now get out of here."

I blow him a kiss over my shoulder as I leave. "Good luck at the races. Lucky will look good in second place."

I grab a cab and head to the Belmont. My family and Ethan are all waiting for me at the entrance.

"You all clean up so good," I say and hug them.

"You are beautiful, Aunt Clem." Missy tugs at my elbow.

I kneel beside her. "I love this yellow dress."

"Grandma made it for me." She frowns.

"Well, it's perfect, and she's smiling down at you wearing it."

"You think so?" She pulls up the brim of her hat and gazes toward the sky."

"I know so." I stand and take her hand. "Let's go place our bets and find our seats. Whiskey's race will start soon."

We wait in the long lines, but finally make our way to the owner's seating area. Daddy sits next to me and Missy climbs in his lap.

"How are the two of you?" I ask him.

"Some days are better than others." He gives me a half smile.

"I'm glad you came."

"Your momma would've loved to see this."

"She's watching." I glance up.

Boone sits in the seat next to me. "Hey, Uncle Boone." Missy waves at him.

"You are so darn pretty," he tells her.

"How did you get this seat? Aren't you sitting with the enemy?" I tease.

"My section was empty, and I wanted to sit by the prettiest girl here."

"In that case, I'm glad."

Instead of watching the horses make their way to the gates, I watch my family. Ethan and Bear are plotting their trip. He's not paid any attention to Ellie, so I guess his trip back home was good for him to get over his crush. Ellie, who's dressed in a pale shade of blue, is chatting with Wyatt. He sees me staring at him and winks at me. I can't help but think about how far he and I have come. He still has his moments when he can be an ass, but he's loyal to this family when it comes down to it. I think he puts on a hard exterior, but I'm betting underneath he has a heart of gold.

We all stand as Whiskey makes it to his gate. He hesitates and walks in a circle. Jose says something to him, and he seems to calm down. When his gate is closed, his head moves up and down, and you can see his body moving. He's not liking it.

When the bugle is blown, he wavers before he races out, putting him behind. Lucky Shot is in the middle.

As they go into the first curve, Lucky moves toward the front. Whiskey is running on the outside, making some headway. We grab our binoculars and watch as the horses make it to the other side of the track. Lucky moves into second position and Whiskey is in fourth and closing in.

"Come on, Whiskey," I chant, and I hear Boone saying the same thing.

They round the next corner with one horse out

in front, Lucky in solid second, and Whiskey on his tail, inching closer.

The last quarter mile, they are all within a nose of one another. The crowd is going wild as they get closer and closer. The jockey on the horse in front by a nose gets too close to the rail, and his horse stumbles, crashing into Lucky. Lucky tries to recover, moving to his right but hits Whiskey. All three horses are down. You hear the crowd go from cheering to an audible gasp. The horse moves around them, avoiding colliding with the horses and the jockey. The horse that was in fourth place crosses the finish line first.

Boone and I are already on our feet, headed down to the racetrack. The three jockeys are standing. The first horse that stumbled and Lucky Shot are on their feet, but Whiskey is still on the ground.

We're blocked from going down on the track. Horse vets are surrounding Whiskey, and Jose is on the ground talking to him.

Fear makes the moment seem like forever before Whiskey gets off the ground. Boone grabs my hand, pulling me through the crowd to the horse recovery area.

Whiskey is limping with Jose at his side. "Are you okay? Is Whiskey all right?" I'm frantic.

"I'm fine, but it looks like Whiskey tore ligaments in his leg. I'm going to get him back to the stable for the vet to get a better look." He takes off his helmet. "I'm sorry, Clem. I tried to keep him from falling."

"It's not your fault, Jose. I'm just glad you're okay and hope Whiskey will be too."

Boone checks on Lucky, who seems to be okay and then follows us to the stable. The vet gets right in with him. The Belmont has all their own equipment brought in for the races, so they are able to take him for an X-ray.

Whiskey comes back with ice packs attached to his leg. "I'm afraid with the damage done, he won't be able to race again," the vet tells me.

"Will he heal?"

"Yes, but he'll live out his days in green pasture."

I'm sad for Whiskey because he loves to run, but I'm happy that he'll be okay. This family doesn't need another loss right now.

"Aunt Clem, is Whiskey going to be okay?" My family walks in the stable, and Missy runs over to me.

"He's going to be fine. He won't race anymore, but he'll live with us on the ranch."

"He'll make for great studding fees," my dad chimes in.

"What are studding fees?" Missy looks up at me.

"That's a conversation for another day." Bear ruffles her hair.

"We're all so proud of you." Ellie hugs me.

"You would've won." Wyatt smiles. "Sorry, Boone."

"Either way, I'm a winner for being part of this family."

Ethan drapes his arm around me. "That was awesome and scary."

I kiss his cheek. "I've missed you, my friend."

"I'm sorry about your mom. I really liked her."

"I hear you and Bear have a road trip to go on."

"Yep, and when we're done, if it's okay with you, I'd like to stay on the ranch."

Daddy clears his throat to get Ethan's attention. "I will have no freeloaders on my property."

Ethan has yet to learn when my father is giving him a ration of shit.

"Oh, no, sir. Bear has taught me how to handle the cattle, and I've been reading up on how to take care of chickens."

I see the lump in Daddy's throat. "Amelia would like that, Son."

"Score one for the city boy." Wyatt high-fives him.

Ellie looks at him like a new man, but he only smiles at her and stays close to me.

"I say we all go out and celebrate. Dinner is on me," Boone says.

"Don't you only celebrate when you win?" Missy is confused.

"We've all won. We have each other." Bear picks her up.

CHAPTER THIRTY SIX
CLEM

"Four months later and 102 is prettier than ever." I hold Boone's hand as we finish the final inspection. We rebuilt it in its old spot, saving the river area for a bigger home.

"Thank god it has indoor plumbing." Ethan opens the bathroom door.

It's two stories now, but still small. There are stairs to the second floor instead of a ladder, that leads to a bedroom. On the first floor, a large kitchen with a living room-dining room combination and an office.

"You setting up shop in here, Clem?" Ethan opens the door to the office.

"I was thinking you and I could go into business together in cybersecurity."

"I thought you'd given that up?" He scratches his head.

"I'd like to have something for myself other than the ranch. It will be extra income for when things are tight around here. We could both do it part-time."

"I'd like that. Beats smelling like cattle every day." He sniffs his shirt.

Boone grabs my shoulders, turning me to face him. "I was thinking maybe you'd like to move from the main house to my house, instead of here. You could still set up shop in 102."

I angle toward Ethan. "I bet you'd like your own place."

He points to the shiny new wooden floor. "Here?"

"Yeah. Sounds like it's going to be empty." I wink at Boone. I'm at his place almost every night anyway.

Ethan picks me up and whirls me around. "Thanks, Clem."

"You're welcome, now put me down." I giggle. "You know you'll be living next to Ellie."

"She and I have come to an understanding. Besides, there's a cute cowgirl working at the coffee house in town who gave me her number." He's all grins.

"Now you'll have a place of your own for entertaining."

Boone glances at his watch. "I need to get to the track. Moonshine has his first run today, and Whiskey is being studded out."

"I'll come with you."

"Hold on a second." Ethan stops me.

"I'll catch up. You go on." I wave Boone off.

Ethan keeps quiet until Boone is gone. "You two getting married?"

"Nope, but it sounds like we're going to be living in sin." I wink.

"Is he still married to Margret?"

"No. Wyatt finalized all that a couple weeks ago. He's a free man."

"Then why aren't you marrying him?"

"Boone isn't ready, and I don't blame him. Just because we're not married doesn't mean we love each other less. Actually, I didn't think I could love him more, but every day I fall for him over and over again. That man keeps me weak in the knees."

"That's hard to imagine. You're one of the toughest women I know, especially when you're wielding a shotgun." He chuckles. "I'm glad you're happy and things worked out for you."

I open the door to leave. "And I'm glad the city

boy is becoming a real cowboy." I point to his new boots. "The women around here are going to love you."

It's a nice day and breezy out, and I enjoy my walk to the racetrack. On the way, I see Daddy sitting on the front porch step, sipping on a glass of lemonade.

"Do you have any more of that?" I direct him to his glass.

"Missy made it for me. You may not want any. I think she forgot to add sugar." He puckers his lips, and I laugh.

I sit on the step next to him. "She's trying to fill Momma's role by taking care of you. I'm going to be spending more time at Boone's. What do you think about Missy staying with us after she gets out of school?"

"I like having her around. Besides, Bear will be moving into 118. He wants to be back at the ranch."

"He's still going to be at the garage?"

"Yeah, but he wants Missy here full-time."

"He's done a good job with her. I know how much of a player he used to be. I thought he'd be the last one of us having kids, but I've got to hand it to him, he's great with her."

"We've all had a hand in raising her, but I agree

with you. She made Bear grow up. He's really stepped up around here. After my heart attack, I thought I'd have to give this place up. He took over and kept his garage going."

"Speaking of this place, have you spoken to Tom? Margret keeps Boone in the loop. He's home, but he doesn't have much longer."

"I took your momma's advice about letting a dead dog lie. The man doesn't want to see my ugly mug, and I'll respect his dying wishes. There's nothing all these years that changed his mind about what happened, so it's better left alone. The property and this family are safe, and that's all that matters."

I stand.

"When are you and Boone going to start building on 116?"

"We're in no rush. I know he wants to build a bridge over the river to the other acreage and let Whiskey River have some room to run. He and I are both going to train Moonshine and plan on getting one of Whiskey's colts. The barns rebuilt, and with the added stables, we'll have room for more horses."

"It will be a good year for the cows. Prices are high, and it will be enough to carry this place for the next couple years. I want to add more cattle for next year."

"Sounds like things are on the right track." I walk down the steps.

"Clem."

I turn to face him.

"I'm glad you found your way back home."

"Me too, Daddy." I make my way to Boone, who's giving instructions to Jose on Moonshine. I put my boot on the bottom rail of the fence and step up to watch Jose working with him. Boone walks over on the other side of the fence and props a dusty boot up.

"He's going to be good. Two years and I believe we'll have another shot at the derbies."

"With the two of us training him, we can't lose."

We watch as Jose loads him in the gate with such ease. "Doesn't look like he'll need Henry." Boone chuckles.

"He's loving life with Whiskey out in the pasture. He still sleeps cuddled up next to him."

He steps up on the rung and is within inches of me. "Speaking of cuddling up, what do you say we head back to the house for a quickie?"

"You're never good at quickies. You always offer, but it turns into an hour-long showdown. Not that I'm complaining." I giggle and hop down. "Come on." I flash him my tits. "That should get your sex pistol going." I take off in a run toward his house across the property. He gets in his truck and zooms by me. By the time I get there, he's standing in the doorway half naked, huge grin on his handsome face, boots are off, shirt torn over his head, and his blue jeans lowered to just where I like them.

I grab his hand as I walk by, and he slams the door.

EPILOGUE

"Is that the last place to sign?" I wheeze through the oxygen mask.

"Yes. I'll file the paperwork, and in thirty days this property will belong to my organization."

"We made a deal. I sell you this land, and you acquire the Calhoun property."

"I'm a man of my word. It will take a little time, but I will own all three hundred acres of Chet Calhoun's land. We'll steal it right out from under him."

"His boy Wyatt is an attorney and a damn good one. You best find a way around him."

"You let me worry about him. He and I have a history, and I know how he operates."

"And what about my daughter?"

"She'll get the money you set up for her, but she'll have to find another place to live."

"I'll die in peace knowing that I've got my revenge on the Calhoun family."

***

A thief and a single father don't bode well. She's snarky, and sexy which can only lead to two broken hearts.

Click here to continue to Stolen Hearts, Book 2

SNEAK PEEK AT STOLEN HEARTS
BOOK 2

WHISKEY RIVER ROAD

KELLY MOORE

CHAPTER ONE
BEAR

I tiptoe onto the porch, hoping like hell my father isn't out of bed yet. The man's up before the rooster crows every mornin', and I'm in no mood for a lecture. Kicking off my boots, I quietly open the screen door, then the front door that always creaks.

Peeking inside the dark living room, there's no sign of him. I make it to the steps before a light flips on, and I hear his deep, baritone voice explode through the room like thunder.

"What the fuck are you doing getting' in this time of the morning? Have you forgotten you have a six-year-old daughter that has to be at school in a few hours?"

"No, I haven't forgotten, but Clem is taking her this mornin'." I press the heel of my hands to my throbbing temples, a grinding sensation looming. The lack of sleep and alcohol consumption are going to be the death of me today because I know him; Chet Calhoun cuts no man slack, including his son, who does all the work on this ranch.

"When are you ever going to grow up?" His voice even gruffer, he stands, rubbing a hand over his gray mustache.

"Could you just for once give me a break?" I take off my hat and toss it on the hook by the door.

He glances at his twenty-year-old watch his father gave him, tapping the glass with the tip of his finger. "You've got thirty minutes before the cattle need to be fed, then you have to repair the fence on the west side of the property. You should be able to get both of those things done in time to take Missy to school."

I stomp by him, muttering under my breath and head to the kitchen to make a pot of coffee. If I'm lucky, ignoring him will set him on a mission to make someone else's life miserable before the butt crack of dawn rises. Evidently, luck is not in my favor today.

"The last time I looked, we kept the cattle outside the house." His boots scuff the wood floor as he blusters in behind me, determined to kick my ass into shape.

The lack of sleep and good judgment escape me at this moment. I slam a mug on the counter. "I do believe you've gotten more ornery since Momma died." I regret my words as soon as I've said them. Not because it isn't true, but I know how much he misses her, and I just poured salt in an open wound.

He steps up so close to me, I can see the color change in his eyes. It's like watching a mood ring change colors from bright to dark, and if I was a smart man, I'd be hightailing it out of here. But no, I've lost all good sense today, and being dumb seems to be my forte in my sleep-deprived, hungover state.

"If me expecting my son to take care of his own daughter and not slack off on his obligations around here makes me cranky, then so be it. Your mother dying has nothing to do with it!" He spits out the last part, and I see him flexing his fist at his sides, trying to rein in his anger.

"I'm sorry 'bout what I said, but I take one night for myself, and you go all off half-cocked, accusing me of not being responsible enough to take care of Missy. Believe it or not, I've got it handled."

"Grown men don't go out partying all night, acting like they ain't got a care in the world." He heads to the back door.

He's walking out. I should just let it go. But hell

no, my dumbass can't shut up. "Have you ever thought I go enjoy myself to forget all the responsibilities I have around here? I've raised a daughter without a mother. I've worked at the garage to help make a life for her, not to mention the long days I put in on this ranch to make next to nothing." I've wanted to say that for so long. I puff out my chest like some proud rooster that just showed the hen who's boss.

He turns around and marches back over to me, wheeling a finger in my face. "You get a fucked-up, young girl pregnant, and you're surprised that you're left raising a child! And, as far as the garage is concerned, we know how you ended up working there!" His brows are drawn so tight his face has lost all its wrinkles.

"Damn, not even six in the mornin' and you've thrown my past in my face." I laugh and walk away from him. "I forget you're perfect. You've never screwed up one day in your life!"

"This isn't about me. You need to grow the fuck up and accept the consequences of your actions!"

"Grandpa, why are you yelling at my daddy?"

We both turn to see Missy standing in the kitchen doorway, rubbing the sleep from her eyes.

"It's okay, sweetie. Go back to bed. It's not time

to get up yet," I say as I walk over to her and brush the hair out of her face.

"You musta done something if Grandpa is using bad words this early in the mornin'."

I glare at my father. "Nothing for you to worry about, baby girl. Sometimes adults argue."

"Then, I don't ever want to grow up." She walks past me and hugs my dad around the waist. "Did you get me a new box for the chicken eggs? I'm sorry I dropped and broke all the eggs yesterday," she says, looking up at him.

"It was an accident, and yes"—he reaches on top of the fridge and drags down a pink box—"I got you a brand new one."

She claps her hands before she takes it from him. "Can we go collect the eggs now?"

"Sweetie, it's early. Why don't you go back to your room until it's time to get up for breakfast?" My head is pounding, and I'm really not ready for her to be awake. All I wanted was to slip in, have a cup of coffee in peace and quiet before I started my day. Whiskey might have been a better choice.

She pouts out her bottom lip. "But this is the time that Grandma and I used to collect the eggs. She'd say, the early bird gets the eggs."

I can't help but laugh. "Momma never did get that saying right."

"I'll take her while you get your shit together," my dad says gruffly over his shoulder, leading her out the back door.

There are days that I don't like him at all, but he's the hardest working man I know, and he expects nothing less from his children. Sometimes I think Clem had it right when she left here. She got to experience life off the ranch and away from our daddy's high expectations. At twenty-six years old, he still scares the shit out of me. I had my share of butt whoopins behind the barn growing up. You'd think it would've kept me out of trouble.

"He can think what he wants. I'm responsible, and I work hard." I jut my chin in the air, grumbling as if he's still in the room.

"Who you talking to?"

I didn't hear Clem come in the house. "Nobody," I say, and fill a mug full of black coffee. "What are you doing here so early?"

"I promised Missy I'd make her pancakes before school today." She sets a bag on the counter and takes out a fresh box of blueberries. "These were Momma's favorite, and I think it makes Missy feel closer to her."

"Life hasn't been the same around here since she died. Daddy's gotten crankier."

"Can you blame him? She was his whole life."

"Yeah, but he seems to take it out on me."

She laughs. "Don't think you're special. He takes it out on all of us."

I pull out a chair at the table and sit. "He thinks I'm still a child and irresponsible because I play in a band and stay out late once a month."

She pours a cup of coffee and joins me at the table. "Ignore him."

"I tried that." I chuckle. "It made things worse."

"Your first mistake was sneaking into the main house this time of the morning. Why didn't you just go home to 118? You've barely been there since you moved back to the ranch."

"It's lonely in the cabin. Missy would rather stay here. I think she thinks Daddy needs her."

"He does, but she's your daughter. Take her home."

"To be honest, she can be a bit much sometimes, and I like the break. Don't get me wrong, I love her, but at times I'm not real good at being a single dad. She asks way too many questions."

She sips her coffee. "I remember Momma always

said she hated the why stage. She'd finally give up and say because she said so."

"Yes! That's what I want to say to her." I throw my hands in the air.

"How about I help you decorate a room for her at your house, and when you need a break, she can come stay with Boone and me."

"She loves that old bastard. I don't think I'll get her away from him."

"He'd never admit it, but maybe he needs a break every now and then too."

"That man is too hard-headed to do anything different. He wouldn't know fun if it bit him in the balls." I chuckle.

She gets up and squeezes my shoulder as she walks by me. She opens cabinets, getting down a bowl. "Maybe it's time for a change."

"You're right. I should take Missy and leave. Move somewhere far away and see what life is like away from the ranch."

"Um...been there...done that...and here I am, back where I started and happier than ever."

I stand and pour a second cup of coffee. "That's because you have Boone."

"You should start dating again."

"I can only handle one woman in my life at a

time, and the short little diva has my hands full at the moment."

"She needs a momma." She flicks me with her finger.

"I'm not great at getting a woman to stick around. They only want me for my body."

Clem spews coffee, laughing. "Good lord, Bear, you sound like a woman."

"Well, it's true. You've seen how the women eat me up at the bar."

"That's because every woman fantasizes about doing the naughty with a lead band member."

I square my body toward her. "Really? Doing the naughty? Is that the best you could come up with?" A crooked smile pulls on the corner of my mouth.

"If you only knew my dirty mind, you'd know that was keeping it clean."

"Damn. No wonder Boone always has a smile on his face." I chuckle. I cross one arm over my chest and tap a finger to my chin. "I heard you and Boone were a little kinky. Tell me how the Saran Wrap works?"

Her face turns the color of a fresh sunburn on pale skin. "Does everyone know about that? Wyatt is such a gossip!"

"I could use some fresh ideas about sex," I tease and jab her with my elbow.

"That's gross. I'm not talking sex with my brother."

"What's sex?" Missy asks, marching in the door.

I inch toward Clem. "Would it be bad if I put a bell on her?" I whisper, only half serious.

"Put the eggs in the fridge and go get dressed." My dad ushers her away from us.

"You two need to watch what you say around her." He points a finger between the two of us.

Clem and I look at each other and burst out in laughter. "You're one to talk, Mr. F Bomb," she roars.

"She's heard curse words since the day she was hatched, but she don't need to know about hanky-panky yet." He whispers the last part.

I continue to chuckle. "First of all, if you think she was hatched, maybe you and I should have the birds and bees talk. Secondly, who calls it that?"

Clem is folded over in laughter.

"I was doing it long before you came along. I don't need no advice in that department." He tugs up his jeans.

"That department," Clem howls, repeating his words.

"I've had about enough of the likes of the two of you." He storms up the stairs.

"Oh my gawd. That just made what was going to be a miserable day, absolutely worth it." I high-five Clem.

"It was, but don't think you won't get your payback at some point today," she says.

"Me? You were in on it too."

"Yes, but I'm smart enough to hide from him." She winks and starts pouring batter into a bowl.

"Hell, I hide, but he always seems to find me."

"You never were good at hide-and-seek growing up. You'd hide, and as soon as the count to ten was done, you'd jump out and say surprise!"

I lean my long frame against the counter beside her. "Seriously, maybe I should try life outside the ranch."

"Daddy would shoot you with his shotgun if you tried to take Missy away from here." She whips the batter as she talks. "Do you like working the ranch?"

"I love it, only second to working on trucks."

"You get to do both of those things. Sounds like life isn't so bad here after all."

"No. Only the six-foot-one grumpy old cowboy makes me want to strangle him every day."

"That's never going to change." She laughs.

"You're right, again." I push myself off the counter. "I'll take you up on that offer to decorate a room for Missy and pack up what things I have upstairs."

"You may want to go deal with the cattle first, rather than the bull upstairs."

The back door swings open, and Boone storms in holding a shotgun. "We've got some cattle missing from the east end of the ranch. I need help trackin' 'em."

"I'll get my rifle." I turn toward Clem. "You got this. Give Missy a kiss for me. Thanks for taking her to school."

"Anytime. I'll go to the cabin and come up with ideas for her room today."

"Thanks, Sis." I grab my hat from the hook and get a rifle from the gun cabinet then snag my boots from the front porch.

Click here to purchase Stolen Hearts

ABOUT THE AUTHOR

"This author has the magical ability to take an already strong and interesting plot and add so many unexpected twists and turns that it turns her books into a complete addiction for the reader." Dandelion Inspired Blog

Armed with books in the crook of my elbow, I can go anywhere. That's my philosophy! Better yet, I'll write the books that will take me on an adventure.

My heroes are a bit broken but will make you swoon. My heroines are their own kick-ass characters armed with humor and a plethora of sarcasm.

If I'm not tucked away in my writing den, with coffee firmly gripped in hand, you can find me with a book propped on my pillow, a pit bull lying across my legs, a Lab on the floor next to me, and two kittens running amuck.

My current adventure has me living in Idaho with my own gray-bearded hero, who's put up with my shenanigans for over thirty years, and he doesn't mind all my book boyfriends.

If you love romance, suspense, military men, lots of action and adventure infused with emotion, tear-worthy moments, and laugh-out-loud humor, dive into my books and let the world fall away at your feet.

ALSO BY KELLY MOORE

Whiskey River Road Series - Available on Audible

Coming Home, Book 1

Stolen Hearts, Book 2

Three Words, Book 3

Kentucky Rain, Book 4

Wild Ride, Book 5

Magnolia Mill, Book 6 Coming Jan 2021

The Broken Pieces Series in order

Broken Pieces

Pieced Together

Piece by Piece

Pieces of Gray

Syn's Broken Journey

Broken Pieces Box set Books 1-3

August Series in Order

Next August

This August

Seeing Sam

The Hitman Series- Previously Taking Down
Brooklyn/The DC Seres

Stand By Me - On Audible as Deadly Cures

Stay With Me On Audible as Dangerous Captive

Hold Onto Me

Epic Love Stories Series can be read in any order

Say You Won't Let Go. Audiobook version

Fading Into Nothing Audiobook version

Life Goes On. Audiobook version

Gypsy Audiobook version

Jameson Wilde Audiobook version

Rescue Missions Series can be read in any order

Imperfect. On Audible

Blind Revenge

Fated Lives Series

Rebel's Retribution Books 1-4. Audible

Theo's Retaliation Books 5-7. Audible

Thorn's Redemption Audible

Fallon's Revenge Book 11 Audible

The Crazy Rich Davenports Season One in order of reading

The Davenports On Audible

Lucy

Yaya

Ford

Gemma

Daisy

The Wedding

Halloween Party

Bang Bang

Coffee Tea or Me